Advance Praise for *Through the Fire*

"A sizzling debut novel from a writer who really has the goods. Shawn Grady is an author to watch."

—James Scott Bell
bestselling author of *Deceived*

"With equal parts drama, suspense, and poetic prose, Shawn Grady weaves a captivating story. The characters are complex and interesting and the story world is so well drawn, I feel as though I've experienced the life of a firefighter. Excellent read!"

—Kathryn Cushman
author of *Waiting for Daybreak*

"Shawn Grady is the real deal—a real-life fireman who can take you into the inferno, scare the living daylights out of you, and drag you back out reeking of smoke and gasping for air. *Through the Fire* is the best fire-fighting novel I've ever read, and there's enough mystery and suspense to keep you scorching through the pages."

—Randy Ingermanson
Christy Award–winning
author of *Oxygen*

"With an expert hand, Shawn Grady delivers a haunting story filled with high-action suspense, intriguing insider details, and characters to cheer for as they navigate deep waters and fiery depths."

—Amy Wallace
author of *Enduring Justice*

SHAWN GRADY

Through the Fire
Copyright © 2009
Shawn Peter Grady

Cover design by Lookout Design, Inc.
Art direction by Paul Higdon

Published by Bethany House Publishers
11400 Hampshire Avenue South
Bloomington, Minnesota 55438

Bethany House Publishers is a division of
Baker Publishing Group, Grand Rapids, Michigan.

Printed in the United States of America

Library of Congress Cataloging-in-Publication Data

Grady, Shawn.
Through the fire / Shawn Grady.
p. cm.
ISBN 978-0-7642-0595-8 (pbk.)
1. Fire fighters—Fiction. I. Title.

PS3607.R3285T47 2009
813'.6—dc22

2009007607

For

My bride, Sarah Beth

The true binding of this book

Midway in the journey of our life
I found myself in a dark wood,
for the straight way was lost.

—DANTE ALIGHIERI
The Divine Comedy, Inferno

CHAPTER 1

Even smoke runs from the fire.

But I find myself compelled to enter hell's havoc and the swirling chasm, to take for my own the taming of the element, screwing my courage to the sticking place. When blackness billows heaven-bent from hallways, and flame tips lick lintels like a serpent's tongue, the Sirens stand singing. Mast ties won't hold fast.

Enter the cloud.

Enveloped by heat.

Vanquish the destroyer.

I come from a family of firemen. And borne into my blood was a gift. It arrives at times in whispers, other times more subtle. But beyond the beckon of skeptical sensibilities I've become convinced.

The fire speaks to me.

I know where it is going. I know what it will do. Some call it heightened intuition. Others credit Irish luck. But I know that it's more.

And it was this very thing, this brash self-confidence, that propelled me down a fateful course one thirty-first of October.

—

Captain Butcher slammed his palm on the clipboard sliding off the dash. He cursed. "We ain't doing nobody no good if we don't get there alive, Aidan."

I winked at him, tightening and relaxing my grip on the steering wheel. His silver-laced moustache rowed back and forth like a set of oars. Our normal driver had taken the day off, so lucky for Butcher, I stepped up as acting operator.

I hung a hard right and the clipboard fell again. This time he missed. He grabbed the side of his door and slung my name with a slew of expletives.

I couldn't help but grin. "Nice alliteration, Cap."

"Nice *what*? Watch out. Slow down."

We threaded through the glowing Reno arch, under its mainstay mantra, *The Biggest Little City in the World*. South Virginia Street stretched out before our blaring Pierce Quantum pumper. I laid on the air horn through intersections and wound the grinder into a high wail. The burgundy hues of the autumn sunset filtered through the foothills, bathing building sides with amber tones and glinting windows.

A pillar of black cloud rose from the south.

Deep into District Three. We'd be third engine in, coming from downtown. I hated being anything but first in. But third was better than second. At least we wouldn't be stuck hooking up water supply.

Static crackled from the radio, "All units, be advised, we have reports of occupants trapped."

I pushed the pedal to the floor. The rig surged like an elephant charging. Cars and businesses passed as blurs. The guys in the back strapped on their packs, cranking open the air valves to the *beep-beep-beep* acknowledgment of the built-in motion sensors. Butcher flipped through the map book.

Another transmission, "Battalion Two, Engine Three on scene, large footprint concrete tilt-up, retail building, heavy smoke showing from the roof. We'll be in live-line operations."

It was McKinley. I heard the strain in his voice. Not high-pitched or excited, but almost muted. Like he was trying really hard not to sound high-pitched or excited. He had been a good fireman, an excellent operator, and now that he had promoted to captain, I knew he'd prove the same.

Butcher directed me down a side street so we'd be out of the way of Engine Five laying their hose from the hydrant.

I pulled us up near the ladder truck. The aerial elevated and rotated toward the roof. The Engine Three crew flaked out their hose line to the front doors. A small sea of disquieted faces gathered in the parking lot, shopping bags in hand, children clinging to shoulders.

I set the brake and hopped out of the rig. The tang of burning wood pierced the air. Fire crackled, spitting and popping. I strapped on my air pack.

Butcher came up to me. "Word is, a mother and her son are trapped in the back. They were last seen by the dressing rooms. Smoke's banked down to the floor."

There was no way they could breathe in that. I grabbed my flathead axe and started with him toward the front doors.

"Truck Three is committed to topside," he said. "Battalion Two assigned us and Rescue One with search, but I need to coordinate with him and Captain McKinley. We'll split into two teams. Timothy Clark with me. You take the new kid and head on in."

"Got it."

"And Aidan . . ." He stopped walking.

"What?"

"I'm trusting you with our probie." He held my gaze for a second longer, then turned and strode over to the battalion chief's rig.

Probie firefighter Matt Hartman's eyes circled wide like china saucers. He pulled on his air mask and tightened his gleaming yellow helmet. This was his third shift.

We advanced to the door. "Ready, bud?"

Fog filled his facepiece. "Yeah," he said with a muffled voice.

"Lightweight truss," I said. "Looks like it's running the rafters hard. Be heads-up."

At the entry I strapped on my mask, the smell of rubber meeting my nostrils as I seated the nose cone. Thick gray smoke hovered in the doorway, greeting us like a silent apparition. A chainsaw started in the parking lot.

I clicked on my voice amplifier and pulled rope out of the small bag on my air pack. I carabinered it to a door handle. "We follow this to get out. Keep a hand on my shoulder."

Hartman nodded.

We crouched and entered the maw. Sounds of the outside faded, and warmth pressed in around my hood. Our flashlights penetrated only two feet in front of us. The sound of hose streams hitting walls rumbled to our distant right. A dull roar like a freeway overpass reverberated above, interspersed with metallic groans. My hands found the smooth tile of a walkway alongside a carpeted section. I trailed a glove and pushed us on toward the back of the store.

Bump. Bump. Bump.

The ladder truck company made the roof, sounding out each step with a tool. I reached out with all my senses.

I listened beyond.

Searching.

There you are.

Rolling like a tumbleweed, tearing through the trusses . . . south . . . southeast.

I stopped.

"What is it?" Hartman said.

I looked behind us. Orange flickers danced through the smoke. "We don't have much time."

We moved on until I felt the rope bag tug on my waist belt. I unclipped it and dropped it on the pathway. "Matt, connect your tag line to mine."

"What tag line?"

"The red bag on your air pack."

He twisted like he was doing the hula hoop. "I don't have one."

We were a hundred feet in, and out of rope to follow back.

The smoke swirled around us. If we ran out of air we'd suffocate. We ran the risk of getting lost in an everyday retail mart, our final breaths taken beside the baby toys and discount-movie bins.

This is how firemen die.

I looked at the rope bag, then ahead into the graphite abyss. Somewhere in that lay a woman and a child.

"All right," I said. "Stick close. Let's go."

Rumbles and groans crescendoed. I quickened the pace, tapping my glove to feel the tile every dozen steps. The temperature elevated.

Two white lights swung through the haze. A pair of firefighters materialized in front of us, a woman's limp body clutched between them.

"You guys Rescue One?"

The firefighter at the head moved backward, struggling. "Yeah."

"Where's the kid?"

"What kid?"

I followed alongside. "We heard there was a mother and a child."

"We . . . searched the whole . . . back there. Nobody else."

I stopped. "No, we heard there was a kid—"

In my mind I saw a vision of a sudden bright flame.

Southeast corner.

Under the roof, by the wall. By McKinley's crew.

I grabbed the radio from my jacket pocket.

"Engine Three, get—"

A tangerine flash filled the room.

I tackled Hartman to the floor. Rescue One scrambled beneath the searing heat, dragging the woman with one hand each. Hartman made his knees and scuttled after them. The store glowed like a volcanic cloud.

"Matt!" I yelled. "Matt!"

He turned.

I motioned toward the rear of the building. "This way."

He stared at me and turned toward the front.

"Matt!"

He looked back again.

A transmission burst from my radio. "Battalion Two to all units, evacuate the building. Repeat, all units evacuate the structure. We are going defensive."

Fire rolled overhead.

"Come on, Matt! We can still find the kid."

He didn't move.

"Matt, come on!"

He pointed to the front. "They're calling us out!"

A thunderous bang hit ground not far from us.

"Now's the time," I said. "Let's get back there."

I turned and crawled toward the back, certain he would follow me.

I felt the frame of a doorway and swiveled my head to make sure I still had him. But he hadn't moved. He knelt, frozen with indecision, as though his knees and gloves were affixed to the floor. There I saw in his face, through the clear curvature of his mask and the gold-lit reflections of fire, the simple look of a child, innocent and uncertain.

And then the roof collapsed.

CHAPTER 2

Sometimes a thousand thoughts fill a second . . .

Hartman.

Rescue One.

The guys on the roof.

My fiancée. My father. My childhood.

All encapsulated in a simple pill.

. . . and then you swallow hard.

Steel framework swung like a pendulum from the ceiling. Debris dumped between us. I tucked tight up against the doorframe, hiding my hands in my helmet, coated by a thick rolling wave of smoke and ash. A large form hit my lower legs, pinning them. The roar continued with a series of objects hitting the floor in syncopated rhythm, slowing in progression until an aftermath of silence.

I groaned and tried to move my legs.

Three long air-horn blasts sounded outside, the emergency

evacuation signal. Pallets of heat pressed in like a sauna. Visibility was zero. I fought and wiggled to free myself.

The wailing cry of a motion sensor pierced the air.

Hartman.

Working the handle of my axe between my legs and the debris, I found just enough purchase to create a space so I could slide out. I pulled free and dropped the axe head to the sound of metal and wood clacking.

"Matt!" My voice dissipated.

I scampered toward the cycling alarm from Hartman's air pack. Raucous radio traffic spilled from the speaker in my jacket pocket. Broken transmissions cut short, voices walking on others.

I felt my way onto a small rubble pile. Plywood. Truss beams. A half-dome light fixture.

The wailing grew louder.

"Matt! Matt, can you hear me?"

My personal light melted into the smoke. I made out fragmented pieces of metal and wood. Then, finally, a glove.

I grasped it into mine. "Hartman. Matt!"

He didn't move. His alarm continued.

I pulled out my radio. The traffic was incessant.

Would everyone just shut up!

Someone took a breath between sentences. I depressed the transmit button. "Mayday, mayday, mayday. Firefighter down."

The radio fell silent.

I continued. "Command, Engine One Firefighter O'Neill with emergency traffic."

Battalion Chief Mauvain came back, "Go ahead, Aidan."

"Chief, I have a firefighter down, unconscious and trapped about two hundred feet inside the structure, toward the C side."

"Copy that, Aidan. Do you have an ID on the downed firefighter?"

"Engine One Firefighter Hartman."

"Copy. A rescue team is on their way now."

I flung from the pile anything I could grasp. I lifted and tossed concrete and metal. Seconds lengthened like oxygen tubing, every moment stealing life from Hartman's vital organs.

Minutes passed. *Where's that rescue team?*

Then I remembered.

We'd left our tag line.

There was no way for them to know where we were. They were wandering in the dark. They could be twenty feet away and still not see us.

"Over here!" I said. "Over here!" The room swallowed my words.

My low air pressure alarm sounded.

Five minutes left.

I had to work fast. I pushed and scooped at a frenzied pace. Every piece I removed replaced itself with another. I stood with a sheet of plywood and, while leveraging it, lost my balance, dropping it and falling open handed on a nail. It penetrated my leather glove, piercing my palm with a searing pain. I shouted and ripped a two-by-four block from my hand.

A distant voice cut through the cloud. "O'Neill, that you?"

On my knees, clutching my glove, I turned to see four spotlights floating like ships through a fog-blanketed harbor. "Yeah. Hey! Over here."

"Hang tight, Aidan."

"Hang on, buddy."

"Command, rescue team has made patient contact."

I waved them over. "Right here, guys, right here."

They say many hands make light work. In less than a minute we cleared the remaining rubble off Hartman and shut off his alarm.

A fine veil of dust coated his facepiece, behind which bowed darkened eyelids and parted lips. I opened the bypass valve on his regulator, flooding his mask with positive pressure air.

"Is he breathing?" someone said.

"Get his bottle off his back."

"Forget it. Just get him on the board."

We logrolled him onto a backboard.

"Let's four point him."

I stumbled backward.

"Aidan, you all right?"

I waved my hand. "I'm fine. Go, go." I moved to his feet.

Someone at the head counted off, "Ready, one, two, three."

I grabbed onto the board, and we lifted and shuffled, bearing increased temperatures just a few feet off the floor. Hartman lay unconscious, and I had the surreal feeling that, as we marched for the door while he still faced the rubble, we were somehow moving his body from his spirit. As though the farther we fled from the spot he went down, the emptier his shell of a body became.

I saw it, with the backs of four turnout coats before me. At his feet I was witness.

Hot wetness soaked through my glove as I clenched the board.

And I knew . . .

His blood was on my hands.

—

The medics loaded the gurney into the back of the ambulance, crimson draping the western sky. The paramedic at the head squeezed a purple bag attached to a tube sticking out of Hartman's mouth. His chest rose and relaxed, lifting and ebbing like an ocean swell.

I watched, helmet in hand, as two firemen climbed in the back, as the doors closed, as the box lit up in a fury, wailing down the road with a police escort. A corkscrew twisted in my gut.

Voices spoke in low tones behind me. "All that weight on his chest . . ."

"He's hypoxic."

"Strong pulse though."

"They taking him to County, like the woman?"

"Yeah."

I turned and brushed shoulders between them. Butcher caught my eye and strode toward me. The acrid odor of smoke and fire wafted from my turnouts.

"You mind telling me exactly what that was, Aidan?"

I ignored him and walked toward the engine.

"Don't you walk away. Hold up. That's an order, Firefighter O'Neill. Hold up."

I stopped and stared at the pavement.

Butcher angled himself in front of me. He spoke in quiet, controlled tones. "You listen to me. Your father was the best fireman I ever knew. And I put up with your reckless and arrogant attitude out of respect for him. I see a lot of him in you . . . but you know what I don't see, Aidan?"

I brought my eyes up to his and set my chin.

"Respect. Your father came from a time when men understood the chain of command. They treated those who came before them with the respect they were due. You know what I see when I look at you?"

I looked away toward the road.

"I see contempt," he said. "And now we got a one-week-old fireman riding unconscious in the back of the bus, intubated and all." He pressed his lips together, his whiskers taut and trembling. He looked at the ground. Then, right to my face, he shouted, "I trusted you with him!"

It reverberated through my chest. Yellow helmets turned, stared, looked away.

Butcher brought his hand up between us, as if to dam up any further flow of indignation. His voice leveled. "Pack up your stuff."

I did a double take between him and the building still spouting gray smoke. "There's still fire—"

"I said pack it up."

"What, are we being released? What about the kid? Are they still doing a search?"

"Aidan"—he pointed behind me—"the kid is sitting in the back of the battalion chief's rig."

Cuffed blue jeans covered dangling legs with Velcro-strapped tennis shoes in the open backseat of Chief Mauvain's SUV.

My mouth hung open, searching for words. "But you said—"

"Things change in fires. We don't always get the best information straight out. You know that. That's why we follow the chain of command. And that's why *we* are not packing up our stuff—*you* are."

I creased my eyebrows and stared at him.

He filled his chest with air. "Pack it up. Everyone else made it out in time. Even the truck guys were off the roof when they were supposed to be. Only you stayed and went deeper in against orders. Hartman shouldn't be in an ambulance right now. He has a wife and a new baby, Aidan." He ran the back of his hand under his nose and glanced at the pavement. "You're on leave without pay. This is straight from Mauvain, not just me. Expect a minimum of two weeks."

I held his gaze in disbelief.

He shook his head. "Just go home, Aidan. You've done enough for today."

CHAPTER 3

Do not pass go. Do not collect two hundred dollars.

I actually caught a cab back to the station. I don't remember the trip. It's as if I woke from a stupor when I pulled out of Central's parking lot in my '83 Land Cruiser. Zeppelin strummed "That's the Way" from the stereo speakers. Gold-tipped trails marked the paths of aspens following creeks down the Sierra's eastern aspects. The day's last silver-lit clouds hung on the horizon.

I crossed Virginia Street just south of the Reno Arch and the narrow corridor of flashing neon and high-rise hotel-casinos. I spun the wheel and crossed the Truckee River at the kayak park. Leaf-blanketed streets led me into the old southwest, past pre–World War II brick homes, thick-trunked oaks, and ailing elms. Ghoulishly clad children trekked from door to door, flashlights in hand, candy bags bulging and swung over shoulders.

My stomach twisted in a knot. I was hungry and wondered if my fiancée, Christine, was available for dinner. I reached into the front pants pocket that held my phone, the skin on my knuckles chafing against the denim. Her line rang seven times and switched to voice mail. I hung up.

Christine worked part time at a coffee shop while finishing up her master's in literature. And though I welcomed the diversion, I wasn't sure I would have been up to a long discussion about Hemingway or Kierkegaard. She dug my love for reading and my understanding of most literary and biblical allusions—thanks to my mother, who had fed me books as if they were milk—but I'd found that her disparaging existentialism inevitably degenerated into musings on the meaninglessness of everything under the sun. That was exactly what I didn't need right then.

I tried to shake the vision of Hartman in my mind, lying in the ER, hooked to a ventilator, grim-faced white-coats standing over him. Part of me felt guilty for even wanting food.

I parked in front of the house and paced up a dark front path. A rotund pumpkin sat in the corner of the porch. I jiggled my key in the lock—up, down, up, down, side to side—until, *click*.

A flick of the front-hall switch spilled light onto honey-hued floorboards and a shadow-laden living room.

Beep.

Beep.

A red light flashed on the kitchen answering machine.

Beep.

Beep.

I sank into a chair by the breakfast table. One hundred and six hours straight. That's how long I'd been at work.

Beep.

Beep.

I pushed the answering machine button. Its computer voice announced, "You have two new messages. First new message."

Christine's voice warbled, "Aidan, I'm in Denver. I'm flying out to New York to stay with my mom for a while. I don't know how long or . . . It's just . . . you have such a hard time saying no to work. I never see you. And when I do see you . . . I'm just fed up with waiting for you to grow up and figure out when you are going to get a real . . . You . . . you know what, just forget it. I don't even know why I'm saying all of this. Don't call me."

I leaned my head back and rubbed my hands over my eyes.

Guess a dinner date is out of the question.

Robert Louis Stevenson stared at me from a framed John Sargent print. Wine hues inhabited his room, his disinterested wife, clad in gold and ivory, reclining in a chair.

The computer voice continued. "Next message."

The doorbell rang. I paused the machine.

On my front porch stood a vampire, a clone trooper, and a black-costumed Spider-Man. "Trick or treat."

"Go away," I heard myself say.

The kids just stood there, cocking their heads like perplexed puppies.

"Ha. Right. Just kidding, kids." I looked back toward the kitchen. "Hold on a sec."

I opened the pantry.

No candy.

I came back with a box of Grape-Nuts, a box of crackers, and a bag of bagels.

"Here you go. Now get out of here."

The three of them strolled back toward the street, staring into their bags. A harvest moon loomed ochre and oversized on the horizon.

Back in the kitchen I hit the answering machine button.

"Aidan, it's Uncle Cormac. It's been too long. How are you doing? Hope everything is well. Hey, I'm calling because I've finally finished the remodel on the guesthouse down here in Baja and wanted to invite you to come stay for a bit—get away, you know? I'd love to have you, so just give me a call. Seriously, you're welcome any time. Call me. Take care, bud."

Beep. "There are no more new messages."

I took a deep breath in and out.

I'd almost killed my partner, my fiancée was leaving me, and I'd just been put on two-weeks' leave without pay. Somehow an impromptu vacation to Mexico didn't feel like the appropriate next step.

Thanks anyway, Cormac.

I had to see Matt. I grabbed a snack and hopped back in the Cruiser. Nightfall draped its chilled swath over the valley. The asphalt lay long and gray on the way to Washoe County Hospital. I parked in an ambulance spot outside the ER. I didn't care. I just wanted to get inside to see him. I'd known the guy all of half a day and already I felt as if I were visiting a relative.

I hadn't taken the time to change. My navy blue department shirt clung to my shoulders and hung heavy with sweat, the scent of smoke trailing off me in a cloud as I entered the ER. I saw a red-haired woman in her twenties standing outside of the cardiac resus room, an infant in her arms. Tears brimmed in her eyes, cheeks flushed and moist as she stared through the door.

Hartman's wife.

A wrecking ball hit me in the gut.

God, I hope he's okay.

Behind the glass, a flurry of scrubs and hands moved about with instruments and wires. I felt frozen, as if my feet were affixed to the floor. I wanted to turn and bail.

A security guard approached. "I'm sorry, sir, but all the firefighters have been asked to wait in the lobby."

Hartman's wife pivoted and looked at me, eyes bloodshot, her baby reaching to touch her chin.

"Sir?" The guard hung close, like a slab of beef in a commercial freezer.

I turned to him. "He's my . . . He's my brother."

"Yes, sir. You're the fifth one to tell me that, and I understand you are concerned for him. But right now the best way you can help him is by waiting in the lobby." He grabbed my arm.

I shrugged. "Get off me."

His expression soured.

"Look," I said. "He was my partner. I was with him when he went down. I was there, all right? He shouldn't be here. It's my . . ." I glanced at Hartman's wife.

Her focus fixed on me. Too much resided in that expression, too many thoughts and feelings and fears. Her bottom lip pushed up. Tears streamed down her cheeks. She shook her head, chin quivering.

"It was my . . ."

"Sir, I'm sorry, but . . ." He kept talking. His voice trailed off.

Hartman's wife kept staring. "Just leave," she mouthed.

The entire ER may as well have fallen silent. The air escaped from my lungs, the light from the corners of my eyes. All I saw and heard was this despairing woman holding her baby saying, "Just leave." She looked to the ceiling, then back. "Please, please. Just leave. Just go."

The guard reached out for me. I stepped back and clipped my hip on an EKG cart. My throat tightened, I couldn't swallow. The room spun.

"Sir, are you okay?" The guard put his face in front of mine. "You look . . . Hold on. I'll call a—"

"I'm fine. I'm fine." I put a hand up. "I . . . I shouldn't be here. This isn't right." I didn't know what else to do. I turned and pushed though the ER doors, digging the keys from my pocket. I walked straight to the parking lot, unable to face the guys in the waiting room.

—

The same dark empty house welcomed me back. I pulled off my shirt and walked down the hallway, stopping at the photo of my father. His affable grin hung frozen in two-dimensional bliss, Irish eyes smiling under a badge hat with a slight tilt, his crisp chalk-blue collar with silver bugles at the hems.

"Five years tomorrow, Dad." I ran my thumb over my palm. "How's that for almost repeating history?"

I got in the shower and let the heated rain wash over me. Steam wafted, pulling soot from my pores. Everything smelled like smoke and ash.

Baja, Mexico . . . I nodded and shut off the water. *All right, Cormac.*

I had no reason to stay and every reason to leave.

CHAPTER 4

After the shower I threw what I needed for a couple weeks into the back of my car and started south. The Cruiser's hundred-and-seventy-five thousand miles were half-life, really, so what was another twelve hundred? The purposeful motion of the road, of having a set destination, freed my mind, helped me relax, and kept at bay the stinging guilt over Hartman and the hollow ache for Christine. The lights of Reno and Carson City soon fled, twinkling in my rearview mirror, swallowed into the vast expanse of the evening. I followed the towering jagged sentries of the eastern Sierra front and wove along the Carson and Walker rivers, amidst the still quiet of Mono Lake and native spirits rising from tule fog blankets.

All Hallows' Eve.

The one night it is said when the boundary between the quick and the dead lay unguarded, when souls walk unfettered to either side. How often had I tread that line? How many times had I run without worry on the fence, balancing over the demarcation of life and death? Maybe I was reckless. Maybe I was missing something my father always had.

Maybe I wasn't the best communicator. Things between Christine and me had been rocky at best over the past few months. I couldn't put my finger on the real problem, but it seemed that everything I did had some ulterior motive in her eyes, and I found myself defending the simplest of things.

My cell phone beeped. I was out of service range. I yawned and readjusted in my seat. My plan was to drive through the night, or at least until I was too tired, to try and make the bulk of the journey to Baja in one big chunk. I'd call Cormac in the morning. It was a bit of a risk, heading off without talking to him first. But knowing him, it wouldn't be a problem. He had always been welcoming in the past. Though it had been almost five years since I last saw him in person. Since he left.

I remember him saying how he just couldn't see himself as part of the fire service anymore, too many things and places to remind him of his brother's death. So he straight up retired and moved to his place down in Mexico.

Too much had happened in such a short time. First his younger brother—my father—had died, and then his father, the department chief at the time, died five months later of heart failure, overwhelmed with grief from the passing of his son. I didn't blame Cormac for needing to get away from it all, but part of me had always resented his decision a bit. As if he were the only one affected by it all. I was right there in the middle of it. It was my dad. My grandfather. My . . . fault.

Hartman's sunken and vacant eyes flashed across my view.

A family of deer trotted across the highway, stealing glances into my lights. I slowed a bit.

I'll never shake the vision of my father lying pulseless and apneic in the back of the ambulance, the feeling of his ribs separating from his sternum as I performed chest compressions, his pupils fixed and dilated, his mouth agape.

Everything went bad on that fire. Large warehouse, unreinforced masonry construction. Rapid, *rapid* fire spread. The explosion and building collapse, the brick wall that broke his neck.

The thing that still prevented any sense of closure was how the department left the official cause as "undetermined." That never set right with me. The head investigator on the case had since retired and they just closed the book on it.

Normal fires didn't burn that hot, that fast, that destructive. My buddy Blake in the arson investigation office made a pact with me that he wouldn't let it rest. Five years later and he still worked on it with me in his free time. Couple times a month Christine and I would make dinner for him. It was the least we could do.

The double yellow line disappeared with the road into a perpetual black. It felt just like the smoke, driving into the dark. An all too common experience for me.

All I could see was what was just in front of my headlights.

CHAPTER 5

Around three in the morning I made it to a veritable ghost town outside of Bakersfield named Red Mountain and paid seventy-five dollars to stay in a roadside motel. I woke around ten a.m. and got ahold of Cormac, to his surprised and cheerful response. He said he'd have dinner waiting and admonished me not to waste a second more in central California.

Cormac also told me that his town of Lazaro Cardenas was just a little south of Ensenada. After hours of driving, I decided he was speaking of *little* in a global sense, because it took me a lot longer than I expected. I was a good quarter of the way down the Baja Peninsula and through my *sixth* toll checkpoint before I finally saw a sign that read *Lazaro Cardenas 25 Kilómetros.*

The town itself, perhaps by virtue of its distance from other cities, retained a nineteenth-century pueblo charm. An adobe mission replete with tarnished bronze bell sat in time-worn grandeur in the city square. Cylindrical timber beams projected from building fronts. A fine coating of sand and dust blurred the street edges.

Eucalyptus trees with painted white trunks shaded a park with a three-level concentric fountain. A dozen men and boys played soccer on a small field of patchy grass. Fading paint on building sides sported dated ads for Coca-Cola and Tecate beer. A couple shops were fronted by wooden carts full of yellow marigolds and what looked like ornamented human skulls and small dressed-up skeleton dolls. I found it quite a bit more intriguing than the standard American Halloween décor, even a bit disturbing.

A winding road took me through rocky bitterbrush-covered hills, westward toward the ocean and my uncle's estate. The peak of the last hill brought with it the unbridled blue of the Pacific Ocean, contained only by the limits of my vision south and by a misty haze creeping in from the north. Cormac's place was easy to find, the only house for a mile in any direction, encompassed inland by horse corrals and a weathered barn, and on the west by an elaborate garden and deck overlooking the water. The word *estate* had never really hit me until then. I was amazed by what the American dollar could buy in a third-world country.

I pulled the Cruiser to a stop on Cormac's gravel driveway, a small dust cloud bypassing the vehicle as I opened the door. The air smelled sweet and humid. A light breeze cooled the line of sweat along my spine. Cormac appeared from around the corner, his thick hairy arms outspread, his grin surrounded by a salt-and-pepper beard. He'd gained weight.

"Aidan!"

I stood trapped in a bear hug before I could bring my arms up. Cormac stood a few inches taller than me. My face squished against his shoulder.

"How's my favorite nephew?"

I managed a muffled "Hey, Uncle Cormac."

"What was that?" he said.

I pulled away and coughed. "Hey, Cormac. It's great to see you."

He shook his head. "It has been too long." He glanced at the gauze wrapped around my palm. "What happened to your hand?"

"This? Oh, you know, nothing. It's only a flesh wound." I laughed, anxious to change the subject. "But you're right, it has been too long. It's weird to see you with a beard after all those clean-cut years with the department."

He waved a hand. "Ah, who wants to talk about the department, anyway?"

I scoffed. "Yeah, count me out."

He stole a glance toward the car. "Christine couldn't make it?"

I swallowed. "Oh. You know. She's swamped with her master's thesis."

His bushy eyebrows crunched.

"Yeah. Something about beatnik writers and grammar teachers. I don't know."

He just stared at me.

I ran my hand along the back of my neck. "She's out visiting her mother."

His eyes crinkled at the sides, just like my dad's. Just like mine. "Say no more, son."

And that was it. Nothing more needed be said. I smiled and patted him on the shoulder. "It is great to see you again."

He stroked his beard, then pointed his index finger. "You must be hungry."

I grinned. "Yeah, actually—"

"Come on. Let's grab your stuff and I'll give you a quick tour. Rosa should have the *pescado* soup done real soon."

"Rosa?"

"You think I can keep this place up by myself?"

"Must be nice living the good life." I grabbed my backpack from the car.

"Yeah. But it comes at a price. My pension doesn't cover everything, so I'm still doing consulting work stateside." He pulled out the rolling luggage.

"Thanks." My eyes trailed over the eastern hills. "So, Lazaro Cardenas. Most of the people here farmers?"

"Miners."

"Oh?"

"The old salt mines down south. Probably still employ sixty percent of the population." He paused outside a thick cedar door. "Well, here we are."

The door opened into a column-lined entryway paved with marble. A small fountain trickled water into a basin with koi swimming under lily pads. The hallways were cool and naturally lit by recessed skylights and transom windows.

"Beautiful home, Cormac."

He let his eyes traverse the room, then sighed. "Come on, I'll show you the garden."

We emerged from the main house onto a large paver patio. The guesthouse sat in the middle of the garden, river rock and mortar walls supporting a ceramic-tiled roof. The inside couldn't have been bigger than five hundred square feet. But it had a kitchen, bathroom, living room, and bedroom. A stone fireplace rose along a side wall.

"What do you think?" he said.

I turned off my cell phone and set it on the kitchen counter. "It's amazing. Just what I needed."

"Feel free to get yourself situated. I'll be on the porch."

"Sounds great." I extended my hand and we shook. "Thanks again."

He stepped out the door, his face half hidden by the frame. "Don't mention it."

Rosa's soup smelled like autumn in a bowl. Fried tortilla strips floated in claret-colored liquid with corn, beans, peppers, and shredded halibut. A dollop of sour cream topped the mixture.

The evening fog moved in on the horizon, bringing with it an unexpected chill that prompted me to zip my fleece jacket up to the neck. The sky melded monochromatic gray, the ocean beneath mirroring its brooding brow.

Papier-mâché lanterns dangled from wire strung beneath the wooden porch covering. A solitary candle on our table flicked in the light breeze. The kitchen windows radiated a warm glow from where Rosa busied herself washing pots. Inside, on the far corner of the countertop, lit candles enshrined photographs of a silver-haired man amid the same yellow marigolds I'd seen in town. Crosses formed from small white bones, tied at the crux with twine, bordered an arched mirror behind it all.

Cormac leaned back in his chair, one elbow on the armrest, the other holding a mug of hot sangria. He stared at the water and the fading sunlight diffusing though the cloud cover. I swallowed a spoonful of the soup, letting the warmth radiate through my chest.

"Did Rosa lose a relative recently?" I nodded toward the kitchen.

He raised his eyebrows. "Hmm?"

I sipped the sangria. Cinnamon, cranberry, and root-stalk earthiness graced my palate. I pointed with the mug. "Did she make an altar for a loved one she lost?"

His mind was elsewhere. He leaned back and glanced in the kitchen. "Oh, that. Yes. But not recently. That's all part of *Día de los Muertos*."

"Part of what?"

He raised one eyebrow, something I could never do. "You don't know about . . ." He made little circles in the air with his hand.

I smiled and shook my head. "No. Not really."

He interlaced his fingers and leaned forward on the table. His pale blue eyes turned translucent, his lips thin and emotionless beneath the beard. "Day of the Dead, Aidan. Día de los Muertos."

Something flicked in those eyes. His expression changed, like someone snapping from a trance. He sat upright. "Matter of fact, tomorrow evening I was planning on joining some compadres in town for the celebration. Should be a good time. You in?"

I swallowed. "Yeah. Sure. Sounds like a good time."

He leaned back in his chair and folded his fingers across his belly.

I stared at my soup, tracing my spoon in a figure eight. "You know, today is the day when Dad—"

"Of course I know. You think I don't?" He paused, wiped his mouth with his napkin. "I'm sorry, A-O. It's just—"

I put up my hands. "No, no. It's fine. Of course you do. I'm sorry. Even after five years it's still hard for everyone."

He put his hand by the candle, warming his palm. "You know . . . this, the fire . . ." He passed his fingers through it, back and forth. Black smoke wisps snaked skyward. "It doesn't care. It has one focus, Aidan. One. To consume." He cupped his hand beside the flame. "It may give warmth. It may give light. But that's not its purpose. Its sole desire is to devour and to consume and to take that which was and to make it no more." He stared at it for a minute, then pinched the wick, extinguishing the flame.

He pushed his chair away from the table. "It's late. You've got to be tired from your travels. Sleep in. Relax. Tomorrow evening we'll celebrate. Tomorrow we'll remember the dead together."

CHAPTER 6

Lazaro came out.

The town emerged, alive in its celebration of the dead. That next night transformed the quiet pueblo into a raucous Mardi Gras conglomeration. A parade filled the streets with fire-eaters and costumed revelers. Macabre floats depicted scenes of death and the departed.

Cormac took me to a bar called La Milagrosa. The custom upon entering was to knock on the doorframe three times, a nod to the bar's namesake who lay with her newborn infant in eternal sleep. A standing-room-only crowd mingled under dim lighting and darkly painted walls decorated with wool tapestries sporting intricate patterns of scarlet and gold. A four-man band huddled in the center, moving fingers with flamenco speed over twelve-string guitars and skin-stretched toms. A light cigarette-smoke haze levitated overhead.

Joining our party were three of Cormac's friends—Virgil, a lanky youth who looked as if he'd fall between the floorboards;

Berto, a shorter stocky man who replied to everything by nodding with a smile and saying "Yes, yes"; and Rodrigo, a local ranch owner who'd migrated up from Panama during the Noriega years and also happened to be fluent in several languages.

We baby-stepped through the crowd, shoulder to shoulder. Virgil led the way, standing a head taller than most and wearing a white cowboy hat.

Cormac turned in front of me. "We still got Berto?"

A set of smiling teeth peeked out between bodies. "Yes, yes."

Cormac put his hand on my back and said something. I leaned my ear by his mouth. "What?"

"I'm going with Virgil to get us some drinks. Hang here with Rodrigo and Berto."

I nodded with exaggeration. "All right."

We huddled in the back third of the bar by a dark hallway. A regular flow of people walked in and out of two separate doors that looked like entrances to restrooms. A wooden sign hung between them from two eyebolts in the ceiling. A long sentence spelled out in Spanish on it.

I tapped Rodrigo on the shoulder. "What does the sign say?"

A smile turned at the corner of his mouth. He leaned near. " 'Abandon all hope, ye who enter here.' "

The crowd encircled around the quartet danced. Two bartenders spun shakers and poured tequila into shot glasses. A small group roared and cheered after several heads knocked back a swallow.

Cormac returned with Virgil, holding several shot glasses. They passed them out, two for each of us. Cormac raised both hands in a toast. "To the white man!"

"Bah!" Rodrigo said. "Make a real toast."

"All right, all right." Cormac paused. His voice took on a somber tone. "To the departed."

I lifted my glasses. "Here, here."

One.

And two.

The five of us downed shots of throat-burning tequila.

Berto exhaled loudly with grinning teeth. "Yes, yes! Ta kill ya! Ha, ha! Ta kill ya!"

I blew out a breath and wiped my watering eyes.

A firm palm slapped my shoulder. Cormac swayed beside me. "What do you think, huh? Funny thing is, Virgil and I already had two at the bar!"

"That was you guys?"

Rodrigo looked perplexed. "Where is Virgil?"

Cormac pointed his thumb. "He went to hit the head, I think. Right, Berto?"

"Yes, yes, señor. *Quieres mas tequila*?"

Cormac laughed. "I like the way you think, amigo. Let's go, you and me. I'll take you on, toe to toe."

Berto grinned and patted Cormac on the back.

"You two coming?" Cormac said over his shoulder.

Rodrigo waved a hand. "I'll be right behind you in a bit. I'm going to say hello to a couple of friends." He spoke into my ear. "*Mi esposa* does not like me coming home . . . how is it you say it in *Inglés* . . . smashed." He winked and straightened.

Virgil returned. *"Vamanos ya!"*

"Already?" Rodrigo said.

Cormac appeared, nodding, taking three steps to maintain his balance. "The horses are here."

Rodrigo's eyebrows elevated. *"Los caballos?"*

Cormac grinned. "Two kilometers to the beach. The whole parade is going. Right now. Virgil had horses brought in just for it this year." He winked at Virgil.

Rodrigo shook his head. "Cormac, not only is it dark, but you are already drunk. You don't even ride so good when you're sober. Now you're going to climb aboard a thousand-pound animal?"

Cormac stared at him, swaying slowly. He burst out in laughter. "You are the best, Rodrigo! That's why I love you, man. Now come on! Let's go!" He hooked my arm and led me over to Berto and Virgil.

"You four have fun," Rodrigo said as he waved. "Perhaps I will see you later tonight."

Cormac waved with his back to him. "That man cannot hold his liquor, always does this. But you and me, we have strong Irish blood! Thick like Guinness!"

I should have eaten something first. My head was already spinning.

—

"If it feels like we're going in circles, we are," Cormac said, mounted on an Appaloosa whose coloring gave the appearance it had rolled around in soot. "But Virgil knows this route, and trust me, this is the fastest way down the canyon and to the ocean." The sounds of distant drums echoed off the hillsides. Flickering torches wobbled with horse hip movements in our caravan. Cormac held a large electric lantern, pale luminescence washing blue over his face. "You be good to old Geryon back there. He is the first horse I bought here."

Horse was an understatement. Beast seemed more appropriate. Geryon's coal black neck flexed thick like sequoia roots. I couldn't remember the last time I had ridden anything not powered by a motor.

The moon hung high and nearly full, lighting our way. My peripheral vision faded into the inky blur of night, my inability to discern shapes exacerbated by the alcohol making a merry-go-round in my head. We passed a sign with an arrow that read *Playa del Séptimo Círculo, 0.2 Kilómetros.*

"We must be getting close," I said.

"Don't worry. Virgil could guide this path blindfolded."

"I wasn't worried," I said. But I don't think he heard me.

The sounds of drums were soon matched with music. The canyon opened up, and we followed a creek down to the beach. Bonfires whipped flames over smooth sand and frothing white waves. Skeleton-costumed dancers pranced around one fire, a crowd clapping behind them, cheering and whooping. Beside another fire, three men twirled batons lit at both ends, dousing the flames in their mouths and then relighting them. Bottles of tequila glinted, masked revelers danced, bone necklaces clattered and flopped. Waves crashed and churned around rock outcroppings to the nearby north.

We dismounted and tied the horses to a log by the creek. Berto split off in a different direction. I followed Cormac and Virgil as they wove their way between the bonfires. Radiant heat burned my cheeks. Someone handed me two more shot glasses. I downed them without thinking. The entire beachfront swayed, the music grew louder, the scene more surreal.

Hartman's face met my mind. His bowed eyelids, his unconscious form laid out on the backboard.

Something like a black hole opened in my chest.

Veiled women, arms ringed with bracelets, snapped fingers in the air, rocked their hips and batted eyes.

I thought of Christine. . . .

Virgil vanished. Cormac was gone. I felt sick to my stomach, dizzy in my head. The whole place hung with the stench of death. What did these people really know about the dead?

Father . . .

A thunderclap woke me from my thoughts. I had wandered toward the water. Bubbles reached my feet, then receded. Up the beach, kids played on rocks. Farther out in the water, long white rollers marked the place of crashing waves. The evening enshrouded, but from what I could make out, the swell had increased, the waves now easily over six feet high.

I saw Hartman again, tubes protruding from his mouth, death's grip now firm and unrelenting. Perspiration surfaced at my brow. I rubbed the back of my hand over it.

What am I doing here?

I turned back toward the bonfires and rubbed my eyes, opening them wide, trying to blink out the buzz. Trudging through the sand felt like lifting lead blocks, each step pulling me to the earth, enticing my resignation down to the dust.

A hooded figure emerged beyond the fires. He had to have been seven feet tall. Sickle in hand. Nothing made sense. I shook my head and blinked. He was gone, replaced by convective heat waving the air.

I squinted and made out the form of Geryon. I could ride back. I remembered the way.

I took three steps before I heard the screaming.

CHAPTER 7

The stake of reality drove down, pinning carelessness to the sand, stilling the drumbeats, and funneling the attention of the entire milieu on four frantic children waving wildly from the rocks, pointing at a youth swept off, now bobbing between frequent wave sets in the open water.

Soberness came like a flash flood. Adrenaline outpaced ethanol, my muscles and mind quickened. I'd learned to harness that epinephrine reflex, to temper it to my advantage. As the better part of the crowd froze with shock and then ran to the shoreline, I stood for a few seconds more, gauging what had transpired. The four kids remaining on the rocks were in immediate danger. The swell was now twice the size of what it had been just minutes before. The moon had peaked, yanking the tide upshore.

I heard a cry from the waves, distant and frantic. *"Ayúdeme! Ayúdeme!"*

I ran along the strip of beach farthest from the water, where the sand was more compact, and outraced the crowd to the rocks.

Waves exploded against outcroppings, blasting foam into the air, spraying my face, the taste of sea salt hitting my lips. Realizing their frail position, the kids scampered to get down, and before I knew it I was knee-deep in the water, Cormac beside me, plucking the children and passing them down a bucket brigade to safety.

The fifth still flailed in the water.

Three men charged out twenty feet, only to get rocked back by the waves. They stumbled ashore, weeping women waving their hands at them. I pulled my shoes off and ran into the breakers. The first few men had exhausted themselves trying to fight the ocean. But instead of trying to go over the waves, I dove in and down. The water was cool, enveloping me as I swam the breaststroke.

An outflowing current channel gave me a good path to swim until I had to duck dive beneath a series of larger waves. I pushed into them, watching moonlit bubbles form and roll overhead. The waves spat me out the back side, showering down droplets. I swam hard during a short lull, the horizon already rolling with the next silver-painted set.

No more than fifteen feet away, hands splashed. I had a matter of seconds before the waves would be upon us.

I may as well have been swimming in place. I stretched my arms and kicked my legs, but the water lifted, the waves came, and the hands I'd been watching sank beneath.

The pit of the first wave swelled and took me under the arms, lifting me skyward. I was caught off guard, and before I could act, the lip flipped me backward. It threw me head over end, knocking the wind from my lungs as I smacked the surface. Underwater it tossed me like laundry. I fought the urge to kick and flail and fight, instead forcing my body to relax and curl into a ball. The inertia pushed past me. I heard the thump of the second wave in the set. My lungs screamed for air. It felt as if someone had poured concrete down my windpipe.

Wait . . . just wait.

The energy passed over again.

A third wave hit. I couldn't wait any longer. I struggled for the surface and broke into the open air, gasping and spitting in a violent tossing of white foam and froth. A smaller breaker crashed over my head. The onslaught of the third wave barreled in. I had to get under it. Filling my lungs, I dove for the bottom, for the sweet sanctuary and calm of the ocean floor. I fought to get under the current and felt it alleviate once I was lower. The salt water made eye-opening easy, my way marked by moonbeams and morphing shadows.

And it was there that—as my oxygen waned and my new goal had become simply to survive—I saw the body of a boy, floating in the pallid light.

I wouldn't lose him this time.

I stroked with everything in me until I tackled his torso, swirling upward, kicking for the surface.

I broke the watery plane, seeing the stars and thinking that I should be able to recognize constellations. I clasped the boy to my chest, trying to suck in air and ending up with a mouthful of salt water, hacking and coughing. For a moment I was holding Hartman.

Water droplets clung to my eyelashes, blurring my vision. Voices shouted nearby. A wave lifted and thrust our bodies forward. We spun underwater. Nothing would separate me from him. Air found my lips again. I saw the dark forms of the rock outcroppings and several men waving and yelling. The tide lifted again, and I wasn't sure how, but my feet found solid ground. The water receded and a hand grabbed my arm. Men had to pry the boy from me. I couldn't think. I just knew to not let go.

But they got him. They ran with him. My strength was sapped. I could barely stand. I watched as the fires flickered and the beach stood aglow with the silhouetted shapes of people, and I felt like a failure because I couldn't take the boy to the sand myself. It was so close. I doubled over and retched, balancing on a nearby rock. I looked up and saw Cormac, his clothes soaked, his eyes wide.

And that's when I realized that I'd waited too long.

I turned to see a wave double my height towering overhead. The rocky surface I stood upon disappeared beneath the brimming mass. I was powerless to act as it lifted. For a moment I felt as though I were ascending.

The earth raced toward me and everything went black.

CHAPTER 8

I blinked and saw two silver-haired men. I blinked again and the duo unified. His hair grouped together in thick, damp strands combed backward. His gray-tipped eyebrows grew high and long, curving under their own weight, hooking back over brass-rimmed spectacles. Crooked teeth accentuated syllables behind moving lips and a clean-shaven jawline. He repositioned his glasses with his forefinger and thumb and glanced at me.

I clenched my teeth down on a plastic tube protruding from my mouth. It extended deep down my throat. I tried to talk but couldn't. I twisted and brought a hand to my face to yank it out.

Señor Eyebrows grabbed my wrist. *"Alaben al Señor!"* His grip was powerful. "No, no!"

I fought, but he held me down. Something like a searing hot cable yanked from my windpipe.

He rolled me to my side as I gasped, hacking and coughing, spitting mucus onto the floor.

Eyebrows pulled a stethoscope from his coat pocket. I felt

the cool ring of the bell housing upon my skin. *"Respira, amigo. Respira."* I inhaled deeply, moving air into the darkest recesses of my alveoli, opening sacs and stretching sinews. The rumblings of fluid sent me into another fit.

I quieted, chest heaving.

"Bien, bien," he said. "*Es* okay. *Es* okay. *Bien.*" He patted my back and sat me up. The room started to turn. My head fell against his chest. He embraced me. "*Alaben al Señor, amigo.* Praise the Lord."

Everything faded into reddish hues.

—

My eyes opened to a warm glow on the horizon. I saw a black-rimmed clock on the wall but couldn't tell time. The numbers didn't make sense. A plump woman in a dark dress stood beside me. I tried to ask if it was morning or evening, but my voice rasped and choked. She squeezed my hand and placed a needle in tubing taped to my arm. I caught another glimpse of Eyebrows, a white collar encircling his neck, an ebony sweater visible through his unbuttoned white coat. My eyes rolled back and my head sank into the pillow.

—

The fifth of November (as I was later told) greeted me like a mountain lake—brisk, clear, and new. No one was in the room this time. The tubing was gone from my arm. I sat up and swung my legs off the bed. Hot needles pricked inside my feet, then shifted to the sensation of heavy sand. I stretched and brushed my hand across a roll of gauze wrapped around my head, a dull throb now present in my skull.

A small nightstand held my personal effects: my wallet, car

keys, and cell phone. My luggage perched on the floor beside it. A total of seven other metal-framed single beds filled the room: four on the far wall, three others near, all empty, the sheets pressed and turned down. Footsteps echoed from a hallway opposite my bed, adjacent to the wall with the clock. Eyebrows emerged, this time without the white coat, only a black priest's garment and a book tucked under his arm. He adjusted his spectacles and smiled. *"Buenos Días, Señor O'Neill."*

I smiled. "Good morning to you, too." My voice sounded hoarse and strange. I took a deep breath, the passage of air unhindered by any rumblings. "So, make up my mind, are you a doctor or a priest?" It sounded like a bad joke.

His eyebrows pinched high on his brow. The plump woman, still clad in black, stepped beside him and placed a hand on his back. They exchanged words in Spanish.

She fixed on me a stare like a second-grade teacher. Her voice was stern, her English carrying only a mild accent. "The Lord is both our healer and teacher. Doctor Juarez merely emulates his Master."

The doctor walked to my bedside and spoke in unsteady English, "Please, call me Abraham."

I rubbed my eyes. "Okay, where am I, Abraham?"

"Está en La Casa de Vida Hospital, acerca de treinta kilómetros de Lazaro Cardenas."

Thirty kilometers. Memories of the beach, of the waves and the rocks . . . "Is the boy . . ."

"He is fine," the señora said.

Doctor Juarez asked her a couple questions in Spanish, a concerned look creasing his untamed eyebrows. He spoke insistently to her in an admonishing tone. She raised a hand and acquiesced, saying, *"Basta. Comprendo."* She pivoted and gave me the teacher stare. "He says that you saved the boy's life."

Juarez nudged her. "And," she said, "no one expected you to wake up. It is a miracle that you are alive. Doctor Perez, the only other physician for a hundred kilometers, just happened to be at the beach that night, fortunately for you. He resuscitated you after several men pulled you out of the water."

Juarez spoke again. Señora Plump translated. "You were dead, Mr. O'Neill. You drowned. Doctor Perez delivered CPR and something called a precordial thumb. With that he jolted your heart back to life."

I ran my hand over my sternum. "Did he bring me here? Where is my uncle?"

Doctor Juarez spoke a couple sentences. Señora Plump nodded, saying, "Your uncle stayed here two nights by your bedside." She pressed her lips together. "None of us thought you would even make it through the first night."

I got the impression that I had disappointed her. The señora was not a woman who liked to be wrong. I rubbed my chin and the bristles of a few days' old beard.

Doctor Juarez produced a folded paper from his pocket. *"Para usted, señor."*

It was a note from Cormac. It said how distraught he'd been. How he'd kept waiting for some positive sign. How he had a prior business engagement he couldn't break. That he'd be back by the end of the week. That he knew I was in the best hands with Doctor Juarez.

I rested the note on my lap and exhaled. My cell phone vibrated on the table, jingling my key ring.

"Excuse me," I said, and flipped it open.

Chief Mauvain's unmistakable voice blurted from the other end, "Aidan, where have you been?"

I cleared my throat. "There's no quick answer to that one, Chief." *Why is he calling me?* "Didn't you put me on a two-week suspension?" I stole a glance at the señora. She squinted a disapproving stare.

"Forget about it, Aidan. You're officially back on. We've been running like the devil up here. Two, three fires a day. The department's staffing extra rigs, and we've exhausted the overtime list. We can't get enough people to come in. So show up for work and we'll consider it early release for good behavior."

I took a moment to process it all.

"Aidan?"

"One sec, Chief." I stood, to make sure I could. The throbbing in my head was marginally bearable. My vision wasn't blurry anymore. I swung my arms across my chest and tilted my head side to side. Self-diagnostic checked out. I was good enough to go.

Juarez put out his hands. *"Siéntese, por favor."*

"Aidan?" the chief said again.

"Yeah, Chief, I'll come in."

"Great. I'll see you downtown in an hour."

I looked out the window, across the dry Mexican landscape. "Um, I'm not going to be able to get there today, Chief."

"What?"

"I'm in Mexico."

"Mexico?"

"Yeah."

"Well, get here as soon as you can. And make sure it's before shift starts tomorrow morning."

CHAPTER 9

Ten minutes after midnight I opened my front door. Candlelight glowed from the kitchen counters. A fire crackled and waved in my fireplace, and the sound of sobbing coursed from the living room. Christine sat on the couch, elbows on knees and her head bowed, fingers woven through raven-black hair cut to sharp angles. Her shoulders shook. A photo album lay open in front of her. An empty wine glass rested on the coffee table with a dark red ring around the base.

I stood where the carpet met the hardwood floor. "Hey."

She looked up, cheeks glistening, eyes red and swollen. "Aidan" was all she could manage, jaw trembling and cheeks tightening.

I dropped the travel bag I'd been carrying and walked up to her with arms out, tentative at first. She stood and embraced me, burying her head in my shoulder.

"It's all right." Words felt inadequate. "Hey, it's all right."

She pushed me away. "No. No, it's not, Aidan." She wiped her cheeks.

"You're right. I . . . I haven't been there like I should. I've been wrapped up in other things. But this, us, this is what's most important." It came out sounding like I was trying to convince myself.

She shook her head, new tears falling. "It's too late. . . ."

"No. Don't say that." I stepped closer.

She put up her hands.

I held mine out. "Let's work this out."

"It's past that point."

"I can fix this, Christine. We can be together. I'll work harder."

She turned aside.

I tilted my head to see her eyes. "Don't give up on us. You're here. We . . . I need you. I need you with me."

"So, it's about you, then?"

"No. No, of course not. It's about us. We need each other." I ran my hands over my chin, tilting my head toward the ceiling. "You have no idea what kind of week I've just had."

"As if you have the slightest idea what kind of *year* I have had."

"I didn't mean that to be a criticism."

She turned to me, brow tight. "Then what did you mean, Aidan?"

My mouth moved, but I couldn't find words.

"How long has it been?" she said. "What, six years? How come I still don't even know you?"

"Of course you know me."

"I don't. I don't get you, Aidan. You . . ." She pointed at my chest. "You've been consumed with something and it hasn't been me."

I felt the pot lid clattering inside. "What, so keeping on with

Dad's investigation is somehow equivalent to putting you on the back burner?"

"This is way more than that."

"I can't believe you are actually jealous. You're being so self-centered. Blake and I are the only reason the case is even still open."

"Don't try to blame this on your father again."

"I'm not blaming it on anyone. You're the one who's being unbending and uncompassionate."

"It's hard to have compassion for someone who's never there, Aidan."

An ashen log broke in the fireplace, sending spark flurries up the flue.

"I'm not an eight to fiver, Christine. You knew that getting into this."

She tightened her lips and looked away.

"You keep trying to fit me into some preconceived notion of a husband in your head."

"Obviously a role you've never seriously considered."

"You have a ring, don't you?" This plane was edging toward a nosedive.

She twisted and pulled on her finger and held the diamond up in front of me. "What is this to you?"

I shook my head. "It's your engagement ring."

"*My* engagement ring?"

"Okay. Ours."

"For engagement?"

"Yes. What? What are you getting at, Christine?"

"Exactly that. That is all this has ever been to you. A never-ending engagement."

"You know that's not true."

"Did you ever intend to actually marry me?"

This was ridiculous. "What do you think I gave you the ring for?"

"I don't know, Aidan. Why haven't we set a date? Are you afraid? Why can't you move forward with anything in your life?" She looked down at the table. "You can't, can you? Not with your father. Not with the case. Not with us." She held the ring over the wineglass and dropped it, clinking to the bottom.

"You're not giving me a chance."

"A chance for what, Aidan?" Her lips pressed in a frown. "You've lost my heart."

I was supposed to fix this. "Let me find it again."

She shook her head.

"Let's start again." I bent my head to catch her eyes. "Let's . . . we can build again." I—"

"Nothing's going to change. Maybe you can't see that. But I can."

"Just believe in me."

"Why, Aidan? Why do I need to believe in you? What do you even believe in?"

Her words stung. "I . . ."

"I shouldn't have to explain this to you. I can't . . ." She exhaled and crossed her arms.

I dropped to the couch and rubbed my eyebrows with the heels of my palms. She was just quicker to acknowledge what we'd both known for some time. What I'd always known deep in my heart.

"If you're not obsessing about your father's case," she said, her voice steady and chilled, "you're working another extra shift, running into fires with no regard for reason or your future. You can't raise a family that way. You're in a self-destructive cycle, and I won't be a part of it. Not anymore."

Wind funneled down the chimney.

"Your father's dead, Aidan. Just accept it."

Anger surged through me. I snatched the wineglass and threw it in the fireplace. It shattered against the brick, shards refracting and flashing yellow.

I stood shaking, turning my hands up in the heat and light, staring at the scar in my palm. I clenched my fist. "I miss him so much."

Hot tears welled. Everything in my life was slipping from my grip. Out of my control. "He . . . he always knew what to do." I took a deep, shuddering breath. "With him . . . in everything. It didn't matter. The world could crumble but he would be standing." I squeezed my eyes shut and tears streamed down. I opened them to see the picture on the mantel of me at five years old, on my father's shoulders, wearing his helmet, him grinning that unfailing grin. Shadows flickered. "But it did crumble." I dried my cheeks with my sleeve. "And now he's gone. And no one knows why." The fire popped. Sap bubbled.

I turned around to an empty living room, the kitchen door hanging ajar.

CHAPTER 10

Captain Butcher's voice called over Station One's loudspeaker, "Roll call."

I crossed the third-floor dayroom and pushed through the blue swinging door to the kitchen. The air wafted warm, filled with the din of laughter and clattering pans and coffee pouring into ceramic cups and the underlying hum of two commercial refrigerators. The north wall was all windows and the city sprawled out beyond with new morning mist and dark diesel exhaust and the quiet motion of small cars on linear streets. Across the room, a red sign with white lettering hung on the pole-hole door: *In Case of Fire Use Stairs.*

"A-O." Lowell Richmond leaned his chair forward from the west wall, his wispy brown hair tousled, face unshaven, with purple crescents doubled under his eyes. He shifted the newspaper into his left hand and extended his right. "Glad to see you survived your purgatory."

I smiled and shook his hand. "Man, if you only knew. This place keeping you busy enough?"

"It's been crazy."

I lowered my voice. "How's Hartman? Heard anything?"

He nodded. "I went in yesterday with a couple guys. He's still on a vent."

My heart sank.

"But—" He coughed. "They said that's only to fully drain the blood from his lung cavities and let the ribs heal up. So they're keeping him sedated."

"So, he's not . . ."

"Gonna die? No way, man. You guys got him out in time. CT scans are otherwise clear. Just the hemothoraxes and a bad concussion."

I took a deep breath and looked around the room. Chris Waits, a stocky Asian man with a black handlebar moustache, strolled over from the coffee maker.

Lowell leaned back against the wall. "Don't let the second-floor Admin screw with you, man. I know you guys were just trying to do your job."

"What's up, Mr. O'Neill," Waits said with a pat. "Good to have you back." He nodded toward Lowell. "This guy already boring you with stories about his tank?"

I looked at Lowell. "You bought a tank?"

His eyes lit up.

Waits sat and placed his mug on the table. "You know, and I'll say it again, there is the world we live in and the world Lowell lives in."

Lowell leaned his chair forward and lifted his hands. "What? C'mon, Chris."

Beside Waits sat John Peyton, a tall, solidly built man in his thirties. He looked up from his paper with eyes tinted red at the edges. He nodded with a smile. "Hey, Aidan."

Lowell looked as if he was fighting to hold back a grin. "And you know what the best part about it is?"

Waits lifted his coffee mug. "I don't know, but I'm sure you're going to tell me."

"It's street legal."

Waits stared at him. "You're kiddin' me."

Lowell shook his head and laughed, tapping the table with his free hand. "And it fits in a standard-sized garage."

"Now I know you're crazy." He took a sip.

"No, see, it's a light-armored reconnaissance tank. They're made for cruising over any kind of terrain. It—" He glanced in his empty coffee cup. "Where's our new new kid?"

"Right here, sir." A slim blond fireman stood at semi-attention by the table holding an empty coffeepot.

Peyton looked at him sideways. "At ease there, son. We'll be in the area all day." He set down his paper. "You from Hartman's class?"

"Yes, sir."

"How is he?"

"I saw him this morning, and it's looking like he may come off the vent soon."

"That's good to hear."

Waits shifted in his seat. "What's your name?"

"Brian Sortish, sir."

"Sortish?" Lowell said.

"Good to meet you." Waits shook his hand. "I'm Chris. Now, let me ask you a question." He motioned across the table. "You believe anything this guy says?"

Sortish laughed and threw an uncomfortable glance at Lowell.

"See," Waits said. "Even the new kid thinks you're full of—"

"We got everybody here?" Butcher called out, holding a sheet of paper.

Sortish extended his hand to Lowell. "Hi, I'm Brian."

"Yeah, I know," Lowell said. "I was right here when you just told Waits. You know how to make coffee?"

"Yes, sir."

"Why don't you?"

I scratched my forehead and glanced at the floor. Requisite rite of passage for a probie.

Brian nodded and spun around. "I'll get on that."

Waits shook his head. "Sheeze, Lowell. You're such—"

"Okay, people, let's get this roll call done so we all know who's where and doing what."

"Don't worry, Butcher," Lowell said. "We'll help you out. You are currently in the kitchen, and today you get to ride on the big red engine with all the yellow hoses. And if you're really good, maybe Aidan will even let you talk on the radio."

A swell of laughter rolled through the room. Peyton shook his head and smiled at his coffee.

"Thank you, Lowell." Butcher stroked his moustache. "Now that I am apparently all squared away, let's go ahead and run down rig and house-duty assignments for everyone else."

Lowell leaned on the table. "You got that coffee made, Swordfish?"

"Sortish," he said.

More chuckles.

"I'm working on it."

"New kid's got coffee, Butcher."

"Yes, all right. Thank you again, Lowell."

Waits lowered his newspaper and looked at Lowell. "Would you shut up?"

Lowell deferred and sat back.

A voice spoke from a far table. "And tell him not to make it rocket fuel like Kat likes it."

Operator Katrina Breckenridge glanced up. She leaned back on the island, silver-streaked hair tied in a ponytail, stirring a spoon in a mug. She squinted her eyes at the man who'd made the remark. "You just can't take it, you big—"

"We're never gonna get through this," Butcher said.

"All right, all right. Sorry, Mark." She smiled at him. "You go ahead."

"Engine One is myself, Kat's driving, Aidan O'Neill and Timothy Clark are the firemen. Truck One is Captain Sower—"

"Where is he, anyway?" Kat said.

"He's tied up talking with Mauvain."

"New info on the fires?" Waits said.

"You know"—Lowell leaned forward— "Mauvain called up here about ten minutes ago, and I swear I could smell the starch through the phone."

Laughs rumbled. The kitchen door swung open and the room fell silent.

Battalion Chief Mauvain stepped in, his football-sized brass belt buckle leading the way. "Morning, all." His tone held the icy candor of someone whose ears had just been burning.

Behind him, appearing to be half his width, stood a slender woman in a white lab coat. A jolt shot through my solar plexus. She had azure eyes that glowed in a frame of light chestnut hair. I was confident that I didn't know who she was, I had no idea of her name, and yet my instinct was that somehow I knew her. Her simple elegance and beauty left Mauvain looking like a shaven Cro-Magnon in a frumpy white badge shirt.

The chief cleared his throat and turned to Butcher. "Captain, mind if we move this meeting into the dayroom?"

CHAPTER 11

I crossed to the wall opposite the windows and sat back in a mustard yellow lounge chair, the kind with a chrome frame and rubber cushions. The more senior guys took up residence in the newer recliners along the walls. Mauvain was all about throwing his weight around, and by changing rooms he'd shifted the momentum. His smug expression showed that he knew it.

Miss Lab Coat stood in front of the chalkboard, her arms crossed. Thin white sunlight traced her profile, lending a crisp brilliance to her features. She scanned the room before catching my eye. I smiled, but she looked away, staring at the glass-framed fire patch collection on the far wall as though it had morphed into butterflies.

My cell phone vibrated.

"Hello?"

"Aidan? It's Cormac. I'm so glad to hear your voice! Where are you?"

"Hey. I'm actually at work."

"At work? I can't believe it. I came back to the hospital and they said you'd already left. I couldn't believe it."

Timothy Clark hit my arm, nodding toward Miss Lab Coat. "You know her?"

I shook my head.

"I hated to leave," Cormac said. "They were talking like the coma could be permanent."

"Come on, now," Timothy whispered. "Do tell, do tell."

"Cormac, can I call you back? I'm in a big meeting right now."

"No problem, bud. It's just great to know you're alive."

"Absolutely. We'll talk later." I hung up and pocketed my phone.

"Beauford Maddox Biltman," Mauvain boomed, commanding the room like a Shakespearean orator. *He'd make a good Macbeth. Or maybe Richard the Third.* He held up a photo of a firebug I recognized from a couple years earlier. "Convicted arsonist in the Fourth Street fires, if you recall."

Lowell laughed. "If that ain't an arsonist's name, I don't know what is."

Mauvain flashed a look at Lowell like an old cat toward a puppy. "Due to certain legalities, a wealthy family with skillful lawyers"—he was counting off with his fingers—"the overcrowding problem at the jail, and I don't know, probably a politician in there somewhere, Biltman, believe it or not, is now free."

Voices muddled through the room.

Waits raised his hand.

"Quiet, please." Mauvain pointed to Waits. "Chris?"

"How long has he been out now?"

"Three weeks."

Kat retied her ponytail. "Is he living downtown again?"

"My understanding is that he's renting a one bedroom off of East Taylor."

Waits folded his arms across his chest. "Right back in District One."

"Yes," Mauvain said. "Which is why I wanted you all to see this. I know we've been getting beat up around here. Some of you haven't been home for four or five days. But I need your eyes and your vigilance. These fires are not only increasing in frequency, but with an intensity that I personally have not witnessed in my career." He motioned to Miss Lab Coat. "In lieu of Investigator Blake Williams, who is still out at the scene of last night's fire, I've asked recently hired prevention analyst Julianne Caldwell to share a bit about the latest test results that support the mounting case for Biltman as the prime suspect."

Julianne stepped forward. Her quiet demeanor gave way to a confident delivery. "Essentially, the latest lab tests conducted affirm that the recent fires are in fact arson, and are related to each other." Her voice stirred in me the sense of hearing an old, old song, like one from an heirloom music box that only comes out at Christmastime. "We still know very little about the incendiary method being used. But we do know this—recent fires have been burning hotter and faster, and the risk for flashover is exponentially higher. One second the fire is in its incipient phase, the next second the entire place flashes into flame."

Timothy Clark leaned forward. "So, we don't know what's causing it to do that?"

She shook her head. "I'm afraid not. Not yet."

The ceiling speaker chirped. A female dispatcher's voice came over. "Battalion One, please landline dispatch."

Mauvain glanced at the ceiling and then at Julianne. "Thank you, Ms. Caldwell." He put his hands together. "Well, that's it for now. You guys are doing a good job. Stay heads-up and be safe." He started toward the stairwell and pulled a cell phone from his belt.

Captain Butcher stood. "All right. Let's get to morning checks and house duties."

Guys stretched and conversation resumed.

Timothy Clark turned to me. "I'll clean the north bathrooms if you've got the south ones."

I nodded. He disappeared down the hall toward the dorms. My stomach growled, so I made for the kitchen and found a couple heel slices of bread wrapped in plastic in the free-for-all bowl on the counter. I pushed the handle down for the toaster and watched the metal wires glow red-hot, feeling the warmth on my face.

"Excuse me," a voice said from across the room. "Do you know where . . ." Julianne stopped when I turned around. "Never mind," she said, and walked over to a set of cabinets, opening and closing doors.

"Are you looking for something?"

"I'm fine." She opened and closed two more cabinets. "Thank you."

"Coffee cup?"

She closed three lower doors and exhaled. She kept her back to me. "Yes."

"Second top cabinet from the right."

She threw her hands in the air and muttered, "Of course, the one I didn't check."

My toast popped up. I grabbed a couple paper napkins and set them on it. "So, sounds like you've had your hands full with the new job."

She pulled down a mug and walked to the coffee maker. "Yep."

I buttered the toast and watched her from the corner of my eye. She poured the coffee and stared at it. Her shoulders slumped.

"Creamer?" I said.

She turned her head to the side and gave a slight nod.

"Fridge to your right. First door."

She fished out the half-and-half.

I set the butter knife down. "You new to this area?"

She stopped pouring and held the creamer carton in the air for a moment, then added a splash more. "I've been out of state for a while."

"Oh. Nearby?"

"Northern California."

I bit into my toast and stared at her, chewing.

"Thank you," she said, raising the coffee mug.

I swallowed my bite. "My pleasure."

She gave a quick polite smile and moved to the door, stopping to look out the window. "It hasn't changed that much."

"Did you grow up here?"

She seemed to be looking more inward than out. "There's always more going on than what you see on the surface."

I stepped to the island. "This probably sounds canned, but . . . you seem really familiar."

She opened her mouth to say something, then shut it. She pushed on the door. "Have a good day, Firefighter O'Neill."

"Wait. How do you know my name?"

She disappeared into the dayroom.

Tones cycled from the ceiling-mounted speaker.

A woman's voice echoed. "Battalion One, Engine One, Engine Two, Engine Four, Truck One, Rescue One with the safety officer to a structure fire—smoke and flames seen coming from the front of a residence."

My heart rate quickened. I opened the kitchen pole-hole door. The brushed-steel cylinder stretched from the ceiling to three floors down. I felt the cool metal on my palms and dropped through the circle of air.

CHAPTER 12

Across the apparatus bay it rained firemen.

My head pounded with my pulse. I stepped into my turn-out boots, pulled up my suspenders, and hopped in the back. Kat shot out of the barn and I threw on my coat, falling back into the rear-facing jumpseat. The ladder truck followed us with the rescue behind it. Chief Mauvain trailed caboose in a screaming train weaving down Evans Avenue.

I worked my arms through the shoulder straps of the seat-mounted air pack, standing to tighten the straps. The engine jerked, and I slammed against the door.

Butcher bent around from the front. "Get seated back there."

I cinched the waist belt and dropped back into the seat. Timothy cranked on his air valve.

Butcher pointed. "Left here on Spokane."

"I got it," Kat said. "I'll get you there. I'll get you water."

She pulled to a stop just past a hundred-year-old two-story

house on my side of the rig. Butcher reported a wood-framed structure with an A-frame roof and heavy smoke showing.

The air brake snapped and hissed. I opened my door and hopped out. Everything felt right, back in step.

Until I saw the fire.

Black smoke rolled out the front door, swirling liquid fire chasing it down a darkened hallway. Two opalescent eyes formed within the flame. The fire morphed, and the world around it shadowed into a Mexican beach, bonfires raging—and there in the doorway stood the sickle-gripping reaper waving with the heat. A vacuum opened in my gut. I stepped back and collided with Kat.

"Look out, Aidan."

I rubbed my eyes. Timothy hopped on the sideboard and put his arm through the hose loops. The fire was on my side, and he had beat me to the nozzle. He yanked the hose load to the pavement and winked at me, taking off up the walkway. The wind shifted and he vanished into the smoke-filled air.

Butcher walked in front of me, radio held by his ear. He slapped my shoulder. "Find the seat and knock it down before this whole thing flashes."

The ladder truck turned the corner, Peyton spinning the rear steering wheel in the tiller cab.

Kat shoved the handle of my flathead axe across my chest. "Am I going to have to do everything for you guys?"

I grabbed the smooth linseeded handle with its familiar dark hickory veins.

My father's axe . . .

She grabbed my jacket and pushed me toward the house. "Wake up, Aidan!"

Kat circled around to the pump panel and shouted, "Water comin'!"

It snaked through the flat hose fabric, swelling it solid. I slid the axe into my belt sheath and strode up the walkway. The nozzle jerked forward in Timothy's grip, pointing at the doorway like a dog to its catch. Timothy pointed it at the side of the house and bled the air from the line with a *hiss-splash.* The heat was palpable. I knelt and strapped on my mask as flames wicked around the doorframe. Timothy crawled in, his boots assimilating into the smoke.

Sheol sucked him in.

I swore I heard laughter. Panic raced down my windpipe. The hose line inched inward like a python.

I couldn't leave Timothy. I pulled on my gloves.

Fire erupted at the ceiling, bulbous and rolling up the building side. I hit the floor and clambered in. Timothy's coat took shape in front of me.

He yanked on the line. "There's a glow back there."

I nodded and grabbed a coupling. We pushed deeper in. Fire rippled above like an inverted river.

Cormac's voice echoed in my head. *"Its sole desire is to consume."*

Timothy took a kneeling position at the doorway to a raging back room. The hallway temperature neared unbearable heights. I held the hose behind him and leaned my shoulder into his back. His torso shifted as he opened the bale and the water stream shot out. He swept it across the ceiling and circled it around the room.

The fire danced. It mocked. It shot from the room with wicked lit fingers, clawing and scratching, curling around my air bottle. It tugged at me, pulling me to it. Flame edges whipped down the walls, forming a sickle in the air, swinging in a slow arc down toward my sternum.

I had to get out.

I turned and bolted, colliding with Butcher, knocking him to his rear. The smoke spazzed and scurried. I glanced back to see the fire darken in the room. The atmosphere cooled, lightening from black to gray. Someone outside broke a window. A fan started on the porch, pushing the haze past us.

Butcher made his feet and stared at me through his mask. He held a radio mic by his facepiece. "Battalion One, Attack Group. We have knockdown." He broke his gaze and walked past me.

Timothy worked the hose line into the room, hitting hot spots with short bursts of water. I stood as the truck guys scooted by, tools in hand. Lead-colored smoky wisps vacillated and wove in front of my mask. I leaned against the wall and took off my helmet.

Nothing made sense anymore.

CHAPTER 13

The wrinkles beside Benjamin Sower's eyes looked like rays of the sun in a child's drawing.

I dropped my turnout boots from the back of the rig to the app-bay floor. "That is definitely a Captain Sower joke."

He grinned, his broad shoulders shaking as he chuckled. "Well now, what else would a cow without any lips say?"

I shook my head and smiled at the floor. "I guess 'Ooo' is it."

He laughed again, the fluorescent lights casting a dull sheen over his bald head.

I climbed down and hung my suspenders over the chrome bar beside the door. My turnout pants were dank and thick with the smell of smoke. "So what did you learn on the second floor?"

He hooked his thumbs under his suspenders. "That I'm glad I work on the third."

I laughed. It sounded like a pressure relief valve off-gassing. "Come on now, Ben. We go way back. What's the inside story?"

"We do go way back. As far back as you go. I was there the day you were born, remember?"

"Strangely enough I don't recall a whole lot about that day."

"Your father's wry sense of humor lives on, I see."

I didn't want to talk about my father. "So tell me."

"All I know is that the pressure from city hall to find this firebug is building."

I nodded. "And today's fire—"

"Probably."

I swallowed. As far as I was concerned, any arsonist could be *the* arsonist, the one who set my father's fatal fire.

Ben shifted his stance. "So, have you seen the garden out back?"

"Um, yeah, actually. That corn looks pretty high. Kind of weird, right there in the middle of the city."

"I'm really happy with that. Last tour someone took off with a couple ears. And that's fine. If they need it that bad, they can have it. I'll grow more. Or *God* will. He provides." His face turned solemn. His voice quieted. "Aidan, on a different note, I have been a bit concerned for you."

Alarms of suspicion rang in my head. He had just come from talking with the chiefs. "*You've* been concerned? Or did somebody come to you who was concerned about me?"

"No. No one came to me."

My face must have betrayed my skepticism, because he said, "My talk with Mauvain had nothing to do with this. I just . . . I haven't had the chance to talk with you since the whole thing with Hartman. I've felt a burden for you in prayer."

He and my dad had been best friends. I had so many memories of him from growing up—Bible studies at our house, barbecues, birthday parties. Even then he didn't have hair.

I patted him on the shoulder. "Thanks, Ben. Really. I appreciate the concern."

He waited.

He knew me too well. I shook my head. "You know, I should have made a better judgment call. We just got into a hairy situation. But Hartman's going to be all right, and that's what matters." Somehow the words sounded false as they fell from my lips, bearing a hollow timbre of rationalization. I was sure he could see through it. I blurted, "I've just been off my game a bit since I came back. I'll get it back though. I just stutter-stepped a bit on this last fire."

Ben sat on the sideboard, nodding slowly, as if he were part of a conference call and listening to another party. He brought his elbow up and rested it on the intake manifold. "It's not like you to feel off your game."

"No. I know. But it happens to all of us, right?" I zipped up my station boots and draped my uniform pant leg over them. "Like a batting slump. I'm just thrown off my rhythm."

"Remember Wade Boggs, Aidan?"

I straightened. "Sure. Yeah. One of the best batters ever."

"Yes. While not a model of moral fortitude, he was in fact one of the all-time best. He was also extremely superstitious. Had to eat chicken before every game. Had to always have batting practice at the exact same time. He had these habits he was committed to following to keep himself on his game. But you know what? I bet you none of that had much to do with why he hit so well."

"Why do you think?"

"Twenty-twelve vision. He could see the ball like no one else. He came built that way. He possessed a gift."

I studied the soot-stained and heat-discolored number 1 on the engine's side.

"So do you, Aidan. I saw it in your father, and I've seen it in you."

An emptiness augered into my gut. I noticed my hand trembling and crossed my arms over my chest. The gift hadn't saved my dad. What hope did I have? I ran my hand over the warped number 1. "What happens if you can't rely on that gift anymore?"

He breathed in. It seemed like a mix between knowing he'd made a connection and realizing that now he had to deliver some answers. He spun the wedding ring on his finger and looked up. "There isn't one of us who doesn't need to learn how to better place his trust in something, or some*one*, outside of himself."

"What if there isn't anyone you can trust?"

"You know there is, Aidan. You've known it since you were—"

Tones.

"Engine One to a medical emergency, seizure. Haley's Casino. Use the air curtain entrance on Virginia."

I threw my turnouts in the back. "I'll see ya, Benjamin."

He stepped back from the rig. "We'll talk later."

I nodded and closed my door. Katrina fired up the engine and Lowell Richmond hopped up into Timothy's seat.

"What're you doing here?" I asked as I pulled on my seat belt. "Waits finally kick you off the Q?"

He threw his turnouts on the floor. "Yeah, I needed a break from rescue, and Timothy owed me."

Kat rolled the rig out and flicked on the lights, looking both ways on Evans. Butcher put us en route over the radio and flipped on the grinder siren. All westbound lanes on Second were stacked, so Kat took oncoming traffic, blaring the air horn. Cars acquiesced by moving to the side.

She weaved the rig through the intersection. "Did the off-going crew mention anything about an issue with the brakes?"

Butcher scratched his cheek. "There was something in pass-on about the mechanic coming to check on a little air leak today. Just make sure you keep her plugged into the air line back at the station."

Kat gave him an impatient look that said, *Please.* "You know I always do."

A white-shirted security guard stood at the casino entrance. We pulled to a stop by the curb.

I snatched the defib and the blue bag from the med compartment that held all the intermediate life-support medications and tools. Lowell swung the red first-out bag over his shoulder with its oxygen bottle and basic life-support supplies. Butcher stepped down to the sidewalk, then turned and climbed back into the cab to grab his small steel clipboard.

"C-P-R, Mark," Lowell said.

Butcher looked up. "What?"

"Clipboard. Pen. Radio. C-P-R. What good is a captain without them?"

Butcher's face changed from surprise to frustration. "I thought you meant we had a cardiac arrest, Lowell."

Lowell elbowed him. "Glad to have me back, aren't ya, Marky?"

We walked from the street through the heated air curtain to the casino floor. Mirrored pillars flashed our reflections. James Brown's "The Big Payback" filled the room from planter-hidden speakers. Stoic-looking overweight people sat and played slots under advertisements of happy-looking fit people playing slots. Security snaked us through to an elevator that another guard kept open with a key.

Butcher turned to the first officer. "The paramedics are still coming, too."

He looked back toward the doors and then spoke into a black microphone on his shoulder.

The guard in the elevator was young and pale with a narrow chin and greasy dark hair. His long bony fingers fumbled with a doughnut-sized key ring that sported about a hundred keys. He talked to himself, turning the emergency operation key left then right. "Ah, let's see. Okay. Well, no. Okay." We stopped at floors three, four, and six to the semi-alarmed stares of hotel guests before taking our nonstop trip to floor seventeen.

Butcher peeked at the run sheet. "Should be seventeen twenty-two."

We filed out of the elevator, Lowell after me, until the door closed, sandwiching him from shoulder to first-out bag.

Bony Fingers flinched and cringed and pushed about six buttons in a frenzy. "Sorry. Oh, right. Sorry."

Lowell worked his way loose. The doors came together behind him. "If that guy's still here when we get back, I'm taking the stairs."

CHAPTER 14

The hallway smelled like air-freshener-suppressed cigarette smoke. A busy flower pattern wove through the middle of a dark green carpet. Butcher stopped by a door on our right. "Seventeen twenty-two. Here we go." He stood to the side and knocked. "Fire Department."

It was a standard practice, standing to the side of the door. You never knew who might be holding some kind of weapon on the inside. The sliding of a latch sounded.

A middle-aged woman with dangling turquoise earrings answered. "He's right in here. Over here."

A man lay supine in bed, wearing a white collared shirt that fell open to the covers. His receding hairline was rimmed with sweat and his cheeks were flushed. Dried blood stained the corners of his lips.

I set down the defib and felt for a radial pulse. It was strong, regular, and rapid—around a hundred and twenty beats per minute.

The television flickered in silence. Meteorologist Mike Alger pointed and drew arrows along the Pacific Coast.

Lowell shook the man's shoulder. "Sir, sir, can you open your eyes?"

I wrapped the Velcro blood pressure cuff around his bicep. He grunted and mumbled and withdrew his arms.

Lowell held open the patient's eyelids and shone a light in his pupils. They were sluggish and about two millimeters. He pocketed the penlight. "What is his name, ma'am?"

"Gregory. But he goes by Greg."

"And what is his last name?"

"Sutton."

He rubbed Greg's sternum with his knuckles. "Mr. Sutton. Greg? Can you open your eyes for me?"

Greg moved his arm to his chest. I trailed after it with the bell of the stethoscope. Lowell flashed me an apologetic look. He fished out an oxygen mask from the first-out bag and placed it on Greg's face.

I pulled the stethoscope from my ears. "One thirty over seventy."

He wrote it on his glove. "Ma'am, what is your relation to Greg?"

She twisted her hands as if they were stuck in a finger puzzle, and her earrings waggled as she answered. "I'm his wife."

"Does he have a history of seizures?"

"Not for some time."

"But he has in the past?"

"Yes."

"Is he taking any medication for it?"

Butcher stepped forward with an empty pill bottle. "Dilantin. Looks like it's due for a refill."

"That's right," Earrings said. "We ran out two days ago, but we don't know any doctors in this area."

Lowell handed me an IV bag and looked up at Earrings. "How long did his seizure last?"

"About a minute, maybe."

"Can you show me what it looked like?"

I flashed a look at him. He had no need for her to actually show him what the seizure looked like. He clenched his teeth, determined not to smile.

"Well"—Earrings stiffened her body and brought her arms to her chest—"first his eyes rolled back, and then it was like this." She tightened her jaw and started to vibrate. The shaking traveled down her arms, progressing into a whole body convulsion.

It was impressive.

Lowell pressed his lips together and nodded. "Thank you. That's perfect. Thank you so much."

Butcher turned his back to Lowell and placed a hand on Earrings's shoulder. "Ma'am, we'll keep your husband on oxygen to clear up his head, start an IV, and check his blood sugar. The paramedics should be here soon, and we'll go from there."

She looked at her husband's face. "I've never seen him this bad."

I bled the air from the IV tubing. Lowell placed a tourniquet on Greg's arm, causing the veins to bulge and swell. He uncapped a needle and guided it to pierce Greg's skin, like a diver into shallow water. He slid the catheter into the vein, pulled out the needle, and placed it on the nightstand. "Sharp out."

I held the IV bag in the air and rolled the white plastic wheel upward, watching the fluid flush into Greg's arm. Lowell taped it all in place as the paramedics walked in the door.

Butcher plunged a drop of blood from the needle onto a glucometer strip. "One fifteen on the sugar."

Earrings rubbed her dangling turquoise as if it were a magic lamp. "Is that normal?"

Lowell smiled. "Yeah. That's just fine."

She exhaled.

Butcher gave the medics the rundown.

Greg blinked and stared at his feet. He pulled the mask from his face to his forehead. "Who are you people?"

"Honey, it's me," his wife said, taking his hand. "It's okay. They're here to help you."

His eyes locked in recognition. "Why? Who needs help?"

"It's the ambulance, Greg. They're here to help you."

"I don't need any . . ." He darted glances around the room. "What's going on?"

His wife patted his hand. "You had a big seizure. You need more of your medicine."

Greg rubbed his forehead. The mask snapped off his head. He stared at it and then the IV in his forearm. He worked to pull the tape off with his free hand.

"No, no, honey," she said, shaking her head. "Don't do that."

The medic held Greg's arm down and put a palm over the IV site.

Greg whipped his head and stared at him. "What are you doing? Don't do that."

I glanced at Lowell. He stood at the foot of the bed, his arms hovering over Greg's legs.

The medic released Greg's arm. "Here's the deal, Mr. Sutton. You need to get your Dilantin levels checked. Why don't you do like your wife is suggesting and let us take you on in to the hospital? She can ride with you the entire way. What do you say?"

He breathed out through his nose, protest written on his face. His eyes turned to his wife, confusion and resignation brimming. But then I saw something I hadn't seen in Christine for a long time. Something foreign yet familiar. It locked between them like a three-corded rope.

Trust.

"Okay." Greg nodded, tears streaming. He squeezed his wife's hands. "Okay."

Lowell patted my shoulder and motioned toward the door. "Let's get the gurney."

CHAPTER 15

The rig jostled over the Evans Avenue potholes on our way back to the station. My cell phone vibrated and I flipped off my headset. "Hello?"

"Aidan, how's it going?"

I recognized Blake's voice. "Hey, man. They keeping you busy enough in Prevention?"

"Honestly, it's crazy. How about you? Nothing like a series of fires for cutting short your leave without pay, huh?"

Nothing like an old friend to hit you where it hurts. "Yeah, thanks."

"How's things going with that? You and old Butcher make up? You like best friends now, or what?"

I laughed. "Right."

"Mauvain knocking on your door, wanting to go fishing and have barbecues?"

"Man, just shut up."

"All right, all right, seriously though. Everything okay? I mean, Hartman and everything?"

I was tired of talking about it. Tired of thinking about it. "Yeah. You know, I'm actually in the rig right now on the way back from a call."

"I got you. Other ears present. Hey, I was actually wondering if we could get together for lunch. There's something I needed to talk to you about, and I'd feel best if we could meet in person."

I had the sensation in my chest that you get on an airplane with a sudden change in altitude. "Oh, okay. Of course. I'm on shift all day today. Can you come downtown? I'm not sure what we're making for lunch yet."

"Right. You just said you were on the rig, too. You know . . . it's probably better that we meet alone. How about tomorrow morning instead? I'll buy you coffee."

What is he guarding? "Yeah, all right. Just give me a ring around eight."

"I'll see you tomorrow."

I flipped the phone closed. What was so private he couldn't risk anyone at the firehouse overhearing?

Back at the station I hiked the stairs to the third floor. Ben Sower stood in the dayroom talking with Julianne. They were focused in conversation and didn't notice me.

Julianne's voice raised a bit. "It's great to see you again, too." She gave Ben a hug and turned for the door, stopping when she realized her path would intersect mine.

"Still here?" I said.

She looked down and to the side. "I was just leaving."

I didn't mean it to sound as if she was unwelcome. "No rush. I mean . . . it'll be lunch soon. You're welcome to stay."

She pulled keys from her pocket and brought her hands together.

"Thank you. That's a kind offer. But I do need to get going. There's a ton of work for me back at the lab."

"Right." I stepped aside. "Of course."

She gave me that same polite smile and walked to the stairwell. Even the way she moved seemed familiar.

"Wait," I said. "Are you sure we haven't met?"

She turned. "I never said we hadn't."

"You didn't?" I cleared my throat. "I mean, we've met before, right?"

Tones.

I tilted my head to the ceiling and sighed. She smiled, this time with a hint of friendliness.

I motioned upward. "It's never the best timing—"

"Battalion One, Engine One, Engine Two . . ."

The dispatcher continued. I put my hands in front of me. "I'm sorry. I've got to go."

She made a quick wave and turned for the door. I twirled onto the pole, spinning around and seeing, just before I descended, that Julianne was still there watching, biting her bottom lip.

The smooth cylinder rushed through my hands, my feet braking in time with the floor. Firefighters scattered to their rigs like bugs from a lifted rock. I made it to the back of the cab as Katrina hit the button for the apparatus-bay door.

She flipped on the rig battery switch to a high-pitched buzz. "Air pressure's down to fifteen pounds." A red light blinked on the dash.

Butcher leaned over. "What?"

Kat pushed the ignition, and the diesel motor grumbled. The ladder truck beside us echoed.

She leaned on the emergency brake. "It's locked out." The

buzz continued. "We're stuck here till the air tanks build up more pressure."

The radio crackled. "Reno, Engine Two en route, clearing another call on the edge of our district."

Lowell flipped up his collar. "That keeps us first due. You want me to hook up the air line?"

I caught a glimpse of the pressure gauge. Both tanks lingered at twenty PSI.

"No," Kat said. "I already had it plugged in. Something's wrong." She swung a look at Butcher that could have transected his head. "I thought you said it was a *little* leak."

Another radio transmission. "Reno, Engine Three en route."

The ladder truck rolled out, followed by the Rescue. Waits waved and smiled as he passed us.

Lowell pounded the wall and cursed.

Katrina revved up the RPMs. The air-pressure needles lifted like bath water. Twenty-two. Twenty-four. Twenty-five. "I can't start moving till we get to at least forty."

I sat in the jumpseat and worked my arms into my air pack.

Lowell cracked his neck. Butcher stared at the ceiling.

We were Labradors on leashes in a park full of Frisbees.

Katrina twisted her grip on the steering wheel. "Even forty will only give us one stop at best."

Dispatch came over the radio, "Engine One, Reno."

Butcher pinched the bridge of his nose and keyed the mic. "Go ahead, Reno."

"Are you en route?"

Lowell sat with his knee vibrating. I stared out the window at the empty apparatus bay. Butcher let out a hard breath.

Katrina placed her palm on the emergency air brake and pushed. "Come on, big boy."

It acquiesced.

The radio chirped. "Engine One, Reno."

Butcher looked at Kat. "We good?"

She shook her head. "That's only thirty pounds . . ."

Butcher ran his thumb back and forth over the edge of the center console.

Dispatch again. "All units responding to the fire at Middlegate Mobile Home Park, be advised we've received multiple calls that there is a child still inside."

Butcher pulled on his seat belt. "Let's hope we don't have to stop more than once." He clicked the mic. "Reno, Engine One's en route."

We flew off the apron like a horse out of the gate. I held the side of the seat as Kat swung us onto Second, barreling east toward Wells. My chest pounded like a war party beating skin-stretched toms.

Radio static. "Battalion One, Truck One on scene with wavers." Captain Sower's voice taut but collected. "Single-wide trailer well involved, one child reported inside."

I leaned to look out the front. Thick, tarry smoke plumed skyward.

"Hang on, boys." Katrina laid on the accelerator through a yellow light.

Butcher pushed the grinder into a screaming wail. The light flicked red with us blaring through. A block away, filtering through the haze, stood a square white sign reading *Middlegate Estates.*

We slowed with the guttural flapping of the engine retarder. Katrina feathered the brake with a squeaking *furp-tiss, furp-tiss* and swung into the park through a curtain of smoke. The rig jerked to a halt beside the truck and a white mobile home with ten-foot flames raging from the top.

"Here's our stop." She pulled the air brake.

I hopped out my door. The odor of burning plastic stung my nostrils. A woman stood screaming in the gravel-lined street. On the trailer's rotting wood porch, from the narrow side doorway, Chris Waits materialized, clutching a little girl to his chest.

Her arms hung limp, gray and soot-stained.

Fire swirled from the rooftop. It curved its neck and glowered over me like a thirty-foot cobra. I blinked to see Butcher charging around the front of the engine. His eyes were big.

He pointed to the trailer. "Get some water on that."

I met Lowell at the sideboard and grabbed a loop of hose. I took off with the nozzle while he flaked out the hose.

Over my shoulder I saw Waits set the girl on a bed of white quartz. I held the nozzle and the empty hose, staring as they pulled out a bag valve mask and placed it over her face. Timothy turned on the oxygen tank. Waits squeezed the bag.

The small frame of her torso rose and relaxed.

Water channeled through the hose line, straightening bends. I looked at the nozzle and the bale bent open. Before I could process the chain of events, a hundred and fifty pounds of pressure shot from the tip and the hose slipped from my grip.

It danced like a Chinese dragon, flipping and taunting. People ducked for cover. I pounced on it, inching my way back to the tip. Flailing spray shook back and forth.

"Shut that thing down!" Butcher yelled.

Katrina pounded a gate valve on the panel. I reached the nozzle as the stream stopped to a trickle.

I made my feet and closed the bale. The fire reared higher, stretching corkscrew tentacles. I stared into its burning gullet, its jaws agape, descending upon me.

Something exploded. A heat wave stung my neck through

my hood. I ducked and spun, catching glimpses of a trailer now fully involved.

Ghoulish figures danced from the flame lengths. Taunting eyes and razor teeth, mocking cackles. The fire folded back, encircling, growing, consuming even the dirt and the rocks as it squeezed in around me.

"Hit that, A-O!" Lowell collided with me and snatched the nozzle. My eyes refocused from him to the trailer. Fire fanned up the branches of nearby cottonwoods.

Butcher backed up Lowell and supported the hose. "Propane tank blew."

Lowell cranked the bale open. "Yeah. No—" Rushing water roared. He spun the nozzle to a wide fog pattern, and the two of them marched forward.

I stood frozen. I felt like a new kid. What was the fire doing? What was I doing? I picked up a section of hose and pushed on it. Butcher and Lowell stumbled forward.

Butcher turned and waved. "We got it. Go help with the girl."

I dropped the hose and stepped backward, tripping on a coupling and falling on my air pack. An ambulance pulled into the entrance. The truck guys worked the girl, still languid, not breathing.

I made my feet and shuffled over to Waits, my new goal to be as little of a liability as possible. "What can I do?"

"Pick her up." Waits squeezed the bag mask. "It's time for us to go."

CHAPTER 16

I wasn't about to let a three-year-old die in my arms.

Never mind that she had breathed enough smoke to make her lungs like leather, that Waits's hand with the bag mask was the only thing keeping her alive.

I cradled her body and navigated the spaghetti mess of hose lines on the broken pavement. Timothy followed with the oxygen bottle. The medics struggled with the gurney.

"Leave it there," Waits said. "We're coming to you."

Smoke stung my eyes, spinning in kaleidoscope swirls of sunburnt orange, amber, and yellow. The girl's straw-colored hair bounced with each step.

I felt like a passenger in my own body. I couldn't think beyond the moment. Everything spiraled beyond my control.

Amid the roaring din of Engine One's pump, the crackle and static of radio traffic, and the hissing recession of heat from hose lines, I whispered to her, "Come on, baby. Come on now, breathe."

From the back of the ambulance the medic reached down. "Bring her up. There you go."

I hopped in and set her on the gurney. Waits kept bagging.

The medic sitting at her head had a slim build, short-cropped blond hair, and a Charlie Chaplin moustache. "Greetings, gents. Let's save us a girl."

Timothy shut the doors and the bus rolled out. Engine one faded in the smoke. The siren wailed. We hooked around the corner and I stumbled forward.

I held the girl's upper arm to wrap it in a blood pressure cuff. Her bicep was thin and cool, like a rubber hose. I squeezed the ball of the cuff and spun the valve, watching the needle descend, waiting for it to bounce, waiting for her pulse, to hear the loudening labor of her heart. It fluttered at eighty with the dull thud of arterial wall knocking.

I pulled the stethoscope off. "Eighty over sixty."

"Thank you, sir." The medic unzipped the intubation kit.

I glanced at his name badge. *Thaddeus McCoy.*

I looked around the ambulance, thinking I should know what to do next. I felt so out of step. "How else can I help, Thaddeus?"

His eyebrows furrowed. "Bones is just fine."

I cocked my head. "I'm sorry?"

"Bones," he said. "People call me Bones."

He placed both hands on the side of the girl's head and tilted it. He nodded to Waits. "Go ahead and hyperventilate her, please."

Waits squeezed the bag faster.

"That's good."

With his left hand around a steel cylindrical handle, Bones inserted a straight metal blade past her tongue, lifting her jaw and shining a light down her throat. With his right hand he held a breathing tube about the diameter of her pinky.

He stared and smiled. "There you be, you pearly gates." He slid the tube down her throat, passing the tip through her vocal cords. "Beauty, eh."

He sat up and held the top between his thumb and forefinger. Waits connected the bag to the tube.

"Go ahead and ventilate." Bones listened over her stomach with a stethoscope.

Waits squeezed the bag.

"Good." Bones listened over each lung. "Good, good."

The driver spoke through the doghouse hole to the back. "A minute out from County."

"Copy, that. Here." Bones placed my hand on the tube by her mouth. "Hold this."

I tightened my fingers on the plastic. *Come on, girl.*

Bones keyed the microphone and gave a report to the hospital. The backup alarm sounded. The ambulance reversed into a space at the ER.

A nurse opened the back doors. "Tube secured?"

Bones finished tearing a strip of tape. "Just about. Okay, all set." He looked at me. "Fine work. You can let go now."

I did and watched the driver pull the gurney out and the nurse take over bagging. They rolled through an automatic sliding door to the ER.

Bones turned and saluted. "As always gentlemen, a pleasure."

I sat head in hands outside the Emergency Department. My hair felt hot on my palms. My coat and helmet lay next to me. Intermittent traffic squawked from the radio.

Waits stood by a planter box, turning a dial. "Sounds like they got ahold of the fire."

I ran my hands over my face and nodded. *No thanks to me.*

The hard *thwup-thwup* of helicopter blades beat overhead. A security officer walked by, keys jangling, his shoulder mic saying something about the bird on the roof. A yellow cab pulled into the parking lot.

Waits motioned with his head. "There's our ride."

I got in the cab, holding my coat and helmet on my lap.

The driver gave us a once over. He had copper skin and a Roman nose, his black hair poofed back like Mario Andretti. "You guys smell like smoke."

Waits nodded. I glanced out the window.

Mario tittered. "Imagine that, huh? So, yeah, where to, fellas? Downtown?"

"Middlegate Estates," Waits said.

"The mobile home park?"

"Yeah, that's right."

"Is that where all the smoke was coming from?"

I pulled on my seat belt. "Yeah."

Mario creased his eyebrows. "Huh." He dropped the transmission into drive. "So, what're you guys doing here . . ." His voice trailed off. He made the sign of the cross and pulled out of the parking lot. "Never mind. I don't want or need to know."

We drove a block before hitting a red light. The meter read three dollars and ninety-two cents.

Mario looked in the rearview mirror. "You guys should be proud of what you do. You do a great job. I couldn't do it." He ran his hand back through his hair. "It's hard to get on with a department though, isn't it?" He flipped the turn signal and spun the wheel with one hand. "I have an ex–brother-in-law out in Elko who was trying to be a fireman. They did a background check on him and found out he was an accessory to a liquor store robbery as a minor. It cost him the job. What an idiot."

Mario slowed to let a bus merge in front of us. "So, same deal as always—you guys sign a voucher and we send it to the city?"

Waits leaned forward. "Where do you need me to sign?"

Mario handed back a white pad of paper with carbon pages. "Just keep the yellow copy for your captain."

We hit every red light for three blocks before we pulled near the entrance for the park. "Here good?"

Waits said thanks and we got out. The cab rolled off.

Waits threw me a look up and down. "You all right?"

I shrugged, putting on my best nonchalant air. "What do you mean?"

"I don't know, Aidan. You just seem out of sorts. But it's everybody though, you know. Hartman in the hospital's been hard on—"

"Look, I appreciate your concern. Really. I'm fine." I took a deep breath. *He's just trying to help.* "What you did for that girl was great . . . it was great. That's what matters."

He eyed me and nodded. "Whatever happens to that girl . . . you know, I can beat myself up that I should've got in there faster, or that I should've gone left instead of right first. But whatever happens, it's not anybody's fault. Except for Biltman . . . I don't know what I'd do if I saw that guy." He stared at the ground, shaking his head. "Just . . . if there's ever anything you need, Aidan, I'm here."

I feigned a confident nod and smile. "For sure, of course. Same for you." I patted him on the shoulder and turned away. I put on my helmet and walked into the trailer park, wondering what wreck-bound surprises lay in wait for me next.

CHAPTER 17

Timothy passed me in the dayroom. "There's an envelope for you on the kitchen counter." He stopped. "Looks like a woman's handwriting."

A woman's? "Oh. All right, thanks."

He smiled. "Come on now. What aren't you telling me?"

"Nothing, man."

He studied my face. "You broke up with Christine, didn't you?"

I shifted my jaw and scratched it. "How could you possibly know that?"

"Please. I saw that one coming a year ago."

So it had been that obvious—to everyone but me, apparently. "Well, yeah. It's . . . I don't know. But I definitely don't know anything about a letter."

"Oh, so it's a letter?"

"An envelope. Whatever."

He laughed.

I shrugged. "It's probably just something from Admin."

"It's not an interdepartment envelope."

"It's not?"

He shook his head, grinning. "Nope."

"Wipe that look off your mug."

"Or what? You'll do it for me."

"Here." I set my feet apart. "Come here a little closer. I want to show you something."

He blew me off and walked toward the dorms. "Don't think I don't know you, O'Neill."

"You better sleep with one eye open."

His voice sailed back, "Bring it. Anytime."

"Don't think I won't."

I stared at the wall with the framed patch collection. A quiet hope grew in me that the note was from Julianne. Not that I'd have admitted it to anyone. I tried to shake off the thought as just a rebound reflex. But there it lingered, just below the surface.

The kitchen smelled like sautéed mushrooms and garlic. Waits lifted the top off a steaming Dutch oven. Sortish washed a cutting board at the sink. I resolved to not even look at the countertops.

Katrina sat by the window two tables in, penciling a sudoku. "There's an envelope for you on the island, A-O."

"Right. Thanks." *So much for my plan.*

Butcher walked up to Kat. "Mechanic says the air line's all fixed."

She looked up. "So we're back in service?"

Butcher nodded. "Yep."

Just beyond him, on the stainless steel counter, lay a white business envelope with my first and last names written in elaborate cursive. There was no way a man had penned that. I lifted the envelope and looked around. Everyone was caught up in activities.

I took a seat at the table by the door. The corner ensured my correspondence remained private. I tore open the seam and unfolded a white sheet of paper.

Aidan,

There is so much more to say than what has been said. You were right about us meeting. I just thought that maybe you'd have recalled it more clearly.

It's hard to explain, but I know a lot more about you than you realize. I know you loved your dad. And I can tell that inside, though you hide it well, you are fighting something.

I just reread what I wrote. You probably think I'm some kind of stalker. That's exactly the impression I was hoping to avoid. But here's the thing. I was still around when your father died. And I know that the cause of that fire remains unsolved. I can only imagine how that lack of closure must affect you.

I think I can help.

If you are interested, meet me at the lab tomorrow afternoon. Earlier is better.

Best regards,
Julianne

"Code seven," Sortish paged over the loud speaker. "Code seven."

Time to eat.

I folded the letter into my pocket. Guys filtered in, filled their plates with Waits's spaghetti, and sat down to eat.

There was a predictable increase in years on the job as they sat away from the windows and toward the pole hole. Captain Sower and Waits sat opposite of each other on the end nearest the pole, Lowell was next over and opposite Butcher, and so on. I sat beside

Timothy Clark in the middle. Naturally, the phone was on the window end and answering it was Sortish's job.

I twirled spaghetti on my fork, finding myself half listening to conversations, half lost in a mosaic of thoughts. Somewhere, in the world of the kitchen table, which lay for me just beyond a veil, Lowell wound into one of his nightly monologues, standing up when he got real excited telling the story.

Segments and phrases met my ears like clips of music when turning the radio dial.

"White Wolf Syndrome."

"That's passé. McCormick's is the cheap stuff now."

I had the strange sensation of not really being there, like a passive observer witnessing everything on a television screen. Seated, but unseen. Present but not participating. I took a piece of garlic bread from a bowl. It looked like bread in someone else's hand.

The table broke into an uproar. I looked up and smiled, no idea what the joke was.

Lowell was out of his seat saying, "So the guy's frantic, pointing and yelling, 'Chicken breath! Chicken breath!' and Butcher's just standing there nodding and thinking we need PD or something when Peyton walks over to the woman and realizes she's choking."

Hands slapped the table and laughter echoed through the kitchen.

Lowell kept on, "And Butcher's still staring at his clipboard with this deer in the headlights look, so I put a hand on his shoulder and said, 'She can't breathe, Mark. She can't breathe.' And just as it dawns on him, I kid you not, Peyton's doing the Heimlich and the lady hocks this fat piece of hot dog right onto the clipboard. Right on it."

Waits laughed so hard he started choking. Lowell faked like

he was doing abdominal thrusts on him, yelling, "Chicken breath! Chicken breath!"

He pointed at Kat. "You know, I used to think Katrina was a good operator, but the more I think about it . . . chicken drive!"

"Yeah, and chicken cook, neither!"

"Yeah, and chicken clean!"

Kat shook her head. "You boys better check your boots before stepping into them tonight—that's all I got to say."

Sower stood and reached for Waits's empty plate. "You all done with that?"

Waits shooed him off. "Get your hands away from there, Benjamin."

Sortish rose, making sure to beat everyone to the sink. I filed out behind Timothy Clark and grabbed a towel to help.

The station, dinner, the guys, it all seemed the same. That was what bothered me most—everyone carried on as though nothing was off. I'd rather have them all furious with me, or even giving me a ration like they did Butcher. But the fact that my faltering was being ignored felt the worst of all. My place at the table now felt like a formality for years served. The respect I valued and desired and struggled for more than anything else was slipping through my grasp like sandstone separating.

CHAPTER 18

Tones.

I spit toothpaste into the sink and glanced at my watch. Eleven thirty p.m.

"Engine One to a medical emergency, cardiac arrest . . ."

I slid the pole. White light . . . wind . . . floor. The night coolness darted in through the app-bay door, wrapping around my knees as I stepped into my turnout drops. We took off down Second Street, the spinning overheads casting colors over the building fronts. A thin layer of autumn frost lay like linen over the parked cars. The sidewalks were dotted with periodic pedestrians, the brash ballast light of convenience stores spilling out into the vacuum of the city. I put on my fluid-barrier glasses and held a pair of latex gloves.

We arrived first on scene outside a single-story brick home. Lowell grabbed the defibrillator and I followed with the other bags. A gray-haired man met us at the door. He stood hunched over, holding a cordless phone.

His lips quivered and he pointed down a narrow hallway. "Back bedroom."

I held the first-out in front of me to keep from knocking down photo frames. A single lamp diffused light over a compact rear room. In the bed, an emaciated woman lost inside an ivory nightgown lay on her back, gaping at the ceiling.

"Let's get her on the floor," Lowell said.

I set down the bags and placed my hands under her legs.

Lowell took the arms. "One-two-three."

We lifted. Her body remained rigid, straight like a plank.

Lowell's eyebrows angled. "Let's put her ba—"

"Yeah," I said.

We placed her back on the bed. Lowell lifted her arm and her whole body moved. Livid purple painted the back of her neck and shoulders. Her eyes were fixed upward, gelled over and dilated.

"I'll let Butcher know," Lowell said.

I thought of the girl from the trailer park. Having lived so little, on the opposite spectrum of life. Her flaccid, dusky arms.

I closed the woman's eyelids with my fingertips. I didn't drape the sheet over her head because it always seemed like burying someone when that was done. I didn't think it right that she should be buried in the bed that she slept in.

I heard weeping from the living room.

Lowell returned. "Fifty-five years."

I picked up the first-out bag. "She looks older than that."

"They were *married* fifty-five years."

I nodded and stared at her.

"The ambulance is here to wait for the coroner."

I walked back with him through the living room. Long shadows cast over thirty-year-old furnishings. The husband sat in a russet brown leather chair.

Butcher knelt beside him and put a hand on his shoulder. The man's sobs sank to laments. An RPD officer stood at the door. The air hung still, the home hollow.

Only one person lived there now.

One living, breathing man, and one shell of a woman he had loved for half a century.

All was quiet back in the rig.

Until Lowell spoke up, of course. "Light as a feather . . . stiff as a board. Light as a feather . . . stiff as a board."

Katrina threw a box of medical gloves back at him. "Would you shut up? I can't believe you."

Butcher stayed silent, staring out the windshield.

Lowell wiggled his fingers in front of him, pointing at Kat in the passing strands of streetlights. "Light as a feather . . . stiff as a board."

She shook her head.

—

Back at the station, the dorms hummed with the sounds of snoring. I lay in my bed, staring at the red digital numbers 12:01 glowing from the walnut-laminated clock in the corner of my cubicle. Three steps from my bed, a curtain hung from a rod balanced above two sets of metal lockers. Some folks had bigger walk-in closets.

I closed my eyes, trying to purge the pestering replay of the day's events from my mind. Wavy images of my father formed in a watery reflection.

His grin. The way he clapped his hands when he was excited about something. A two-story brick warehouse took shape behind him, framed by an empty blue sky. A light breeze moved across shady porch steps.

I knew this place. The Reno Fire Museum.

I knew this day.

He spoke with animation, describing at length the intricacies of gilded design on the doors of the restored American La France aerial. Bringing that ninety-year-old truck from its rusty, overgrown farm-lot condition to its state of cherry preservation had been a passion to which he'd dedicated a fair portion of his own sweat and dollars.

He had picked me up after shift in his '72 Dodge Dart, itself a labor of love. Folks had asked about it so often while I was growing up, I had memorized his standard response. "She's got a three-forty with a six-pack Holly carb, seven-twenty-seven tranny and posi-traction rear end." After which the usual response was a whistle and a nodding of the head. As a kid, I had no idea what they were talking about, but I knew that car was no simple grocery getter.

And there I was, all of twenty-two years old, still riding shotgun on Sixth Street with the windows down, the exhaust muffler grumbling, the whole car seeming discontent with no one to race.

He talked about how there were only a few guys in the whole country—no, the whole world—who could replicate the intricate designs on an antique fire truck like the '17 La France. How fortunate the restoration team was to find and hook up with this guy from Ohio, and how I just had to see what had been done with it. It was the final touch. It was finished and show ready.

They'd brought it in the back doors of the museum the day before, and he wanted me to be one of the first to see it on display, under can lights and behind thick scarlet ropes with shiny brass pedestals.

We walked through the front doors into the black-and-white checkered-tile entryway. Artifacts and apparatus from the department's history filled the broad footprint of the first floor. About midway down, in the center of the room, stood a wide red-carpeted staircase that led to an upstairs showroom. And just to the right of that, spanning fifty feet from nose to tiller, sat the hard-wrought work of firefighting art.

"There she is, A-O."

Replete with wood-spoked wheels with hard rubber lining, a short visible stretch from the pioneer wagons that carried families to Reno in generations past. Brass rails and bells and buttoned black leather seats. And the ladder! A hundred feet in four sections, sanded and stained, glowing like new, all bedded beside pristine iron gear wheels, pulleys, and hand cranks.

I whistled. "How'd you get her in here?" Apart from the front doors, the only way into the building was through a raised loading dock.

He grinned, proud. "We had to build a ramp that stretched from the tow bed." Putting a hand behind his neck, he admired the truck in its new home. "That's what she looked like, Aidan, when they ran with her almost ninety years ago. Responding down these same streets. Over the same river. Bells clanging and guys hanging off the sides. Can you imagine?"

Tones.

I sat straight up in bed.

"Engine One to a medical emergency. Subject down, unknown problem . . ."

I walked bleary-eyed to the pole.

No one spoke as we drove down Virginia. Kat pulled alongside an unshaven man passed out underneath the glowing Reno Arch.

Lowell nodded at me. "How come you don't ever see that on the postcards?"

The man woke with a sternal rub, and with almost admirable

ability, stood, brushed himself off, and walked heavy-legged north on the sidewalk.

Kat shrugged. "At least he's headed to District Four."

We got back in station at 2:05. Fatigue filled my muscles. I climbed back into bed, letting my head sink into the pillow. The carousel of rising and sinking stresses again spun down with waning inertia. Before I was even aware, sleep fell upon me.

Tones.

Blood rushed through my chest.

"Engine One . . ."

I grunted and rose, slipping on my tennis shoes for the pole.

We exited the barn, responding to another medical.

This patient was sleeping by the side of a building in a vacant lot off Sixth Street. He could stand and somewhat walk, so the police took him in their wagon to the "drunk tank" at the county jail.

We pulled back into the station as Rescue One rolled out for a call. I climbed back into bed, sleep hitting hard and fast.

Tones.

Another medical. Another drunk. The ambulance beat us there. A four-fingered wave from them was all Butcher needed to clear us to return back to the station. Code four: They could handle it.

I fought to keep my eyes open on the short ride back, the potholes in Evans Avenue keeping me awake. At 2:50 I trudged to my cubicle and sat on the bed.

Tones.

Pole. Boots. Headset. Another medical. Difficulty breathing in a casino hotel room. Lowell gave a nebulizer treatment to alleviate a woman's wheezing. I took vital signs. He did the talking. We transferred care to the medics and got back at 3:15.

Back upstairs. Back to my cube. I stood at the entryway and

stared at the bed. Peyton's somnolent sawmill was in full production next door.

Truckies.

I slid under my warm covers. A current of colored lines washed over me. Images of people moved like old film actors speaking in sepia silence. A deep breath expanded my lungs. My conscious mind relented, and a nebula overtook me, tugging me, drawing me into its depths.

Tones.

My eyelids flashed open.

"Battalion One . . ."

CHAPTER 19

Butcher keyed the mic. "Reno, Engine One en route to the fire on East Taylor."

"Ten-four, Engine One."

Kat swung onto Second, laying on the accelerator.

Lowell stepped wide with the motion, swinging his coat on. "Whoa, you're not in a bad mood tonight, are you, Kat?"

She couldn't hear him with her headset on. He pulled his on and I followed.

"What are you yappin' about back there?" she said.

Lowell positioned the mic by his mouth. "I said, 'You're not in a bad mood, are you?' "

Butcher opened the map book. "This'll be one block east of Wells Avenue."

"Got it." Kat varied the siren tone as we approached an intersection. "Why do you think I'm in a bad mood, Lowell?"

He strapped on his air pack. "No. I didn't say I think you're in a bad mood. I was just wondering if you *were* in a bad mood."

"Why were you wondering that, though?"

"Clear right," Butcher said as we slowed for a stop sign. "It's a small apartment complex. There's a hydrant on . . . the north side it looks like."

Kat hung a hard right.

Lowell steadied himself with a hand on the door. "Well," he said. "Obviously now you are in a bad mood."

"I am not."

"Okay, you two. Watch these pedestrians up here."

"Right, I see 'em."

Lowell leaned toward me and pulled off his headset. I moved mine away from my ear.

He nodded. "I find it's always best to stay seated when she drives angry."

"I heard that," Kat said.

Butcher stared through the windshield. "It looks like we've got smoke up ahead, guys."

My chest fluttered, vibrating all the way down through my knees. I kicked each foot to shake it out.

Cool air fed through my cracked window. The moon shone bright, unobstructed by clouds.

As we crossed Wells Avenue I smelled the smoke.

—

Gray ribbons wrapped around a second-floor walkway. Lowell put a hand on his door handle.

A man in boxers and a white T-shirt ran to the rig, waving his arms. "Gun! He's got a gun!"

Butcher yelled to the backseats, "Hold up. Get back in." He glanced at Kat and picked up the mic. "Let's pull forward. Reno, Engine One's on scene, two-story cinderblock multifamily residence with gray smoke showing from a first-floor unit. Advise all incoming units to stage out of the area—we have a report of a suspect on scene with a gun."

Kat pulled us past the rear alleyway. An apartment's back window shattered with fire spitting out of it.

"There," Katrina said, pointing in her side-view mirror.

A pale, lanky man hurtled over a juniper hedge and scrambled down the sidewalk. He wore a pair of tight black jeans and an unzipped polo jacket that flapped behind him. Two RPD patrol cars skidded to a stop in front of him. He hesitated and tried to double back, jumping over the hood of a parked car. He hit his boots midway and then slipped off headfirst onto the concrete. Kevlar-covered chests pounced on him like wasps on a barbecued chicken wing.

"That's him," Katrina said. "That's Biltman. They got him."

"All right," Butcher said. "Let's get in there."

Kat backed up the rig. Rolling coal-colored curtains flowed from the first floor. I hopped out and stretched a live-line to the door. Kneeling with the nozzle between my legs, I strapped on my mask.

I was forgetting something.

My axe.

Lowell walked up, helmet in hand. "Let's do it." He seated his helmet and hoisted his axe, busting out the window beside the door.

Tarry shadows shifted inside, levitating like specters. Owl eyes blinked from the blackness.

Keep your cool, Aidan. Keep your cool.

Butcher held his mask in one hand and motioned with the other. "Swirl us some water in there, A-O."

I shot the stream in the cloud. It shook and hissed. Lowell

pulled more of the hose to the door. I shut down the bale. Butcher checked the doorknob. It didn't budge. I felt around my belt grasping air. No axe.

"Watch out," Butcher said, nudging me aside. He turned around and burro-kicked the door.

Wood cracked. He kicked again, pounding out splinters. A third kick. The frame snapped and the door flew open.

Smoke snuck surreptitious glances around the corners.

Lowell twirled his axe over his hand and sheathed it in his belt. "I could've got that, Marky."

Butcher motioned with his head. "Let's get in there."

I hesitated. Lowell nearly snatched the nozzle, but I yanked it away.

He strapped on his mask. "Wet stuff on the red stuff, A-O."

I put a hand on the doorframe and crawled inside. Lowell lifted the hose line behind me. I swam forward as though under murky water.

The image of a giant wave flitted through my mind.

Focus, Aidan. Focus.

The temperature heightened. The front of my helmet hit something large and hard.

"Keep going." Lowell said.

"I can't."

I felt around to both sides. A hard flat object on my left, to my right something softer. I pushed and it moved enough for us to squeeze past.

An orange glow lit the black fog beyond. The heat forced us lower.

Again, the laughing.

My breathing quickened, ineffective and shallow.

Lowell pushed me on. Flames fanned around a shut door. I

crawled to it, clenching my teeth. He reached in front and shoved it inward.

The room lit like concert lights. I sucked the air from my mask. Waves of fire rolled overhead.

I cranked open the bale. Water hammered the hose and knocked me to my rear. The line snaked and slithered back. I grasped the nozzle tight.

Don't lose it again, Aidan!

Lowell burrowed his shoulder into my back. I balanced off him and made my knees, hosing the furnace, whipping the water stream in a broad circle.

The ceiling darkened and the doorframe flickered down. Lowell pushed the hose forward. I steadied myself with a hand on the floor.

He nudged my back. "The seat of the fire's in the bathroom."

"I know, I know." My knees kept sticking to the melted carpet.

I penciled overhead with short bursts of water. We crept forward and found a door to a small bathroom burned halfway out, everything beyond involved in fire that shot out a high rectangular window.

The flame seemed to form horns and turn its head.

It saw me.

Regrouping itself, it grew and intensified, coming for me.

I brought one knee up and unleashed the water stream. It screamed and hissed, blowing ashy smoke back over us. Everything became lost in the cloud. I saw myself standing before the towering wave, it sucking me up, lifting me, clenching me in its indomitable fist, its arm cocked, ready to drive me back to the rocks.

A terror-filled yell choked out in my throat.

Then the atmosphere cooled, smoke color shifting to a thinning gray. And the vision fled.

Lowell patted my shoulder. "All right, buddy. Let's shut her down."

Fans roared from the front door. Flaming speckles dotted the doorframe. Smoke streams flowed out of the bathroom window. Sweat bullets ran down my cheeks. My chest heaved. Additional crews came crouching under the rising smoke line, setting drop-lights and throwing salvage covers over furniture. Lowell busted holes in the drywall, exposing charred studs. I followed behind and bathed the wood with the bale cracked open.

The apartment cleared of haze, and I saw a scorched couch sitting cockeyed in the living room, our hose line winding behind it. A wall heater with a dent hung where I had hit my helmet. A kitchen counter rose beside it. Everything plastic sported elongated drips stretching to the floor in suspended animation. A television pouted, having folded in on itself.

The truck company went to work pulling ceiling. Lowell and I regrouped with Butcher outside. I peeled off my mask.

Lowell peered back in the doorway and motioned to Butcher. "Mark. Check this out."

On the kitchen counter rested a shotgun barrel and a hacksaw. The remains of a wooden table lay broken and splintered on the floor.

Butcher pointed to the stock of a gun sticking out of a box on the floor. "An improvised sawed-off shotgun?"

Lowell looked into the box. "This thing's full of cartridges. We crawled right past it."

My stomach knotted. I ran my fingers through my hair and glanced around the living room.

"Let's tape this off until the investigator gets here," Butcher said.

A dark-haired cop with a Tom Selleck moustache walked over to Butcher. "You guys get the story on what happened?"

Butcher wiped his brow. "No. We saw you catch our arsonist, though."

I loosened the shoulder straps on my air pack.

The cop folded his arms. "Good old freaky Biltman. Turns out this is his place."

That got my attention.

"Did you know he's also a meth addict?" he continued. "He owed money to some gang members who, he said, were waiting for him outside this apartment with automatic weapons." He rested his hand on his gun. "He doesn't have phone service, so he figured he'd set a fire to cause a distraction and bring help."

Lowell shook his head. "Hacked up his table and set it on fire in the tub."

The cop nodded. "His neighbor came downstairs with a fire extinguisher and Biltman shoves a gun in his face and tells him that if he puts it out he'll kill him. The fire spread faster than Biltman could handle and so he bailed. That was when you guys pulled up."

"Great," Lowell said. "That's just great."

Butcher nodded. "That neighbor must have been the guy yelling at us when we first got here."

The cop scratched the back of his head.

"Good times," Lowell said.

The cop smirked. "Yeah. Good times."

CHAPTER 20

I flipped open my phone and dialed. It rang a couple times as I walked to the Cruiser.

Blake answered, "Investigator Williams."

"You just like saying that, don't you?"

"What's up, you hose dragger?"

"Where are you right now?"

"I'm over at Prevention. Trying to make some headway."

"You still want to meet this morning?"

"Yeah. Yes, absolutely. In fact, I was just packing things up here and was about to call you. How was the night?"

"I don't even want to talk about it."

"Well, I'll buy your first cup of coffee, then."

"Sounds great. Dreamer's or Java Jungle?"

"Let's do Dreamer's this time."

I rolled out of Central and crossed the Virginia Street Bridge, its century-old concrete weathered but stalwart, and parked by the coffeehouse in the old Riverside building. I took my coffee outside and sat at a table along its brick-lined walls and watched the dry-suited paddlers in the kayak park, marveling that the brisk autumn air did little to dissuade them.

There is something discernable in the human spirit when fatigue has flooded the synapses. Time slows. Perception floats. I'll hear leaves rustle, sense wind currents, notice light refracting off the dew-laden legs of an insect. A couple yellow boats sank and surfaced, spinning and turning off the standing waves. The sound of the water and the gentle rustle and dance of the Riverwalk trees proved a refreshing alternative to the Station One walls and the windows that wouldn't open.

One hour of sleep. The same sun I'd seen rising on my way to work had risen again, but *my* day hadn't ended. Lowell said it was like the sun was mocking him.

A man and woman walked past wearing long wool overcoats. Coal for him, tan for her, along with a scarlet beanie. She laughed, their fingers intertwined and swaying in rhythm with their steps. I took a sip and thought of Julianne.

I still couldn't place her. But something about her seemed . . . right. Like home.

I had a clear view of the corner loft in the Park Tower where I had lived when Christine and I started dating. She'd moved in there after I bought my parents' house. It was a cool little flat, all four hundred and forty square feet—not including the balcony, which is what really made it great. The summer festivals, the concerts, Artown movies at night in Wingfield Park. I remember having ice tea with her while we watched *The Wizard of Oz* from a pair of chaise lounges we found at the Salvation Army store. If Reno had a heart, this was it. It was where mine fell for hers, six years prior. And that first year was good.

Then my dad was killed.

It made everything different. I know it shouldn't have. But I became so caught up in the investigation. I wanted to know, needed to know, every fact about that fire. I read and reread every report typed by every captain and chief and investigator. Not to mention news articles and editorials. Stacks of papers cluttered up corners of my flat. When Christine came over after classes, we'd be less than ten feet from each other—me at the desk, poring over incident narratives and her on the couch, cross-legged and hedged in by a book. She read Ayn Rand a lot. That should have been my first red flag.

Folks were full of wisdom for me. "Sometimes bad things happen, Aidan." "It was just his time, Aidan." "Believe me, Aidan, God doesn't have anything against you or your father. Firemen die sometimes, and there's nothing we can do to stop that."

That last shining nugget had come from Butcher.

I stopped going to our church. It seemed as if every time someone saw me it made them think of my dad. I couldn't walk from the foyer to the sanctuary without half a dozen "caring" and inquisitive comments about me and my mom and my grandfather. It was just easier not to go. So I didn't. If I wasn't at work, I was at the Prevention office with Blake, and if I wasn't there, I was sitting on a stool nursing a Guinness, listening to stories about my great-grandfather and the San Francisco quake told by Patty McDonough, who was so ancient I couldn't believe he still had the strength to pull the tap handle.

Somehow, the stories soothed me. My father had died, but our family legacy hadn't.

My mother, amid her own heartache, still walked with a strange peace through it all. She encouraged me to talk things out. But I'd dodge her invitations, giving her clichés about how it didn't work that way for guys. We fix our own things. We don't ask for directions. We retreat to the cold dark shelter of our caves and concoct charcoal-laid plans for overcoming the beast.

My solitary grieving eventually ran its course, and Christine graciously welcomed me back. She understood I had needed time for healing and resolution. Problem was, I'd never found any. I was just as confused and angry and frustrated with God as I had been when it first happened. We never really talked about how my father being crushed by a fallen brick wall affected me when I tried to go to sleep, or when I went on fires. Because I wanted to make sure that she and everyone knew that I wasn't going to give in, that I wouldn't meet the same fate. I would beat it. I would always know what the fire was doing. I would sense a structure before it collapsed. I would hear the fire before it flashed. And I would not be God's next example of how firemen just die sometimes and there ain't a thing anyone can do about it.

I looked back at the river and swallowed lukewarm coffee, the heat from my cup already lost to the autumn air.

Christine had come from an affluent upbringing, her sights always set a bit higher than mine. "One day when we have our home on the lake . . ." she'd say, meaning Tahoe. And, "Ooh, A-O, have you seen the new Porsche?" Which of course, I hadn't. Or if I had, I sure wasn't taking notes to decide what color to pick out.

At times I would stop her midsentence and in all seriousness say, "Babe, I am a *fire*man." I would elongate the word too, and associate it with the phrase "glorified garbageman." And she would laugh as if I had just said the funniest thing in the world, and by the way, did I like her new Coach purse and wallet? She got the wallet on sale, only three hundred forty-eight dollars.

What had fueled her persistent disassociation from reality? And what convinced me that it wasn't that big of an issue?

The fact that she had been in school had probably delayed the inevitable. As she neared completion of her degree and contemplated establishing her life as she had pictured and footnote-captioned it in her mind, the clear lens of reality started taking focus.

She was engaged to be married to a fireman.

No home on Lake Tahoe.

No fancy foreign sports cars.

No high-society art fund-raisers.

A brisk breeze spun dried leaves in an eddy on the sidewalk.

Someone spoke behind me, "What's up, loser?"

I turned to see Blake, his dark wavy hair combed with a pomade gloss, crisp lined collar under a tailored suit jacket. A slight fold betrayed the piece holstered at his flank.

I took a deep breath. Sometimes a friendly ribbing found the space between the bones.

CHAPTER 21

What's up, Gary Cooper?" I stood. "You get a lot of chicks walking around in that getup?"

He swung his arm wide and gave me a hearty handshake. "You look like you've been sleeping under a bridge. Somebody beat you up before I got here?"

"Yeah, you know. Engine One nights. But I can still get chicks looking like this."

He grinned. "It's cold out here. You want to go inside?"

He was right, even my clothes felt cold. I followed him through the front doors.

Espresso wafted through the room. Blake bought me a refill, and we found a seat by the windowed wall. A girl sat at the baby grand piano playing something somber.

Blake's news came sudden and unexpected. "I lost my house, Aidan."

His clean Brut-basted jawline defied what he was saying. It was like Pierce Brosnan telling you that he wasn't really James Bond.

I had expected him to unveil some sort of striking discovery and inroad on my father's case. "What happened?"

He leaned back in his chair and undid a button on his coat. "I did some pretty aggressive real estate investing. I got overextended and had to short sell three houses. Now the bank has foreclosed on my primary." He shifted his lower jaw to the side and shook his head. "I screwed up, man."

I leaned forward with an elbow on the table and rubbed the back of my neck. "Wow. I had no idea. It all came down that quickly?"

"About half a year ago I knew I was in trouble. But the market . . . you know. So . . ." He looked out the window. "I just needed to find somewhere, so I—"

"Hey, if you need a place to stay you can always have the extra room at my house."

He shook his head.

"I mean it," I said. "It's no burden."

He let out an embarrassed laugh. "You don't make things easy, do you, A-O?"

"I'm sorry?"

He swallowed and looked out the window again. He rubbed his forehead. "Look at me, huh? Here I am straight off talking about myself. Tell me what's going on with you. How are you? I heard all about that fire with Hartman." Then quickly, "I hear he's getting better, though."

I ignored his questions. "Blake, it's all right if you're in need, man. That's what friends are for. Whatever it is, just tell me and I'll help."

He exhaled and nodded. "Right. Thanks. You know, I've actually been rooming over at the Cairo for the last couple of weeks. It's not so bad."

"Last couple of weeks? You're already out? What about your stuff?"

"In storage."

"Why didn't you tell me sooner? I could have helped you move."

"You know, I kept thinking I'd find a way out of it."

I glanced at the earthy brown liquid in my mug. "So . . . how's the room service at the Cairo?"

He released a laugh. "It's just great, Aidan." He lifted his cup and mouthed a curse at me.

I rubbed the scratch of day-old stubble on my jaw. "Look, man, I really mean it. I have that spare bedroom—"

"Aidan, I can't impose on you like—"

"Don't even." I raised a hand. "The truth is out. Blake Williams actually needs help." I stood and mock proclaimed it to no one in particular. "Blake Williams actually needs my help."

A man behind a laptop raised a disinterested eyebrow.

I sat back down. "You can't backpedal now. You don't have anywhere else to go. Look, I could just as easily be in your shoes, and I don't even know if I'd have sense enough to just go to a buddy and ask for a hand."

He jutted out his chin and stared at the table.

"Just consider it payback for all your research on my father's fire. You've done so much for me. Christine reminds me of that all the time."

"Heh. Right." He sat up straight, a buoyed expression on his face. "You're a true friend, Aidan. I'll give it some thought, okay."

"All right."

He glanced at his watch. "Hey, about your dad's fire."

"Yeah?"

"I do have to get going here, but I will say that we're close."

"Last time we talked you said you'd made inroads with some calculations."

"You're talking about the ones on the wall's structural integrity?"

"Yeah."

He adjusted his watchband. "Oh, this goes far beyond that."

"But that was significant, right? That brick shouldn't have collapsed that fast."

Blake nodded. "And your dad knew that. When James went into that structure, he expected, and rightly so, to have more time than he did. Even with unreinforced masonry, those rafters were all cut and stack, not lightweight trusses. Their integrity under those fire conditions should have been way longer than today's gang-plated stuff. That fire with Hartman, you guys would have—"

"I know, had much more time with a solidly built roof. I know that. We pushed the envelope for—"

"You don't have to justify what you did. I'm just talking about the difference in construction. My point is, that the wall in the fire James was fighting should not have fallen as quickly as it did given the conditions." He drank the last of his coffee.

"So don't go spreading this as gospel," he continued, "but the pieces are lining up. More and more of them with each day."

"Each day?" I said.

"With each fire."

"So these current fires and my father's—"

"Are related. Yes. I believe so. Now, there are still missing pieces. And I'm still studying the findings from last night's fire, but—"

"Did Biltman set my father's fire?"

Blake pushed his lips together. "I'm not quite at the point where—"

"What point are you at? I need to know, Blake. If that guy—"

"I know, Aidan. I know. Listen, I'm busting my butt working on this." He stood and buttoned his coat. "I've got to get going, all right? You're just going to have to trust me."

CHAPTER 22

I felt as if I'd just walked onto the set of *CSI.*

To be fair, everything at the Prevention office that afternoon was brighter. But phones rang, and people shuffled around desks with flapping papers in hand, glinting badges pinned to white-collared uniform shirts. An investigator stood at one end of the room, suit coat haphazardly draped over a swivel office chair, leather handgun harness hanging loosely under his arm. He scribbled on a large whiteboard decorated with circles and arrows and black-and-white photos of unshaven suspects. Business was hopping in the fire prevention world.

I didn't see Julianne, and Blake wasn't anywhere to be found. I stopped short of clamping down on the arm of Prevention Officer Jim Schaeffer as he passed me in full stride. "Hey, Jim."

He glanced at me without slowing, returning his eyes to his route. "Hey."

"No. Hey, Jim? Quick question."

He stopped and turned, eyebrows raised.

I put my hands in my pockets. "Have you seen Blake or—" I cleared my throat—"Lab Analyst Caldwell this afternoon?"

His eyes deviated to his right and down. I tried to remember from detective shows if that meant he was fabricating an answer to my question or if he was actually searching his memory. "No. No, I haven't seen Blake. But Julianne should be around here somewhere." He waited as if I had just thrown a ball and he needed my permission to chase it.

"Thanks."

He sped off, staring at the papers in his hand.

I rubbed my neck, taking a few steps backward.

A sudden "Oh!" and the clanking of glass told me my presence had elevated from nuisance to interference. I turned and caught a surprised Julianne by the shoulders. She held a wooden tray, and her lab glasses had fallen forward to the tip of her nose. She shifted her elbows and her shoulder in an effort to right the glasses.

I stepped back. "Hey. Wow. I'm so sorry. Here. May I?" I pointed to her glasses.

She glanced at them, then back at me. "Please." She leaned her chin forward and up. I pushed the frame to the bridge of her nose. "Woo," she said. "Thank you. Much better."

I grinned. "Everyone is in quite the hurry."

"It's been this way for days. Nonstop. Admin is bringing down the hammer. City manager's breathing down the fire chief's neck, and it all rolls its way down here. It's been an interesting first few weeks."

I realized I was still blocking her way. "I guess I should let you take your beakers to the lab."

She laughed. "These aren't beakers."

"That's right. Those are . . . the cylindrical glass . . ."

"Test tubes?"

"Yes. Test tubes. I was getting there."

She smiled.

"Thank you for the note," I said.

"I'm sorry I wasn't more friendly before."

"No, no. It's okay."

She studied my face. "You still don't remember me, do you?"

"That's not entirely true. I remember you. I just have no idea where from."

An awkward silence transcended the small gap between us.

"I remember seeing you," she said, "on TV at your father's department funeral. I remember wondering if what was going through your mind was anything like what I was going through." She pressed her lips together. "I'd lost my father a week before that."

I shook my head. "I'm so sorry to hear that."

She made a quick scan of the room. "Have you spoken with Blake recently?"

"Yes, actually. This morning we—"

"Follow me." Motioning with her head, she led me across the room to a door and asked me to open it. "Thank you. Come on in."

We entered a large laboratory. A protected hood system stood to one side. Tables held vials and droppers and microscopes. Labeled cardboard shoeboxes lined wall shelves next to binders with laminated page protectors.

Julianne set down the tube tray. She peeled off her gloves and propped up her glasses. "I'm Julianne, by the way." She offered her hand and shrugged. "Just to make it official."

I shook. Her grip felt slender and smooth. "Aidan O'Neill. Pleasure to officially meet you."

"Grab a seat if you'd like." She pointed to a tall table bordered by metal stools. She pulled up a seat from a different table and glanced at the closed lab door. Specimen refrigerators and a host of electronics hummed.

Her feet paired on a rung. She leaned her forearms on her knees. "So much more peaceful in here, don't you think?"

"Your little enclave?"

She nodded and then took a deep breath. "So you really don't remember, do you?"

I shook my head.

She played with a button on her lab coat. "You were on the island. At the Celtic festival."

"At Wingfield Park?"

She nodded, eyes glinting.

I searched my memory. Images entered like a flood. . . .

Dancers on stage hopping to the rhythm of fiddles and drums . . . A young woman leaning on the bridge railing, watching the Truckee River pass beneath. Her deep blue eyes met mine and she smiled.

I looked up at Julianne. "You were on the bridge."

She nodded again.

An older man behind her had looked pale and tremulous. He was holding his head. She took his arm and walked him to the edge of the bridge. When he stepped onto the island, his knees buckled.

"You were the one," I said. "The one who helped that man who collapsed."

Her expression saddened.

I felt as if an album of old photos had opened in my mind. "I came over . . . and you were shaking his shoulders and saying something. I said—"

" 'I'm Aidan O'Neill with the Reno Fire Department. I can help.' "

"That's right. I knelt by his head and opened his airway. He was unconscious but breathing shallow."

She wiped her eyes. "Yes."

"He . . ." I stared at her. "He was your—"

"Yes."

"Your father."

I watched the scene replay in my head. The medics coming. Me standing on the island by the entrance to the bridge, watching her cross with them.

I put my hands on my head and looked at the ceiling. "So that's how we first met."

She folded her arms and gave a tempered smile.

"I'm so sorry," I said.

"It's okay." She shook her head. "I am, too. For your loss."

The second hand ticked on the wall clock.

"Did you go away after that?" I asked.

"Yes. But not far. I went through school at Davis before coming back for this job." She stood and set her lab glasses on the table. "I'm not satisfied with the 'undetermined' conclusion, either. Blake told me. I know you feel the same way."

I leaned my elbows on the table. "I'm really glad to have him on my side. He's refused to put this thing down."

She clenched her teeth behind closed lips, slowly nodding. I couldn't tell if it was from agreement or just acknowledgment.

I scratched my cheek. "Where is he right now, anyway?"

She scoffed. "Good question." She walked over to a wall where dozens of generic brown shoeboxes sat in organized rows. "I'm not sure what Blake has told you, but I think I may be able to help you with your father's fire."

I watched her trace her fingers under the white box-end labels. I stood and pocketed my hands. "Do you think these recent arsons are connected?"

"Yes, I do." She stopped at a box and tapped on it. "And I am also convinced that Biltman isn't the one setting them."

CHAPTER 23

Each box label bore a date, ID number, and investigator name. She stacked two at a time in my arms. "You can put them on the lab table if you'd like."

I laid them out, counting fourteen in all.

She waved a palm. "Each one of these is a separate fire. This one is the department store that collapsed on you guys." She stole a furtive glance toward the door and lifted the lid. One small ziplock bag lay on the bottom.

I reached my hand out. "May I?"

"Sure." She nodded. "Just don't open the bag."

I lifted the plastic into the light and let my eyes focus on a cubic centimeter of glassy black char. "Is this all the evidence you have from that fire?"

"That's everything."

"Out of all that?"

"That's it."

"Blake find this?"

She nodded.

I placed the bag back in the box. We moved to the next.

"This was from an apartment fire on the fourth of this month." She shifted an inquisitive glance toward me as if to say, *"Were you on that one?"*

I shook my head. "I wasn't on duty that day. I was down in Mexico."

She squinted her eyes in mock misgivings. "A likely story indeed." She raised two plastic bags from the box, both containing fragments like shiny dark pebbles.

"And these?" I said.

"Same as the first. Blake says they may be incendiary residue. I've run them through the IR spectrometer and haven't found anything conclusive. Just carbon. Transformed end products of incomplete pyrolysis."

"Char."

"Yeah. Glassy char."

We moved through all fourteen boxes, nothing more revealing than the first.

"I almost forgot." She walked back to the shelves, tracing her hand farther down the row, squatting by a box near the floor. "Your father's fire."

She held it with two hands close to her abdomen. A torrent of memories rushed in. I saw his face in images tied together with onion-layered emotions that made my eyes well up. I turned, squinted, and pinched the bridge of my nose. I blinked out the moisture and acted as if I had removed a piece of debris from my lashes.

Julianne slid the box onto the tabletop, then stepped back and motioned with her hand. I placed my fingers on the lid and lifted it to the sound of smooth cardboard separating.

A dark coffin of air lay beneath.

I looked up at Julianne. "It's completely empty."

"I know. There's nothing."

"That's your connection between this and the recent fires, *nothing*?"

"It's a stretch, I know. But you've got to realize that out of all the boxes on this wall, this is the only one with absolutely nothing in it. The closest ones to it are these fourteen." She walked back to the wall and returned with two others. She lifted the lids. Both boxes held a heap of evidence bags. "These two are from Biltman's last fires before he was caught a few years ago."

"Overflowing."

"Right. Not hard to notice the difference between his fires and these fires. But the pressure from Admin right now is to prove progress with these recent arsons. Mauvain got wind that we found a connection between the recent fires and jumped at the chance to link them to Biltman, the obvious and known fire setter."

"So, this fire last night . . ."

"Tons of evidence. The work of a mentally unstable amateur."

"Unlike these other fourteen and my dad's."

"All, I believe, the work of a highly intelligent, experienced professional."

"But why would Blake go along with Mauvain in molding the case to point to Biltman? He could clearly see that the evidence doesn't support it."

"Good question." She took a seat. "There is one other thing. Did you happen to notice the investigator's name on the boxes?"

I checked the labels.

B. Williams. B. Willliams. B. Williams . . . Every single one.

I looked at her sideways. "What exactly are you suggesting?"

"Look, I'm not one to slander or even talk about other

people. I'm really not." She got up and paced. "I get along with everybody—"

"Just say it."

She pressed her lips together and nodded. "All I'm saying is that Blake is under tremendous pressure to deliver results with this. He's on the promotion list for Prevention chief. They want decisive action." She folded her arms. "Aidan, you seem like a great guy. Just be heads-up, all right?"

"Just what?"

The lab door opened. A brass-badged Prevention chief leaned in, his pear-shaped torso pushing his belly over his belt. I stared at the boxes on the table and glanced at Julianne. She raised her hand slightly and gave a shake of her head to say it was all right.

The chief cleared his throat. "Julianne, I'm afraid I need you to process a new set of samples."

She smiled. "Straightaway, Chief."

He cleared his throat again. "That's my girl."

She walked past me and winked.

"Make sure to bring a jacket," the chief said. "It's a bit cold out there this morning."

Julianne stopped. "Jacket?"

"Yes. I need you to go straight to the fire scene."

She cocked her head. "The Biltman fire?"

"No, actually. There's been a string of new fires this morning. Investigator Williams was at the scene of the first and marked the items he wants you to bag and test."

"Blake's already been there?"

"Right."

Julianne looked around the room for her coat. "Okay. Where is it?"

The chief handed her a paper and looked over her shoulder. "Young O'Neill, is that you back there?"

I raised my eyebrows and smiled. "Chief. Hey. Long time no see."

"How are you all hanging in downtown after that roof collapse?"

"We're getting along okay, Chief. Thanks." It was like reciting lines. "Sounds like Firefighter Hartman is making a strong recovery."

"Glad to hear it." He held up a key ring for Julianne and dropped it into her palm. "This is for the Chevy. No running the lights and sirens now, young lady. And take this just in case we need to reach you." He handed her a radio, then turned and left.

Julianne doffed the lab coat and pulled on a mahogany brown vest. She twirled the keys into her palm. "Care to join me?"

CHAPTER 24

Brick university buildings looped like film reel. Julianne leaned forward, gripping the ribs of black vinyl on the steering wheel.

"You know," I said, "you can actually go a full twenty-five through here."

She scanned through the windshield. "Quiet."

"What?"

"I'm trying to concentrate."

I leaned my elbow on the door. "Watch out for that student."

She let off the gas. "What?"

"Oh, my bad. False alarm."

"That's not funny."

I reached toward the center console. "I bet this siren switch will get us there real quick."

She slapped my hand, returning her own with ninja-like quickness to the wheel. "Don't you dare!"

I held my hand up and stared at it. "Who hit me?"

A smile creased the corner of her mouth.

We passed the planetarium and wove our way into the adjacent neighborhood. I read off a series of directions from the chief's notepaper and looked up just as Julianne slowed to a stop near the fire scene. An RPD patrol car blocked off access to a court where a single engine and ladder truck sat parked. Firemen moved with the slogging pace of overhaul, pike poles and drywall hooks in hand. Vapid steam meandered off the roof.

"I know this house," I said.

"You do?"

"Yeah. As a kid. Isn't this Todd Youngman's house?"

"I don't know. Wasn't Youngman a battalion chief?"

"Yeah. He's retired. He and my dad used to fish together. He had golden retrievers."

"Does he still live here?"

"As far as I know. I haven't seen him since Dad's funeral." I opened my door to see Battalion Chief Anderson approaching in a huff, as if he'd just finished blowing out the fire by himself.

"Blake just left half an hour ago," he said to Julianne. No introduction. No *"Hi, how are you?"* He pointed to the rear of the house. "The probable origin is taped off in back. You got gloves and bags?"

Julianne produced a silver briefcase. "All set to go, Chief." She half-curtsied and smiled.

Chief Anderson's face did what looked like a hard reboot. His affect sweetened and changed, as though he were looking at his daughter or grandchild. "Well, that's excellent. Now, you just let me know if you need anything."

"Sure will, Chief. Straightaway." She motioned with her hand, hooking it in front of her like Shirley Temple saying something with determination. I had to look away to keep from guffawing.

Chief Anderson started back toward the scene. "And there's coffee and drinks at the back of the safety officer's rig if you'd like."

Julianne waved again, like only a girl can wave, wiggling fingers and all. Chief Anderson returned the gesture before he realized I was watching. His face fell into a frown. "Morning, Aidan."

I stifled a grin. "Morning, Chief."

He disappeared behind the ladder truck. I walked around the hood of the Tahoe. "How do you do that?"

She clipped the handheld radio on her belt. "Do what?"

"You're like a snake charmer."

She smiled and put a finger by her lips. "Shh. You'll reveal my secret." She started toward the house, briefcase in hand.

"Here," I said. "Let me get that."

She pulled it away. "I've got it."

She walked on and I stared at her for a moment. I quickened my pace to catch up. "Is it the *straightaway* that gets them or the curtsy?"

She stopped and twisted her lips, looking up to her right. "Probably a combination of both. But the *straightaway* seems to give the whole thing a sort of British flare that just melts their butter."

I laughed, shaking my head. "That's so awesome. You're like the Chief Whisperer."

We suction-cup-stepped through mud along the side and back of the house. Yellow fire-line tape cordoned off an area that, from the looks of the scattered concrete pillar foundations, had once held a wooden deck. A large black triangle stained the building side, showing where the flames had lapped up at the soffit and attic vents. Three little orange flags, like the kind used to mark damaged turf on a field, stuck out from the charred debris on the ground. Julianne flipped open the briefcase and pulled out a digital camera. I stepped back as she snapped several photos.

She donned exam gloves and picked out a pair of tweezers; a long, thin scalpel-like device; and three plastic bags. As she bent under the fire-line tape, I leaned forward to hold it up for her, watching as she took care to place her feet only in the existing footprints in the mud.

I let the tape back down. "You're a natural at this. What a crime to keep you cooped up in a lab."

She hunched over the first flag and tilted her head with a dismissive shrug. "You should see me when I get things cooking indoors."

Whoa. Deep breath. "So . . . what do you see?"

She poked around with the long instrument. "Looks like another one of Blake's interpretations of a suspicious char fragment." She opened a ziplock bag one-handed and used the tweezers to pluck and deposit the piece.

The next two didn't prove to be much different. She retraced her steps and I again held the tape as she ducked and returned to the briefcase. She opened one of the bags and transferred a kernel into a test tube.

I sat on my haunches. "Now what? Chemical tests?"

She uncapped a small vial and plunged fluid from it with a pipette. "I'm starting a series of algorhythmic experiments to test the reactivity of the unknown. The sooner you do it, the better chance you have of detection before it decomposes or evaporates. You'd be surprised at how fast a little heat and humidity can eradicate evidence." She said all this as she worked, deliberate and methodical, exacting in her measurements and procedure. She gave a swirl to one of the tubes. The liquid changed to a faint amber.

I raised my eyebrows. She looked at me and nodded. "Could be something."

She drained the test tube and returned the fragment to its bag, marking the outside with a pen. "All right." She capped the vials and placed the tools in a separate plastic bag. "These will need to be cleaned."

"Wait." I stood. "What is it? What about the other two pieces?"

She shook her head. "There are further tests I need to do." She shut the briefcase. "We need to get this back to the lab."

CHAPTER 25

She drove with hands at ten and two, staring straight ahead.

I adjusted my seat belt. "What is it?"

"I keep thinking I'm forgetting something. I bagged the samples, the scooper; I have the radio . . ." An alarm beeped from her wristwatch. She glanced at it. "Oh. Dad." She stopped at a light and played with the zipper on her vest.

Dad? "You need to make a stop?"

"Do you mind taking a detour?"

"No, not at all. Whatever you need to do."

"It might take half an hour . . ."

"That's fine. It's no problem."

She switched on her blinker and glanced at her watch again. We drove for about ten minutes before pulling into a parking lot with a sign that read *Pathways Memory Care.*

She shut off the engine and exhaled, staring at the steering wheel.

"Your dad," I said. "I thought he was . . ."

"Dead?"

I nodded.

"No, he's alive. But I did lose him. Just in a different way. That week before your father died, that time on the bridge, he hasn't recognized me since."

I ran my finger across a fine layer of dust on the center console radio. "Alzheimer's?"

She shook her head. "Stroke. Massive bleed."

"Does he remember anything before the stroke?"

"Some scattered things. But not me, so far." She pressed her lips together. "He can't walk anymore."

"I'm so sorry."

"Don't be. I'm . . . I just can't believe that I almost forgot to visit my father at a memory care." She smiled.

I chuckled. "You know, I'll wait here. Take as much time as you need."

"No, I'd . . . If you want, I was kind of hoping you'd come in." Her eyes met mine, and I realized that she was inviting me inside—not into a building, but into her garden, into a recess of her heart.

I nodded. "Okay."

Ornate woodwork and flower patterns adorned the entryway walls. Gilded-frame prints hung throughout, broad representations of the European impressionists. The air held the odor of an aerosolized garden scent.

At the front desk we met a joyful round-faced woman with a curly cloud of white hair. She wore a thick aqua blue cardigan joined in the front by three big buttons. The youthful glow of her cheeks and the brightness of her eyes marked her too young to be in her eighties, but she was too respectfully aged to be less than sixty.

"Julianne." Ruby-colored reading glasses dangled from a black-beaded string around her neck. "Missed seeing you at church Sunday. How are you?"

Julianne leaned over to give her a hug. "I'm doing well, Pearl. How have you been?"

She took a deep breath through her nose and tottered her head with contentment. "Just wonderful." She gave the impression that breathing air was like sipping sherry.

Julianne squinted. "Have you fallen in love?"

She laughed and placed a hand on Julianne's arm. "Dear one, *let* me tell you. His love is better than life, His presence sweeter than wine." She walked around the desk and gave me a once-over.

Julianne stretched out a palm. "Pearl, this is my friend Aidan from the Fire Department."

She shook my hand. "A pleasure to meet you." She smiled and paused. "Well, your dear father. Let me take you to him."

Julianne followed alongside. "Is he playing pinochle with the guys again?"

Pearl stopped, running her fingers along the cuff of her sweater. "I'm afraid he hasn't been playing with them this past week."

"What has he been doing?"

She looked at the floor and considered. "Thinking, I'd say. Thinking, and perhaps a little praying, too."

"Has he been in his room the whole time?"

"Oh no. Of course not. He eats his meals and everything just like before. But late afternoon like this, when he usually plays cards with the other gents, he's instead been sitting out in the atrium, gazing at the flowers and the fountain. I make it a point to chat with him. He gets very quiet out there, but I know he likes me talking to him. I pray with him and give him a hug, and I know that he knows he's loved. At dinnertime, it's as if his period of afternoon quiet is over and he goes back to his normal routine."

"Why wasn't I contacted? Has the doctor been to see him?"

"Yes. And that's why I didn't call you. He says this is normal, that the stress on the mind of feeling lost and without bearing can become too great over time. Sometimes the body's normal and healthy reaction is to seek the quiet of something familiar, something grounded."

I looked at the floor. An instant later I found myself embraced in Pearl's thick cardigan, squished with Julianne in a group hug. "God has a plan for him." Pearl squeezed us tight. "He does for all of us." She straightened her glasses, which had gone cockeyed. "Now, let me show you the way."

I watched Julianne in the atrium with her father. She studied the lines and angles in his face, searching for any sign of recognition. After a while she just sat with him, placing her hand over his, watching a fountain spill water from staggered bronze leaves into a shallow basin.

I wondered what kind of pain that brought, and how it differed from a loved one's sudden death. It was a form of loss either way. The doctors were unable to fix what had happened with Julianne's father. I was unable to stop what had happened to mine.

None of it seemed right. None of it seemed just.

All of it was out of my control.

CHAPTER 26

The gray shade of dusk pulled over the city, blurring the edges of the high-rises. I left Julianne to her tests back at the lab and picked up some items I needed from the store—fresh basil, portabellinis, fettuccini, sun-dried tomatoes. My mother would be over for our weekly dinner soon.

At home I rinsed the basil in the sink and stared at the detached garage beyond my small patch of browning grass. Colors melded and shadows shaped images. A translucent figure morphed into Christine emerging from the door, book bag slung over her shoulder, keys jangling from an index knuckle, tilted-up oversized sunglasses diverting the flow of her hair. Her face wore the serious expression of a metropolitan woman moving in the pace of city life and Starbucks-instigated *New York Times* urgency. She followed the flagstone path to the back door . . . and vanished.

Water streamed into the sink. The basil in my hand bent low, sopping wet.

The doorbell rang.

I grabbed a towel and walked to the front door. The old brass knob squeaked when I turned it. "Hey, Mom. I—"

Cormac stood on the doormat. "I had to see you with my own eyes."

"Cormac. Wow. Come—"

My face mashed against his shoulder. He pushed me away and stared at me. "How's your vision? Been getting headaches?"

I wiped my hands on the towel. "Good to see you, too. . . . I didn't expect you here."

His beard had been trimmed down to a long bushy moustache. He ran his hand along a smooth jawline. "I had to make sure you were all right. How do you feel?"

"I'm all right. You know my head is a little—"

"It tore me up that I couldn't be there when you woke up." He walked in. "I heard you'd left the hospital and I couldn't believe it. This morning I drove to San Diego and caught the first plane I could get out here."

"It's good to see you. Come in. Yeah. Do you have a place to stay? I mean, you're welcome to the guest bedroom."

"No, no. I'm good. I've got a hotel. I'm only here for the night." He put his hands on his hips. "Wow. Look at you. The eternal hourglass turned upside down again."

I shook my head and glanced at the floor. "Well, I definitely feel fortunate."

He stood there smiling, cool air feeding in from outside.

"Hey, come on and have a seat." I closed the door and took his coat. "Mom is going to be here any minute."

"Alana?"

I smirked. "Yeah. Unless someone changed moms on me."

"Aidan, I didn't realize I was interrupting plans."

"No, don't mention it. I always make plenty for dinner."

He strolled into the living room and sank into the leather chair. Dad's old chair. I'd kept a lot of the furniture when I bought the house from my mother. She couldn't see staying there alone after my dad died, but couldn't see parting with it, either. Seeing Cormac there was a bit surreal. I was pretty sure he hadn't talked with my mom since he'd left to live in Mexico. She, too, had been upset with him for leaving, but there was something more than that, an awkwardness that hung between them.

I uncapped two bottles of Guinness and handed one to Cormac.

"Thanks, Aidan. House smells great, by the way. What are you cooking up?"

"Irish fettuccini alfredo."

He cocked his head. "Really? What makes it Irish?"

I tipped my bottle in the air. "I drink this while I'm cooking it."

The doorbell rang.

My mother hugged me at the door, Gaelic eyes smiling over rosy freckled cheeks. "How's my boy?"

I kissed her on the cheek. "I'm all right." I motioned toward Cormac. "Guess who was able to make it up for dinner."

She saw him and tensed. "Cormac. How are you?"

He stood. "Very good, Alana. Thank you. I'm much better now that I know Aidan is okay."

I gritted my teeth. "Let me take your coat, Mom."

"Oh yes. Thank you. I read about the roof collapse. How is your partner, sweetie?"

"He's getting better. I—"

"Roof collapse?" Cormac said.

I started toward the kitchen. "Yeah."

"When was this?"

"It was this large footprint department store. Trusses failed. I actually need to check on those noodles."

"Wait," my mother said. "Isn't that what you were talking about?"

Cormac shrugged. "First I've heard of it."

"Mom, would you like a glass of wine?"

"Aidan, what was Cormac talking about?"

Cormac glanced between us. "I'm sorry. I didn't realize she didn't—"

"I was at a beach in Mexico and got thrown onto a rock by a wave. It knocked me out and I woke up in the hospital. I'm fine."

Cormac shook his head. "Aidan here is too humble about his recovery. I saw it all. No breathing. No heartbeat. It wasn't until that doctor—"

"All right, all right," I said. "I was just trying to spare her the details."

"Aidan, I can't believe you didn't tell me."

"I just didn't want to make a big deal of it."

"You dying is a big deal."

"Well, I didn't die, Mom. See, here I am."

"Your heart not beating sounds a lot like dying to me."

"He was dead. And now he is alive." Cormac made a fist. "The incarnate will to power."

I put my hand out. "Cormac."

My mother's eyebrows knitted. "How could you keep this from me?"

"I don't know, Mom. Did Dad come home and tell you about every near miss?"

"How many near misses have there been, Aidan?"

"It's not like that. I just didn't want to worry you."

"I already worry. Do you think I don't already worry? Twenty-four years with your father and I worried every time he left. I don't think you quite understand what it's like. Have you told Christine yet?"

"That is a different situation altogether."

"No, it is not." She turned and looked over the living room.

Cormac forced a jovial tone. "Well, fortunately, Aidan doesn't take well to dying."

I shot him a *just shut up* glance.

My mother ran her hand over the edge of the leather chair. "Every night that James was at work, he called me. And I would sit here and answer the phone and hear his voice and he would always say how he would see me in the morning. Every night. Even that last one." She blinked away moisture in her eyes. "He wasn't lying. I know that I will see him again, when I am with the Lord. I have peace in that. But not knowing is the worst. Promise me you won't keep things like that from me."

"I've never understood how you could be at peace with God when He took Dad from you."

"I wasn't ready for your father to go. And I'm not ready for you to. I pray for you so much. But you have to trust in Him. Your father did."

"And look where it got him."

"God has plans for you, Aidan Paul. He may have to take you through the fire to accomplish them, but listen to Him. Have faith in Him. Stop being so stubborn and wise in your own eyes."

A pot lid clattered on the stovetop.

"I've got to get that."

We spent the better part of dinner in silence. Conversation stayed simple and polite. Cormac did the dishes and left right before my mother did, shaking my hand and wishing me well. I walked my mom to her car. She put a hand on my cheek and then drove away. Behind me the front door hung open. An amber hallway, warm but empty, waited within.

CHAPTER 27

The next morning gave me all of five minutes at work before the tones went off. The dispatch printer etched in a frenzy.

"Battalion One . . ."

Here we go.

I pulled on my turnouts as Kat slid down the pole beside me. Butcher jogged across the app bay. Peyton slid the pole by the ladder truck's tiller cab. A loud smack sounded off like pieces of wood clapped together. Peyton yelled, clutching his ankle on the floor.

"What happened?"

He winced, squeezing his eyes together. "Pole was wet. My foot slipped."

Engine One growled to life. Butcher shouted out his window. "Let's go."

Sower saw Peyton lying on the floor. "We need a tillerman?"

Peyton stood, using the pole to pull himself up. He yelled even louder when he bore weight on his ankle. He cursed again.

Sower motioned to Butcher. "You guys go. I'll take Aidan to tiller."

"Go," said Peyton. "I'm out, man. Go."

Engine One drove off. In its empty bay, the Nederman exhaust tube swung like a giant dark elephant trunk. My eyes trailed to the buildings along the horizon and the dark column of smoke rising beyond.

My pulse sprinted.

Sower climbed into the captain's seat of the ladder truck and threw his helmet on the dash.

I swung on my coat and climbed the ladder to the tiller cab. Throwing on the headset, I wrapped my hands around the steering wheel.

"All set back there?" Donovan's voice met my ears.

"Yeah." I stepped on the floor ignition button to allow him to start the truck. Through the channel of the ladder bed I watched the tractor cab shudder.

"All right. Pulling out." Donovan accelerated onto the apron. "Whoa. We do got us a fire."

Sower said, "You didn't see that before?"

"No. The Cairo, right?"

"Yep, I'm pulling the preplan right now."

The rig bounced into the street. Donovan cranked the cab right just as the tiller box cleared the app-bay door. I clung to the open cab door with one hand, and with the other I spun the tiller wheel left and then back to center, bringing the trailer in line with the tractor. A visceral blast of brisk air rushed past. The sound of tires on the dirt-littered road, the roaring transmission, and the wailing siren all tore through the air.

As a kid I'd always wanted to be an astronaut or a tillerman.

"Sixth floor, south side," Sower said.

Donovan replied, "Copy that."

We turned west and screamed down Fourth Street, air horn blasting across intersections. From the corner of my eye, I caught a glimpse of Christine's car going north down a side street, a dark-haired man sitting in the passenger seat.

Blake?

The radio clicked. I blinked and looked forward, turning the wheel just in time to follow the tractor into the hotel parking lot.

Butcher transmitted, "Battalion One, Engine One on scene, multistory high-rise, heavy smoke showing from the C and D sides of the building at the sixth floor. We do have occupants visible in the windows. Engine One will be heading to the fire floor."

"Battalion One copy. Break. Truck One, Battalion One."

Sower responded. "Battalion One, Truck One on scene at the C-D corner of the building. We have a visual of the occupants on the fire floor."

"Copy that, Ben. You think you can get the stick up from where you're at?"

"That's affirmative, Chief. We'll be in aerial rescue operations."

"Battalion One copy, break. All units, Battalion One on scene. This'll be Cairo Command, Chief Mauvain IC. Command post will be by the fire control panel."

Donovan set the air brake. I put on my helmet and climbed down from the tiller cab. Sirens echoed through the streets. Gray smoke weaved wraithlike overhead.

Six floors above, a window shattered. A chair toppled to the parking lot below.

I cinched my helmet strap tight.

The rig's high idle kicked on. I moved to the front of the captain's side and assisted with extending the outriggers. Four horizontal legs stretched from the sides of the truck and dropped at an angle to plant on the pavement.

I grabbed two ladder belts from a cabinet. Sortish climbed out of the cab with his glowing turnouts.

Great. Another new kid not to kill. I tossed him a ladder belt.

"Thanks," he said.

I strapped mine on, looking at the fire floor. Several windows were broken. Thick smoke poured out, rolling upward along the building side. People were hanging over the edges to suck clean air.

"I count three so far," I said. Behind one of the leaners, a bobbing orb swam in the smoke. "Make that four."

Sortish squinted. "I see 'em."

The truck whirred with hydraulic effort. Donovan stood atop the turntable, elevating the ladder from its bed with a steady hand on the lever. I climbed the tiller cab and spotted him. "You're clear."

He worked two levers at once, elevating and spinning the ladder toward the building. I descended and met up with Sower.

He held a radio by his ear and looked at me. "Go on air, and climb the stick with our mudflap as soon as Donovan's ready."

No comments about trusting me with the new kid. What other choice did he have? I reached my right arm around and twisted the valve on the bottom of the air bottle. High-pressure air swished through the lines. The motion sensor chirped to life with the regulator vibralert purring acceptance.

Donovan sighted the sixth floor as if he were aiming a gun barrel. Leaving his eyes on the building, he extended the fly sections, coaxing them forward like a skilled conductor wooing a sustained note from the string section.

All seemed silent save for cables and pulleys stretching for life.

An ethereal haze waved in the air. Red lights spun in alternating time. A flurry of activity swamped the street as a blazing crop of heat broke forth.

And then the first body fell.

CHAPTER 28

He hit the pavement like a pumpkin.

I turned away, as though I could shield my mind.

Sower motioned. "Go, go, go."

I strapped on my mask. Donovan feathered the stick under the first window. Orange illumination flickered in the dense smoke rolling from the unit. A woman lay on the sill. The ladder tip positioned directly beneath her—so close she could have climbed onto it on her own.

"She's hypoxic," Donovan said.

I left my facepiece regulator dangling and climbed the first of the four fly sections. My father's axe dangled from my waist strap, clanking with each step. My leather gloves moved over the grip tape–covered steel rungs.

Looking back from the second section, I saw Sower starting in on the first, Sortish still on the turntable. I guessed he didn't want to chance another probie with me after all.

My chest burned. Condensation filled my mask. I clicked my regulator in place and defogged the lens.

I couldn't climb fast enough.

By the third fly section, spectators below looked like larva, and the ladder truck like a monster film–sized insect angled for attack.

Above, two bodies straddled the next window over, sitting upright, waving, vanishing and reappearing with the erratic tide of smoke.

The first room flashed.

Glass shattered in an explosion of flame. A cloud of heat disseminated overhead.

The woman fell from the edge and landed on the rails of the ladder.

Her clothes were on fire.

My quads burned. My calves swelled with blood. I pulled with my arms.

No water. No one on the ground had a hose line ready. My axe was useless.

The ladder section narrowed as I worked up the fourth fly.

She began to slide.

My legs and arms felt like lead.

Just let me get there.

I had to. For her. For me. For Hartman. For Julianne. For my father. For every reason and none at all, my sole desire was to reach her in time.

But the angels let go.

No.

My voice never left my facepiece.

She cascaded like a meteor down to the ground, slamming into a car roof.

I squeezed my eyes and gritted my teeth.

Keep moving, Aidan.

I pushed upward. Charred and flaming debris littered the ladder tip.

The radio in my jacket clicked. "Hang on, men."

I leaned into the rungs and carabinered on. Donovan worked the controls. Sower clung to the second fly section. The ladder jerked and swung toward the next window. The two occupants straddled the sill, doubled over, gasping for air. The tip halted between them and swayed from side to side. I unhooked before it steadied and climbed ahead.

Ten feet away. Let's do this, A-O.

I craned my neck to keep them in view. The back of my helmet knocked on the top of my air bottle. Both still conscious, they reached for the ladder, grasping at the air as if they could reel it in with invisible cords.

Five feet.

"Hang on! Hang on!" I said.

Two feet.

Dusky arms outstretched.

An explosion erupted from the room. A pumping tide of smoke engulfed us.

Come on.

One foot.

I stretched out my hand to the man on the right.

"Take my hand! Take it!"

His form disappeared, his body swallowed by the fog. Five digits extended.

Like finding a light switch in the dark, his fingertips met mine.

I lurched, seized his wrist and pulled back. His body tumbled toward me. He twisted and caught his legs on my knee, grasping for the rungs.

I squeezed him tight to the ladder and looked up for the other. Starved for oxygen, he could fall any moment. Pumping smoke obscured my vision.

Sower appeared in the smoke behind me.

"Pass him down. I've got him." He positioned himself behind the man, arms under his, knee between his legs, and started a careful descent.

The heat bore down. I locked my leg into the rungs near the ladder tip and swam through the darkness, reaching with both hands.

Come on. Where are you?

A dull thud sounded.

Little eruptions let loose from the smoke, flashing and fading with the locomotive chug.

I found the window sill and felt for his body.

Nothing.

I bent under the smoke line. Sower stood with the first victim at the top of the third fly.

"Ben!"

He looked up.

I motioned. "I'm going inside."

I am?

Sower shook his head and undid his ladder belt, strapping it around the man and clicking him to a rung. He waved at me, but I wasn't about to argue. I turned and climbed back up to the tip. My hands found the sill and I brought my leg up.

Here we go.

I pushed off the ladder and flailed into the room. I fell with my bottle toward the floor, something cushioning my landing. An arm protruded beneath me.

The smoke belched so thick I could barely see the window I had just come through. I struggled to my feet and pulled on the arm. It felt like lifting an anchor with a bungee cord.

His torso lifted and slumped. My hands slipped. I careened backward, knocking over a lamp and crashing to the floor.

The heat pressed in through my turnouts. Fire rolled above me, spattering like cloud-to-cloud lightning.

I made my hands and knees and crawled forward until I hit a wall. I felt upward for the sill but found only more wall. No window. No exit.

Swiveling my head I searched in vain. Where was he? Where was I? I moved to stand but was forced to the floor by the temperature. I crouched and gritted my teeth.

Then from the cloud, the fire seemed to form faces. Razor teeth like a blacksmith's irons, a wall of glowering eyes encircling me.

It's not real.

My earlobes burned through my hood. I squeezed my eyes open and shut. The Mexican reaper again waved before me. The dark expanse of the ocean enveloped me.

I shook my head and exhaled forcefully.

A circle of flame tightened around, an insurmountable wall of fire.

I closed my eyes.

Help me, God.

I took a long, deep breath.

Think, Aidan. Think. You're just in a room.

The window should have been at my side, behind me. I swam in reverse, feeling with my limbs the objects around me. It was taking too long. I had to get out.

My leg hit the bed. I kept moving and felt something soft with my foot. I pivoted and felt the shape of a torso, neck, and face.

Behind him was the wall. I felt the sill above that, and as thick-stranded smoke streamed out the window, I glimpsed the faint veiled sunlight.

I slid my hands under his arms and sat his slumping frame against the wall.

The low-air-pressure bell clanged on my pack. The facepiece regulator vibrated.

Almost out of air . . . again.

I squatted low and lifted with my glutes. I lost my balance forward, pinning him up against the sill. His head flopped back through the open window.

His arms bowed and he sank.

No, no, no.

He slipped to the floor, his body listing to the side. I caught him with my knee.

I grabbed his shoulders and then the smoke stopped pumping. Like a visceral coda, or the sudden cessation of a gusting wind followed by a poignant silence.

Air sucked into the room with one sudden motion, racing past my head like a quick deep breath through narrowed lips. The wool cloud separated. Alpine mountaintops came into view. An amber haze ensconced the sun. The steel ladder lay beneath the sill, Sower leaning from the tip waving his arms.

"Aidan! Aidan—"

A blood-orange burst swathed my sight. A pressurized heat wave pounded past. Piercing stinging encircled my wrists and a searing iron pressed upon my neck.

I dove headfirst for the ladder, grasping for metal. Sower bear-hugged my body as I slid against him. The ladder jerked away, and he pinned me to it. I grabbed a rung while we swiveled from the window. A raging blowtorch shot from the opening.

I brought my legs in and found solid footing. We swung out from the smoky curtain, Sower slapping flames from my turnouts.

"Get water on 'em!" Someone shouted from the street.

Three firefighters, like yellow ants, scrambled with a hose line, arcing water up to us. Cool liquid pellets bounced off the building, showering down, hissing and steaming. Sower kept his arm around my back, pinning me to the ladder.

He spoke in low tones, barely discernable over the tumult. "I've got him, James. I've got him."

I leaned my facepiece against the rung, my mouth too dry to swallow. Water fell like rain in the desert. We were overtaken and drenched.

And as broad daylight passes, acquiescing to a storm, there was nothing left to do but hold on.

CHAPTER 29

Chief Mauvain's voice boomed behind the closed door to the captain's office. "It was your job to stay on him!"

The second voice was faint, a barely audible rise and wane of tones.

Mauvain retorted, "I don't want excuses."

This time the other voice rose before dissipating. "I didn't agree to be your . . ."

I looked both ways down the dorm hallway. Everyone else was in the kitchen, eating a late lunch. I stepped closer to the door and leaned my ear toward it.

"If you're looking to . . . I suggest you reevaluate that position."

"That's not what we agreed to." Recognition of the second voice flashed. *Lowell.*

"You will agree to what I tell you to. Is that understood?"

A long pause told me it was time to get moving. I turned the corner at the end of the hall just as the office door opened.

I slid the pole with a slow twirl, stopping midway to take in the view. The light of the setting sun poured in through the app-bay windows. The ladder truck sat next to Engine One, the light rescue truck next to that, all facing forward in quiet anticipation. I relieved my boot tension on the cylinder, finishing with a slow, straight descent to the floor.

I hopped up on the engine's diamond-plate bumper and watched a flock of starlings launch from rooftop to rooftop, swirling and swaying in the air currents above.

The ring of my shirt collar chafed my burnt neck. I ran my fingertips lightly over the blistered red rings encircling my wrists. Second-degree handcuffs. Having no desire to fill out a volume of paperwork, I'd hid them from the safety officer in the morning.

Those rooms should have been sprinklered. There's no way the fire should have spread that fast and that violent. Three citizens were dead, and I'd nearly joined them.

The sun slipped behind the high-rises, silhouetting their forms and turning linear edges radiant. I thought of how the workday was ending for most. How folks would make their way through traffic back to their homes and their couches and TVs. They'd see their dog, or their kids, or whatever they had waiting for them. They would draw the curtain on their day and prepare for bed and fall into the twilight existence of sleep, waking to a new day, a new world, with new air and challenges and blessings and all the things that make up a life.

Somehow, I'd awakened in Mexico with a different life, a different set of rules. No longer buoyed by air-bottle bravery or side-slung angels heaving couplings over curbsides. Now I struggled and clawed with fear and trembling through the task I'd once conquered with ease and indifference.

I'd been assigned back to the engine, sure that any confidence Butcher had in me, any respect he'd allowed himself in his toleration of me, had all but faded. I felt the uncertain stares of others, the twisted freak-show curiosity of the half-horrified, half-pity-filled onlooker.

I couldn't hear the fire anymore.

I was being hunted by it.

—

Ben worked a hoe with soil-stained hands. His one-hundred-fifty-square-foot garden patch looked out of place behind the station—cornstalks and pumpkin vines beside fuel pumps and chain-link fencing. He straightened when he saw me, sweat glistening across his brow. He wiped his forehead with his arm. A trace pattern of dirt clung in its wake.

I put my hands in my pockets. "Beautiful time of night to garden."

He sniffled. "Isn't it?"

"You need a hand?" I said.

He picked up a bag of seed. "I'll make a shallow trench and you drop one of these in where I show you."

I poured tan pellets into my palm. "What are we planting?"

"Stuff for next season. This is green cabbage."

The color drained from the city with the waning light, artificial blinking bulbs and neon tubes becoming the disparate alternative.

"Something's wrong, Ben."

"No, you're doing it fine."

"No, I mean something's been wrong. With me. I'm sure it's obvious."

He stopped working the dirt.

"I can't . . ." I looked away. "I don't know what's happening. Everything is chaos. It's crazy. I feel like the fire . . . is out to get me."

Sower placed both hands on top of the handle. "Funny you'd say it like that. Because you've seemed lately like you're *trying* to let the fire get you. It's like you've been on this self-destructive rampage, Aidan. It's not safe for any—"

"Ben, I can't hear the fire anymore."

"What about reading the smoke, Aidan? You're so bent on beating the fire that you're neglecting to respect it. Like I said, it's as if you're—"

"What's wrong with wanting to beat the fire?"

"Nothing, in essence. But it has to be balanced. Unless something's changed, you are just a man, Aidan."

"And fire is just an element."

"That is created by God."

"A God who is indifferent to death and suffering."

"You know that's not true."

"It's not?"

"No, Aidan. It absolutely isn't."

"Then why'd He let Dad die?"

He stared at the cornstalks. "The Lord gives, and the Lord takes away."

"Not if I don't let Him."

He laughed and shook his head. "I think I'm finally starting to get you."

"Are you now?"

"You have such a chip on your shoulder. You think you know better than God."

"That's not what this is about. You haven't even been listening. I'm saying I'm off my nut, Ben. I think the fire is out to get me. Me. Personally."

"And you think you can't hear the fire anymore?"

"I know I can't."

His broad shoulders lifted with a deep breath. "Or could it be that you've finally realized that you can't control it?"

I shook my head. Talking to him had been a mistake.

"Have you seriously considered the opposite?"

I folded my arms. "What opposite?"

"That maybe you *can* hear the fire. That maybe you're hearing it just fine. That the fire is, in fact, out to get you."

"You're funny." I glanced at the seed in the dirt. "You know what? Forget it." I turned away.

"I'm just asking if you've considered it."

The white walls of the station stood shadowed and quiet.

"You have a God-given gift, Aidan, just like your father. Things like that are irrevocable."

Tones.

"Battalion One, Rescue One, Engine One, Engine Two, Engine Three, Truck One with safety officer to a business on fire, multiple reports of heavy smoke coming from the front."

—

We screamed down Second toward Wells. A towering column stretched to the sky, atramentous against an achromatic canvas. My backup set of turnouts felt stiff and unnatural, the charred first pair having been succinctly snatched up that morning by the safety officer. I'm just glad he didn't see my helmet, all blackened and soot stained, the visor tarry and warped at a tented angle.

The rig bounced over an intersection. I clicked the waist belt on my pack. Lowell cranked on his air bottle.

The Jake brake fluttered. Kat pulled past a single-story concrete block structure—Simmon's Medical Supply. Pitch-colored clouds poured from the front door. An Asian man holding a white shirt by his face stumbled along the sidewalk.

I hopped out and met him. "Is anyone inside?"

He shook his head. "My business. My business."

I grabbed him by the shoulders. "Are any people in the building?"

"No, no. Stop the fire." He hacked and coughed. "Stop the fire."

"Go sit over there," I told him, pointing down the block.

Lowell met me at the sideboard. "Alley pull?"

"Let's do it." I grabbed the big loop and the nozzle. We split ways and paid out the hose. Kat sent water through it lightning quick. It whipped and jerked, and the nozzle pointed, ready for attack. I knelt by the smoke-filled doorway and bled the air from the line.

The front windows stood blackened. Somewhere in its lair the beast slumbered, smoke undulating in tarragon stertor. The sweet acrid scent stayed in my nostrils as I donned my mask.

Breathe.

Breathe.

I saw a serpent uncoiling, lithe and lambent. Its basilisk breath engulfed the threshold.

I shut my eyes. *Read the smoke.*

I opened them to see intermittent flare-ups bursting above.

Lowell knelt beside me. "Ready to go?"

"Look at the smoke."

"What?" He couldn't hear me.

"Look at the smoke. I think it's going to—"

Fire erupted, shattering the glass. We tumbled backward. I pulled on the bale and widened the pattern, circling the water around the doorway and then to the windows.

Lowell cursed about the heat. He tucked his helmet near my shoulder, his weight bracing my back.

Engine Three arrived and pulled the larger two-and-a-half-inch line. Behind us Butcher called for a defensive strategy. Truck One elevated their ladder. A cannon stream shot from its smoothbore tip, deluging a thousand gallons a minute.

Surround and drown.

The fire receded, retreating to its lair, roaring and hissing the entire way.

CHAPTER 30

A frigid breeze breathed through the birches, the morning air crisp on my cheeks outside the Station One lobby. It had rained lightly overnight, leaving the asphalt dark and glistening. Something in it made me think of Christine, the way her hair reflected light like record vinyl, framing her face while she held a Hemingway novel. She'd swap quick coy glances from my dad's chair in the living room. "Am I your Catherine?" My response always the same. "Yes, Christine Patricia Allen. *You* are my Catherine."

A forlorn vacuum opened inside me.

What had Blake been doing in her car? For that matter, why was he leaving the Cairo as we all were arriving?

My cell phone vibrated. "Hello?"

"Aidan?"

"Yeah?"

"It's Julianne." Her smooth voice cooled my loneliness like salve on a sunburn.

"Hey. How are you?"

"I've found something new."

I pulled out my car keys and switched ears. "With the fire at Chief Youngman's house?"

"Well, yes and no. I'm at a fire scene right now, and there's another connection. I don't know why I didn't see it before, but this is one of several I've documented in the last two days." She was quiet for a few seconds. "Can you meet me here?"

"Sure. Yeah. Who else is there?"

"It's just me. I'm over on Wells Avenue."

I stuck the key in the ignition. "I know exactly where you are."

—

A faded red Bronco and a stretch of yellow fire-line tape were the only signs of the department that remained around Simmon's Medical Supply building. No engines, no truck, no chiefs.

The windows were boarded up. Through the front door I saw Julianne standing, sans lab coat, wearing dark slacks, a white blouse, and dark suit coat. She stared at the burn patterns across the walls.

I ducked under the fire line and walked through the front door, crunching glass shards along the concrete. "Don't you look the part?"

She gave a measured smile. "I'd much rather be looking through a microscope, believe me."

I nodded. "Battlefield promotion?"

She let out a quick laugh. "Sort of. Just temporary, you know. 'Acting Deputy Field Inspector.' "

"I see. Do you get to have a gun?"

"No. No. But I'm ready to taser the first firebug I see."

"That's impressive. No pepper spray?"

"Oh, I've got that, too. I'll tase 'em and then I'll pepper spray 'em."

I chuckled and trapped a drywall nugget under the ball of my foot, scribing a white semi-arc on the floor.

"It's good to see you again, Aidan."

I looked up. "You, too."

She crossed her arms. "I saw news footage of the Cairo fire. I saw you climbing the ladder."

I bit my cheek and nodded.

"When you went in that room, I didn't know if you would come out."

I avoided her eyes. Racks of elongated medical supplies hung frozen in their melted state. "You know, you should probably have a helmet and a HEPA mask in here."

She creased her eyebrows. "You think I need it any more than you?"

Touché.

She motioned down a hallway. "Come on back here. I'll show you what I found."

I followed her to a large back room with a single window on the back wall that lent pale light. The space was empty save for the skeleton frame of a metal filing cabinet sitting in the corner. It looked like Wile E. Coyote with a blown stack of dynamite.

"This," she said, "was the office."

"Nothing but ash."

"Yes. And no."

"More of nothing to add to the not-so-heaping stack of anti-evidence?"

She wasn't amused. "This time I've managed to find something in that nothing." She pointed down and made a circular motion. "Take a few steps back."

I scanned the floor. Encompassing the room's perimeter, where the cinders had been swept clean, the smooth finished concrete was interrupted by a ring of cracks and chips. "What caused this?"

"Think Johnny Cash."

"A Boy Named Sue?"

She smirked. "No."

"What? Okay. The Man in Black?"

She shook her head. "Think what, not who." She circled her finger, pointing at the floor.

"The Ring of Fire?"

"There you go."

I studied the spalled concrete. "How?"

She knelt and pinched fine flecks of the aggregate. "Something burned here so hot and so fast that it instantly fragmented the concrete."

"And the room's contents with it?"

"Gone. Almost entirely consumed. As if a veritable wall of fire shot up and out, devouring everything in its wake."

My eyes followed the scorched sediment.

She stepped closer to me. "It seems to have burned out and away from the starting ring. The little that was on the inside here probably didn't go up until later." She drew her jacket together. "But it's not just this. A closer look at the sprinkler system showed that the water flow had been shut off at the riser."

"Any fingerprints or DNA?"

"Absolutely nothing, so far. Even the tamper alarm is clean and unactivated. Whoever this is, they're wise to detection methods, both automated and investigative. So I decided to start searching for patterns, and I think I may've found some commonalities among the occupancies."

I played connect the dots in my mind with the recent fires. No picture emerged. "What do you see?"

"This one is the most obvious, but I wouldn't have made the link except for when you said that house the arsonist targeted two days ago was retired chief Youngman's. This business here is the primary supplier for oxygen-related equipment to our department."

"So, both are department related. What about the fire Hartman and I were on?"

"I looked into that. Turns out they are the parent company of our local uniform store."

I scratched my jaw. "What about the trailer park fire?"

"That I don't see a connection with occupancy. But I do with geography. Engine One was on the initial attack string for that fire."

"And it was on C-shift."

"Right. As roughly ninety percent of the arsons in the last week have been."

"There was an A-frame fire I went to when I first got back."

"Which was in District One and happens to be a rental property belonging to another retired RFD chief."

"And the Cairo?"

"Again, Station One on the first alarm string." She walked to the window. "I know. The department connection might be a reach. But what we do know for sure is that each of these fires burned hot and fast and left little evidence. And the majority have been on your shift and in your first due area." She turned and stared at the floor. Shadows cloaked her body. "There's . . ."

"What?"

"There is something else."

"Tell me."

"I don't know if I should—"

"Yes. You should. Come on now. You brought it up."

She swallowed. "It's about your friend."

"Who? Blake?"

"Yeah."

"Go right ahead."

She tilted her head and looked at the ceiling. "There is a history there."

"A history with . . ."

"Between."

"Between who? You and him?"

She nodded. "We were dating for a time."

A memory awakened. "You're Julie?"

"Some friends call me that. Did he talk about me?"

"Was this like . . . six years ago?"

"Yeah."

"He mentioned going out with a girl named Julie, that it didn't work out. That was about it. I never made the connection."

" 'It didn't work out'? That's rich." She angled her lower jaw and shook her head. "We'd been dating for a few months. Things were getting more serious. But he'd just been telling me everything I wanted to hear." A ripple traced over her eyes. "He's your friend. I shouldn't be saying this."

I narrowed the space between us. "It's all right. Believe me. It's okay."

She brought her lips together, looked to the side and back. "I had to work late one night waitressing. When I left it was dark and as I sat at a light on Fourth Street I looked over and saw Blake walking out the back door of a strip club with two women clawing at either side. They all got into his car, his Fire Department vehicle, and took off." She shook her head. "Aidan, I feel so awkward telling you this—"

"No. It's fine. I didn't know that about him. Thank you for telling—"

"I'm not done."

"Go on."

"This one is a much, much bigger jump. I hardly know you, so what do I have to lose, right?" She mumbled, "Except maybe my job." She folded her arms. "If you look at the circumstances . . . I mean, if you really examine the current situation. There is a possibility . . . And this is just conjecture, really . . ."

"Julianne please, again, just say it."

She shifted her weight. "All right. I just found out that Blake had been passed over for the promotion to division chief in Prevention. And this wasn't the first time. It was the third. That's got to sound like a death knell for his hopes of climbing the ladder. Something like that is bound to stir up resentment." She straightened her jacket. "That's all. Infer what you'd like. I just needed to tell someone. It's hard to know who you can trust right now."

I didn't know what to think. I shook my head. "Why, after what you've been through with him, would you even consider taking a job where he works?"

"I know. But I'm all my father has left. The opportunity presented itself, so I took it to get back here." She took a deep breath. "You should also know—" She pressed her lips together.

"I should also know what?"

"You should also know that I, personally, can't—" She stopped, tracing fingers over a jacket button. "Aidan, I want you to have the closure you need with your father's death. But how can you expect that finding the arsonist will really change anything for you?"

"It will bring justice."

"Yes. But in your heart. Your fight is with more than just a murderer. I think you can't accept death."

"He shouldn't have died."

"But people do. Of anyone, you should know that."

"Doesn't make it right."

"And will catching an arsonist change that?"

Anger blended in my gut. "I don't have to listen to this."

"Why, Aidan? What are you so afraid of?"

"Who said I was afraid?"

"Are you? Where is your peace?"

"We make order out of chaos. That's the job."

"So you're always the hero and never the victim?"

"We stop loss."

"Enough with the slogans. Some things are beyond your control."

"And what if I can't accept that?"

"You can."

"What if I won't?"

She breathed deeply. "You'll have to." Her eyes locked with mine. "You need to. Or life will move on. It will. And you will miss out."

I looked away. "I don't need this."

I turned and strode down the hall, out into stark daylight and the chill city air. I blinked against the brightness, seeing a red-hued vision of Christine's car with Blake sitting in the front.

"Hard to know who you can trust right now . . ."

I glanced back at the building.

That it was.

CHAPTER 31

I took a long walk down Wells, strolling for at least an hour, maybe more. My feet led me to Patty's. I looked at the thick weathered-wood door and leaned on the sidewalk pay phone. Something twisted in my stomach.

Why am I here?

Going in was neither a healthy nor wise choice. I wouldn't find any answers in there. No healing. No rest.

I turned and faced the pay phone. Tagged with black marker, torn white sticker residue covered the tarnished and keyed up chrome. If I dialed Christine from it, her caller ID wouldn't indicate me. I fingered a couple quarters in my pocket and put a palm on the handset. I held the coins by the slot.

Who will answer?

I dropped in the quarters and dialed her number.

It rang three times.

Four.

Five.

Six.

I pulled the receiver from my ear.

"Hello?" A man's voice.

He repeated. "Hello?" A woman asked a question in the background. It sounded like Christine. I heard chafing sounds like a hand over the receiver, then a muted, "I don't know, babe." A ruffling sound was followed by a clear "Hello?"

The voice was unmistakable. I wished it hadn't been.

I slammed down the handset. My quarters jingled deep in the machine.

Patty's beckoned.

My dim-lit sanctuary. Where the passage of time either slowed or sped, the metered course of mortality bending to the will of the imbiber. Eleven fifteen on a midweek morning, but to no surprise, there stood Lowell beside a stool, monologuing with arms outstretched, the messiah of malt liquor. Chris Waits sat two stools down, his grin broad between his handlebar moustache, eyes angled with the aged understanding of a Japanese elder. A couple other bodies at the bar laughed and grinned. I scooted up to the rail.

Patty wiped his hands on a towel hanging from his waist. "Well, if it isn't the estranged O'Neill boy."

I folded my hands on the counter. "Estranged?"

"It's been nearly two months, lad."

I pulled back. "No way. A couple weeks, maybe."

"Don't you lecture me on the passage of time." He wagged his finger in the air. "You're not going to win that fight, Aidan-boy. So ya might just as soon—"

"All right, all right." I raised my hands in surrender. "Man, Patty. Go easy on me."

"Go easy on ya?" His motor was started.

Here we go.

He whipped the towel from his apron and held it in the air. Then he cracked a smile at the corner of his mouth, and crinkled his eyes in acceptance. He placed the towel on the counter and leaned forward. Reaching up with one hand he grabbed the back of my head and brought my forehead to his. "Good to see ya, lad." His breath exhausted the thick stench of whiskey. He straightened. "Have you been eating enough? Are you hungry?" He pointed his towel at me. "Remember when you were a boy and you asked why I always drank Guinness?"

"I remember your face looked like I'd just spit in the holy water."

"And what did I tell you?"

I licked my lips and looked up to recite. " 'Cuz it's a meal in a glass.' "

He slapped his thigh and cackled. "That's right, and don't you forget it, Aidan-boy."

Lowell seemed to just notice my presence. "Aidan." He placed a hand on my shoulder, his eyes already glazed by a couple pints too many.

I wondered what deception lay hidden in his gesture. What truths lay behind that veil?

Waits waved from down the bar. He asked Patty to pour me a pint. I nodded. "Thanks, Chris."

Lowell continued with his stories. I nursed my stout, running my thumb along the sweating glass sides. Down the bar, the lines of age drew on flushed faces, quivering lips looking for nurture at the rim of a glass. I took back a mouthful, letting it sit on my palate before swallowing its slow mind-numbing medicine.

The pint stood like a silent cone-shaped monolith, my own personal idol. This place . . . my own dark sepulcher.

Was it Thoreau who said the tavern will compare favorably with the church? I'd let this brass-railed bar become my altar, a murky draught my living water. Repetition and ritual.

Ancient.

Revered.

And powerless to change a hardened heart.

All were accepted. None were healed.

—

I opened my eyes to see streetlight edging through the window blinds. It diffused into the dark of my room. I rolled off the bed, a dull throbbing in my head arguing against uprightness. Separating the shades with my fingers I saw the Land Cruiser parked out in front, straight and proper by the curb. I felt my front pocket for the keys but found only flat denim. The cranial pounding moved to my forehead. I pressed my palm against it.

Green digital numbers glowed from the nightstand: 6:37 p.m.

I stumbled to the kitchen, found a glass, and filled it with tap water. I forced myself to drink it all and ate a piece of bread. Back in the bathroom, my fumbling hands found an aspirin bottle. I threw back three and swallowed, sipping from the tap to wash away the chalky residue. Leaning back against the doorframe, I stared at my vacant bed. A gaping emptiness gnawed at me.

My stomach churned. I dropped to my knees and vomited in the toilet. The cool porcelain felt firm under my palms, the tile hard on my patellas, my heaving stale breath putrid and humiliating.

I wiped my mouth with the back of my hand and pushed aside the shower curtain. I crawled into the tub and lay my head back—sinking into a deep, hollow, dark slumber.

CHAPTER 32

Look, Aidan. See Daddy?" Steam lifted from the iron resting on the end of the board.

I held a smooth wood block over my building. It was as tall as the table, as tall as I was. I threw a quick glance at the television. A long ladder stretched into a smoky sky. A fireman carrying an axe climbed it. I peeked at my swaying tower.

"Look, Aidan."

I squeezed the carpet with sock-covered toes. "Is that Daddy?"

"It sure is. See him on the ladder?"

"Is he in the sky?"

The iron exhaled a hot vaporous sigh. My mom turned over a chalk-blue collared shirt, one Dad wore at work. "He is very high up."

"As high as the mountains?"

"No, not that high. About a quarter of the height of Circus Circus."

When we went there I got lots of quarters. They had these heavy brown balls that when you rolled them and they went up in the holes, then you got lots of tickets. "The quarters of the game place?"

"That's right. Good memory."

I set the block on top of my building. It fit perfectly on the phone-shaped one. The building leaned a little, so I shifted the block and it balanced. I let go, and the tower swayed slightly. I measured with a flat hand from my head to it.

"As tall as me, Mom."

"The building?"

"Yeah."

"I don't think so, dear. That building is hundreds of feet tall."

My chest swelled with pride. "I know. Look."

"Oh. Right. Very nice work, Aidan."

"It's hundreds of feet tall."

"Maybe in pretend feet." She turned the shirt over again. She didn't have the white basket with all the pants and shirts. Just that one.

"That's a special shirt."

She stared at the TV.

"That's a special shirt, Mom."

"What, dear?" She looked over and smiled.

"That one takes a lot of ironing." I smiled back.

The iron breathed out. She stopped smiling. A sad look filled her eyes.

"Mom, you're squeezing the shirt!"

She looked at her fist and set the iron down. She draped the shirt on the board and turned away into the kitchen. "Aidan, don't touch that. It's hot." Her voice sounded warbly.

I itched my nose and stared at the ironing board.

She loved to iron blue shirts.

I'd almost forgot about my building. I sidestepped around it, then ambled down the hallway, finding the creaky boards. I could make it to my bedroom in five creaks.

Warm sunshine shone through the high window in my room. It made a rectangle on the floor that half covered my circle carpet with all the colors and half covered the wood part of the floor. I laid down in it. The sun made rainbow circles when I squinted my eyelashes. Sometimes if I looked long enough I could see invisible things floating around like little hairs or worms or bubbles. When I lifted my hand and shielded the sun, I saw some different dark clouds that were only in one part of the sky. They were black like the wax paper you can write on with toothpicks.

Under the window sat my mud-colored toy box. He-Man was in there, probably on the bottom in the corner next to the rubber turtle and my disc guns. I lifted the lid and dug my arm in.

Nope . . . Nope . . . There he is.

I ran from my room and skidded down the hallway all the way from the bathroom to the living room, jumping on the carpet where the wood floor ended.

I landed, and my building swayed. I stood perfectly still, holding He-Man by the waist. When it settled, I stretched out on my belly, looking up at the tower the way He-Man saw it.

I brought him up to one of the blocks at the bottom and cocked back his fist.

"Oh, dear Jesus!" my mom cried out.

She cupped her hands over her mouth, standing at the edge of the kitchen. She stared at the TV.

I didn't like it when she was so loud. The TV picture was smoky and orange and shaky. "Where's the ladder, Mom?"

She said something so quiet I couldn't hear.

"What?"

She shook her head.

"Mom, I can't hear you. Take your hands down."

But she just stood there.

"Mom, what did you say?" I looked at the TV. The ladder appeared, and a fireman with an axe climbed down through the smoke. "Look, Mom. Is that Daddy?"

Her hands moved to her chest. "Oh, Lord. Thank you. Thank you, Jesus. Thank you, thank you."

"Are you praying for the food?"

She came over and knelt in front of Dad's chair, her arms held open. "Come here, baby."

"One sec. Watch this." I aimed He-Man so he would strike the block. He swung a mighty swing, toppling the tower to the carpet. It was awesome.

I hopped over the blocks and jumped into my mom's arms. She held me tight, swaying back and forth. She smelled like my blanket and bear. I liked long hugs.

I played with her earrings. They were gold with little white marbles. I tried to get the marbles out. "Aren't you so glad you saw that?"

"What, dear?"

"Aren't you so glad you saw that crash?"

Her eyes crinkled. Each side had four lines. "Oh, yes. That was a really strong punch by Conan."

"That's He-Man, Mom."

"Right." She sniffled and smiled. "I love you, Aidan."

"I love you, too, Mom. Is it time to eat yet?"

She looked up and ran fingers under her eyes. "Oh. I guess it is."

"You know that four plus four is eight."

She blinked and gave a curious look. "Very good, Aidan."

"Will Daddy be home tomorrow?"

She put a hand on my cheek and kissed my hair. "Yes, bug-a-boo. Yes, he will."

CHAPTER 33

I stood in a stream, my feet ankle-deep in warm muddy water. The wetness climbed my pant legs, rising, flooding, then raging. A *hiss-splash* of pelting water shot over my face.

My eyelids unlatched under blurring rivulets, refracting white tile and incandescent light.

"Wakey, wakey, A-O."

The shower shut off. I blinked away droplets. My wet plastered hair dripped water down my temples. I wiped my face and stared up into the purple moon judgment of Christine's countenance.

"You know," she said. "Yi Jing once spoke the ancient proverb, " 'He who wants warm, dry rest ought not to sleep on a riverbed.' "

I pushed myself over the edge of the tub and slosh-stepped past her to the bedroom, stripping off wet cotton.

She scoffed. "Top of the mornin' to ya, laddy."

I turned and threw my sopping shirt. It hit the wall beside her, leaving a wet shadow imprint on the plaster.

She stared at the shirt and then at me. She held a small cardboard box filled with miscellaneous items and dangled keys on a finger. "Here are your house keys. I'd like my apartment key back, please."

"I . . . I don't know where my key ring is."

She let out a derisive laugh, then turned and walked out. "And if you're going to insist on not answering your own phone, have the department take me off your emergency contact list. It's C-shift today."

I glanced at the clock. 9:05 a.m.

I was already late.

"Don't expect me to bail you out next time," she yelled from the entryway. "You're not my problem anymore."

The front door slammed.

—

Mauvain's office.

There were few things I enjoyed less. I typically made every effort to avoid setting foot on the second floor, and I worked even harder to avoid entering a chief's office. Lowell called the entire floor a commonsense black hole. Spend too long in administrative management and rational thought got sucked from your synapses.

Butcher wasn't a happy camper when I'd walked in at nine thirty-five. But in the sea of other items he had to tackle that morning, my issue was set adrift, only to be snatched up by Mauvain, who happened to be walking down the stairs as I made my way up.

I stewed in the chair opposite his desk and chewed on the inside of my lip. The chair's height adjustment was stuck on low, exacerbating the already present feeling of being a kid in the principal's office. Mauvain's large leather chair sat empty. I stared at his wall of framed certificates.

He walked in holding a flopping stack of papers, leaving the door open, and settled behind his desk. He didn't look up but set the papers down, clicked the mouse for his computer, and lifted his head to read the screen. I looked out the windows, across the parking lot and the train trench to the bleak urban tones of downtown.

"O'Neills and punctuality." He typed and stared at the monitor. "Close the door, Aidan."

I wasn't quick about it, but I stood and complied, and then slowly made my way back to the low-rider seat. I could just see him after hours with that chair upside down, working with a screwdriver to sabotage the height adjustment. I didn't know where he was coming from with the "O'Neills and punctuality" comment. My dad had made a habit of showing up a half hour early for every shift. Now, awards ceremonies . . . that was a different story. He may have missed one or two of those.

Mauvain sat back, folding his hands. "You are aware that we have an arsonist on the loose?"

My head was still pounding. My mouth felt like cotton. "Yes, sir."

"And, you are aware that we start work downtown at eight in the morning."

We started work at every station at eight in the morning. He was the king of condescension. "Yes, sir."

He raised his eyebrows and ran his tongue along his teeth, making a suction-release sound. He wanted an excuse. And any reason I gave would only open an opportunity for him. I kept quiet and stared at him. His face drew down. I was making him work. Time for a new tactic.

He pushed his chair back and walked to the window. "That was quite a fire at the Cairo."

I kept silent.

He stared into the distance. "Interesting, Aidan, how things seem to fall apart around you. First Hartman. Then a couple flashovers. Your unpredictable behavior. Folks have been talking."

There it was, his next weapon, the power of the opinion of some indefinable group. He wanted me to ask what "they" had been saying, who "they" were. But I wouldn't learn from him anything I didn't already know. Guys couldn't figure me out. How could I blame them? I couldn't figure me out.

He turned, leaving his thin façade of cordiality on the sill. He leaned both hands on the desk, staring in my eyes. "Spitting image." He shook his head and breathed out through his nose. "Same look. Same insolence. Same arrogant attitude." He straightened. "The apple certainly hasn't fallen far from the tree."

I held his gaze. As far as I was concerned, he'd just paid me a compliment.

"You should know that Biltman's a bust. He set his own place off. That's it." He sat down and framed a tent with his fingers. "But of course, you knew that, right?"

I cleared my throat. "Why would I know that?"

He rocked his chair back and forth. "How was your time off?"

"Short."

"Get everything done that you wanted?"

"What makes you think I had anything I wanted to do?"

He parted his hands and shrugged. "Guy like you that works a lot. Must be things you want to take care of."

"I was in Mexico."

"Right. Right." He scratched his temple. "You have anyone who can account for that?"

"May I ask what this has to do with my being late?"

"I heard that you were at the Prevention lab the other day."

"And . . ."

He leaned forward and lowered his voice, as if he were letting me in on a little secret just between the two of us. "Folks down there are swamped. This investigation is high priority, and there is a lot of sensitive information surrounding it. It's probably in your best interests to not get in their way, if you follow me."

"No, I don't follow you."

"Stop showing your face around Prevention."

I pulled out my phone. "Maybe I should have a union rep here."

He put out his hands. "Please. I don't think we need to take it to that level. Just having a chat." He stood, this time walking to his awards wall. He pocketed his hands. "James never saw the value of recognition. A certificate to him was just a piece of paper. But you know what these are, Aidan?" He motioned toward the wall. "These are rungs. Each one lifting the smart and diligent worker another step higher. Some folks are jealous of that. Some resent an individual's efforts to better himself. They feel threatened. Belittled. But knowledge is power. Isn't it?"

He waited for me to respond.

His face betrayed a subtle twinge. "Knowledge *is* power, Aidan. And don't think I don't know you. You've been lucky with these recent fires. It would be unfortunate for that luck to run out." He walked back to the desk. "Tell you what. I'll be sure to keep watch over you." He picked up the paper stack and thumbed through it. "Your next paycheck will show three hours docked, absent without leave." He looked up. "I'll make sure that gets in your file."

Looking back at the papers, he waved toward the door. "Leave it open on your way out."

—

The black leather punching bag creased and retreated from my fists. Blow, blow, blow. Combo jabs and palm-heel thrusts and dorsal-foot-plane side kicks. That afternoon gave me Station One's basement gym to myself. My iPod blasted The Who from a set of connected speakers. Roger Daltrey wailed "Won't Get Fooled Again."

What was Mauvain's angle anyway?

Front kick. The bag chain clinked and shook. Front kick. Sweat flipped and sprayed from my face.

Did he really think I had something to do with the arson fires? Directing suspicion toward me would be a convenient smoke screen for him, especially if he was involved with it all.

Who could I trust anymore?

I pounded the bag with gut-born aggression. Jab. Jab. Hook.

Not my ex-fiancée.

Jab. Jab. Hook.

Not Blake.

I stood back, chest heaving hard-blown breaths, clenched fists at my sides. My pores stank of secreted ethanol. And there, amid the ruins of what I'd known as my life and the state of things, a dust-settling clarity fell into place.

Blake had been staying at the Cairo the day of the fire.

Every one of the serial arson evidence boxes bore his name.

He'd been passed over for promotion.

And I saw him . . .

In her car.

I heard him . . .

In her apartment.

I turned away from the bag and stretched my neck, pushing open palmed against the ribbed surface of my fist.

The ensuing thought, like a disturbing image, edged its way through the doorway of my mind.

If Blake was tied to the current arsons, and if the current arsons were tied to my father's fire . . .

CHAPTER 34

I walked through the rest of the workday with the drugged calm of conviction. And with my empty-handed capitulation came solace.

I stood in the kitchen and stared out the windows. The colors of the evening spilled across the sky like an overturned drink onto a tablecloth. Swirling dust devils danced in a vacant lot. A lingering expectation of a tempest hung in the air. And I knew the day's moment lay at hand.

I walked to the pole, slid to the floor, strolled to the engine, and took a last look at the transient tawny light suffusing the streets.

Tones.

The dispatcher delivered, monotone, methodical. Something big was going down. The string of rigs ran long.

Brush fire.

In the hills. Threatening structures.

The wood thud of doors closing sounded from the pole holes above. One by one firefighters squeak-slid to the floor. I unzipped my brush bag and pulled the lighter weight yellow pants over my station blues. Kat appeared in the front seat. Battery on, ignition switch flipped, motor rumbling. Butcher swung on his brush shirt and climbed into the cab.

Lowell stepped in holding a bowlful of boiled eggs. He dropped into his jumpseat. "I hate brush fires."

We shot westbound on I-80, the Pierce's diesel motor more than apt on the incline. At the line where the eastern Sierra foothills meet with the sprawling home developments of the valley, a dark gray plume pitched skyward.

Engine Five gave an initial report, "Rapid fire spread moving with two fronts—one toward the timber, the other toward the houses."

I tied a bandana around my neck and strapped on web gear holding water bottles and an emergency foil fire shelter. My heart charged with the rig, aching to approach, drawn to the destruction.

Bring it.

Lowell stuffed his mouth and pulled on his yellows. I double knotted the laces on my brush boots.

"She's running the draws," Butcher said. "Let's watch those downslope winds."

Kat took the off-ramp to McCarran Boulevard. "Good ol' Washoe zephyrs."

Two other engines met us as we exited the freeway, and we traveled together, with us taking point. The sunlight dimmed as we neared the hilltop, gray glowing smoke hovering over the roadway, traffic at a standstill in both directions. Butcher grabbed the PA. "All right, people, let's part the waters. Let's do this." He rested his elbow on the center console and held up the mic like Moses' staff. A wave of motorists made for the sides of the road.

Kat navigated the opening channel of pavement. The rigs behind followed in her wake. We wound through the intersection, turning west past the RPD patrol cars blocking the street, and crested a small hill leading to the subdivisions.

A ghost-town air lingered in the abandoned streets. Kat maneuvered amid thick curtain waves of backlit smoke. Jagged ash strips whirled in the gutters.

One hand in the map book, Butcher pointed south. "Head up this street here."

We throttled around until the flashing reds of Engine Five broke through the cloud. Operator Lent arced around the back of his rig, flipping a glance at our engine and pointing to two houses closer to us.

I brought my goggles down and opened my door, the street slowing under the rig. I waited for it to stop and caught a glance of the fire between the stucco houses. A wall of flame stretched and flicked up the canyon side beyond the backyards.

I was tired of being taunted. Fatigued with the inexplicable. I wasn't about to sit and let harrowing images of Hades overtake me. I'd call it out. I'd meet it in the streets. Let it consume me.

What do I care, anyway?

Butcher looked to the back. "Deploy the progressive hose packs."

The air was heavy with burnt sage and juniper oils. I snagged a Pulaski axe and sheathed it through my web gear, the flat grubbing end hanging on the belt. Lowell tossed down two bulging green canvas hose bags. I shouldered one and turned so he could loosen the top flap. He yanked the coupling out and connected it to a discharge port.

He patted my shoulder. "You're good. Go."

I charged across a driveway, hose threading to the ground.

A cedar-paneled fence door blocked my way to the backyard. I pushed on the latch.

Locked.

I dropped the pack and pulled out the Pulaski. I rammed it against the one-by-six edge. Two blows busted the bolt free.

Smoke eddied over and around a low black metal fence on the far side of the yard. I bent to pick up the pack when the oven door flapped open.

I felt a sudden searing on my cheeks as the fire mounted the fence and rose on its haunches, a half block of burning bearlike aggression. It stretched and grew, twisting in a vortex. Back on the lawn Lowell pulled on his face shroud, twirling his finger in the air. "Water comin'!"

I fastened my shroud around my mouth and nose. The flames folded over and down toward the house. I dropped to my belly, gripping the nozzle, sucking air between grass blades.

The flush of water shot up behind me and under with squirt-gun streams spurting from the couplings. I twisted the nozzle.

Left for life.

Air escaped and flitted past my helmet. I took a quick breath before the rush of water came. I fanned it into a fog stream shaped like an umbrella. Lowell crouched behind and lifted the hose. We duck-walked forward.

Come get me, beast.

A shower of droplets covered my goggles, colors blurring through the water fan. The fire shook, flipping back and straightening. Surprised by the onslaught, angered by the imposition, it rolled inward and then unfurled out along the ground. I narrowed the stream and dug in my heels, sweeping from side to side. Flame fingers hissed, vanished, leaving blackened smoky wisps. It regrouped and rose back by the fence.

I moved in, the soles of my boots burning beneath. "Get back to *Gehenna*!"

Lowell leaned in. "What?"

I kept my helmet tilted, shielding my face from the heat, peeking out just enough to see my water stream evaporate into the air, confused spastic smoke shaking and coughing like a car motor searching for the right flammable mixture.

I had it off balance. I wanted to knock it over the edge, force it to scurry back down to the pit from where it came.

Kat transmitted over the radio, "We're at quarter of a tank."

I closed the bale halfway and held our ground. The engine only carried seven hundred fifty gallons. Seven hundred fifty separating the fire from the house. Seven-fifty keeping the fire from us.

A minute later, Butcher announced, "Kat's got the hydrant. Show no quarter."

I opened the bale and pushed us forward. Lowell stretched a second hose line connected to a gated valve from the hose pack. We flanked with two fronts. The fire retreated to the opposite side of the fence, sneaking glances in and under the bars. It tried to slither through, wicking in every way possible, fighting to keep its fingertip grip on the ground it had gained.

But it relented. We had it. The smoke lightened to gray. The last remaining fire disappeared into the draw, swallowed by a blackened smoky moonscape dotted with flickering sagebrush torches.

Lowell coughed and spit. I doused white root ash to the sound of bubbling bellows.

Butcher strolled through the waning fog, radio held close to his ear. He staked his shovel handle in the smoldering grass. "Don't get too comfy, boys. Sounds like the other side is losing it."

CHAPTER 35

Talk about snatching defeat from the jaws of victory.

The fire had taken two wood-shingled houses and was well on its way with a third and fourth by the time we redeployed. We got there quickly, but Butcher had been ordered by an overzealous staging manager not to move until they sorted out incoming rigs.

Fortunately for the neighborhood, a favorable wind shift drove the fire up the mountain and away from the houses. It spread into the timber and into high, rocky, and inaccessible-by-engine topography.

I sat back in the hose bed with Lowell and watched the Army Guard Chinooks hover like upended phone receivers, twin rotors fore and aft beating the air above the head of the fire, dropping thousand-gallon bucket loads of water. Single-engine air tankers played chase with smaller lead planes, following them in low and banking descents to blanket the hillsides with scarlet slurry lines in the sand to retard the fire's forward progress.

"That was old Captain Peterson's house right there," Lowell said.

I stared at the empty ash piles off-gassing, angled pipes protruding through a steamy and littered foundation. A simple fireplace and chimney stood surrounded by rubble. "That house right there?"

He nodded.

Then, in the most twisted and fitting way, I found myself entirely unsurprised to see Blake's gray-suited form scuffling and searching through the silt of the foundation. He wore rubber turnout boots and a white Prevention helmet, his leather gloves sorting and separating charred debris.

A sense of reckless empowerment came over me. And crazy in the way that abandonment comes, I climbed right off the rig with a beeline trajectory for Inspector Blake Williams.

Lowell shifted. "Where you going?"

I didn't look back. I stepped into the cinders and the temperature lifted.

Man's floor, hell's roof.

Blake bent over by the chimney, staring into the fireplace. I stopped a few feet away, unnoticed.

I wondered what was going through his head. Did he find and dispose of the incriminating evidence? Did anyone have the slightest suspicion? He probably thought he was home free. He was Irish Spring, clean as a whistle. Nonchalant. Unassuming.

Not an arsonist . . .

Cheater . . .

Murderer.

He scraped in the back corner of the firebox.

I spoke louder than normal. "Looking for evidence?"

He jerked his head up, striking his helmet on the upper hearthstone. "Ow. Hey, Aidan. How's it going?"

"How does it look like it's going, Blake?"

His expression flicked like the pixilation of an image. He grinned. "Right. I guess sometimes they get away from us."

I took off my helmet and scratched my head. "It can only get away if someone lets it loose in the first place."

He stared, his expression traversing from confusion to suspicion. He shifted his focus to the charred scraps at his feet. He knelt and started picking them up. "So. Were you guys on these ones here?"

I stared at him. I wanted to see him sweat, to see his pores open on his cheeks and brow. How long had he been sneaking behind my back? How long had he been at all of it? Did his deeds date back . . . to a warehouse, and a brick wall, and to me compressing my father's chest in that mad midnight ambulance ride?

"Why'd you do it, Blake?"

He shuffled the debris between hands, still looking down. "I'm sorry?"

I crouched to his eye level, adjusted my helmet. "I know you did it. I know all about it."

He froze in profile. He swallowed, took a deep breath, and straightened. "Do you, now?"

I stood, arms just out from my sides. "Is it for the rush? You like seeing all the pretty lights and sirens? You like watching people's stuff burn?"

He stepped closer. "Aidan, lower your—"

I shoved him, both hands into his chest, knocking him backward against the chimney. "You don't get to speak."

"What is your—"

"You don't!" I shoved him again. "How long?" I brought my helmet rim to his. "Let me be even more specific. Where do I start, Blake?"

"Aidan, I do not know what you're talking about."

I gripped tight the lapels of his suit beneath his open fire coat, his silk Armani lapels. Always so proud of his image, his status, his look. "Christine tell you to buy this one? Is that it? She your personal fashion consultant, Blake?"

"Aidan!" He brought his arms against my chest and tried to push me away. "Get. Off. Me." But I had him off-balance, my weight leaning into him like a steel strut. He grunted and relaxed.

I pinned him against the brick, my elbows over his shoulders. "How long? How long have you been cheating with her when I was at work?"

Hearing myself say it pulled the drain plug on my indignation. Swirling despair sank in my chest. I loosened my grip and stepped back. "Why'd you do it, Blake?"

His right hook surprised me, landing on my cheek and sending me reeling. A second strike knocked me flat on my back. My helmet tumbled off. I shifted to my feet and drove a solid fist into his gut. He let loose a sound like a balloon deflating.

I rose over his bent body. My jaw numb and hot. "You did it, didn't you? Couldn't get what you wanted from the department, could you?"

He turned to look at me, and I struck his face, knocking him down.

"Get up!"

He placed his gloved hands in push-up position.

"Get. Up."

Thick crimson ropes dangled from his nose. He spit into the ashes. "You've got it wrong, Aidan."

"Get up!" I wanted to hit him again. I wanted to pound into him and out of him every anger and boiling hate inside of me. "You think you can take whatever you want, Blake? If they don't give it to you, you burn it. Is that how it works, Blake?" I used his name like an invective. "So what is it? Was it good for you, Blake? What gave you more pleasure? The fires? My fiancée? Or my father's funeral?"

He pushed to his knees, shaking his head. "You're wrong, Aidan."

"Shut up!"

"You're wrong."

I kicked him in the side. It sounded like branches snapping. He buckled.

My legs trembled; my torso shook.

Blake gritted his teeth, pushed himself up on one knee, and with an arm around his abdomen rose to his feet.

I shook my head, my lips quivering. The gray powder beneath us lifted with a strong gust. It spiraled up and over our heads. I shut my eyes as dirt pelted my face, filling my hair. I blinked through specks and eyelash grime to see Blake squinting, a hand shielding his forehead.

The wind settled. Salt streams cut the dusty chap on my lips. My voice found little volume, only simple conviction in a straightforward sentence. "You're setting these fires and sleeping with my fiancée."

Blake shook his head and pulled the fingers of his gloves. "You're wrong, Aidan." He wiped blood from his mouth with the back of his hand. "You're wrong about the fires."

CHAPTER 36

A voice echoed from a distant corridor. "Hey, buddy. Hey, you can't sleep here. Hey."

My eyelids opened to a blur of blue shirts, haloed streetlights, and Gerald Montegue's unmistakable stare, his deep Basque eyes like sheltered caves.

"Aidan?" He bent at the waist and put a hand on my shoulder.

Why did I have to be woken by A-shift?

"Aidan, what the—"

I struggled upright. "It's all right." My words slurred as I spoke. I wove a hand in the air and then brought it to my numb face, feeling with my fingertips the diamond pattern of the bus stop bench I'd passed out on.

Other guys on the crew laughed and shuffled. I felt humiliated. How many drunk patients had I run on like this? What day was it anyway? How'd I get there? I stared at my clothes for clues. "You guys seen my car?"

"No way."

"I think he's gone from Guinness to McCormick."

Gerald straightened me with arms on my shoulders. "Come on now, buddy. This isn't you. What're you doing down here?"

I opened wide my eyes and blinked. Memories slinked in like late-arriving guests. "I . . . I think I was walking home from Patty's?"

Montie said something to a fireman behind him. A captain with a clipboard nodded. With the streetlamp backlight I couldn't make out his face. The fireman Montie spoke with came into focus.

Timothy Clark.

"Hey, Timoshee," I said. "Working overtime?"

He came beside me and put my arm over his shoulder. "Just a straight trade, bud."

Montie lifted my other arm. "Let's get you a bed inside." They stood. I tried but felt myself slipping between them. "Come on now, bro. There you go."

I don't remember getting into the back of the engine, or how I ended up in my cube on the third floor of the station. I woke a couple times to the sounds of alarms but quickly faded into sleep, unable to make sense or understand my place in it all.

—

The sound of diesel engines jostled me from a dream, something about skeletons selling suits on a beach. I was an empty-pocketed traveler. The brightness of the day inhabited the dorms, a clear reminder that the earth kept turning regardless of my schedule. I couldn't stand up straight without a kettle ball knocking inside of my head, so I hunch-walked to the showers to cleanse the sweat and stench from me.

My knuckles were scabbed and my jaw clicked when I opened

it. The washing of water brought a recollection of events. Like wiping dirt from a page, the story came clear.

After the fight with Blake, I didn't go home when shift was over in the morning. I had stalled in the station kitchen, drinking coffee and reading the paper and not really talking to anyone. The C-shift crew disappeared. And among the oncoming A-shift guys my stay outlasted the easily excused. Questions kept popping up like, "You working this morning?" or "What rig are you on today?" and "Did you get a full twenty-four hours of overtime?" So I slid the pole and slipped out the back while the A-shift crews held roll call in the dayroom.

I had sat in the Cruiser with no destination in mind, but somehow my autopilot steered me to Patty's, where I had to knock on the back door. He let me in and I helped him clean and prepare his few grilled and deep-fried menu items. He didn't once ask why I was there, just swapped stories and shot the breeze and toasted a shot every hour on the hour.

The rest is fuzzy, with progressive dimming, like details of a landscape that slip away with the dusk. I had retired to the backseat of my conscious mind, setting cruise control to navigate the rest of the evening. Little flicks of images and flashes of feeling appeared like power poles and billboards through slanted back windows. The world went dark until I opened my eyes to see a four-man engine company staring down at me.

And there I was on this morning, drying from a shower. A-Shift leaving and B-Shift coming on. I called a cab to take me back to my car still sitting at Patty's.

I arrived at the bar parking lot and tipped the cabbie. It wasn't until I sat behind the wheel that the sense of despair again ripped open. The pounding in my head receded and now felt like a thick mesh of cotton, and I wasn't honestly sure that I could even be considered fully sober.

I wasn't going into Patty's again. I inserted the tip of the key into the ignition.

A rap on the door window startled me.

Ben Sower looked in, smiling, hand raised with two knuckles protruding. I pulled the key out and rubbed my eyes.

He knocked again.

"All right, all right," I said. "Hold on." My voice was hoarse. I unlocked the door. He opened it.

He gestured palm up for me to exit. I looked at him, knowing that he wasn't asking. With no energy to argue, I swung my legs out and leaned my elbow on the steering wheel.

"Come on, now," he said. "All the way."

I exhaled and complied. When I made my feet, he snatched the keys from my fingers.

"Hey."

"You won't be needing these for a bit, son."

I glanced at the street and put my hands in my pockets. What did he want from me? I was tapped. I didn't have anything more to give. He stood as a monument to my inability. I couldn't measure up. Not to my father. Not for my fiancée. Not for Julianne.

Could I even measure up as a fireman anymore? My focus fell to the faded white parking lot paint.

He brought his head down to make eye contact. "Come for a ride with me."

Those unchanging eyes, rimmed with lines. I felt like a kid who'd been grounded, the outside world off-limits, my only avenue to accept my discipline. "Where are we going?"

"Watch your leg there." He ushered me away from the door

and shut it. "Where you are going is exactly what we have to talk about." He put a hand on my shoulder and gave it a squeeze. "You're not in trouble, Aidan. Wipe that penitent look off your face. Come on. I want to take you somewhere you haven't been in a very long time."

CHAPTER

37

The moment I figured it out, I went from reluctant to agitated.

Ben took the long way, finally puttering his old Ford pickup along the McCarran loop north of Rancho San Rafael Park. He kept me talking, reminiscing, even laughing a couple times at his ridiculous jokes. So when it snuck up on me and I realized what he was doing, I felt betrayed, foolish, and incensed all at once.

"You can turn this truck around right now."

His expression projected a strange confidence. "It's been half a decade, Aidan."

Gray clouds gathered over the hills. "Take me back."

"The only way for you is forward."

Everything in me wanted to strike the dash, to break a window. Skin stretched taut over my scabbed knuckles, white and purple in fists clenched tight. I was at a point where all options seemed spent.

Ben turned onto the narrow road leading into Our Lady of Sorrows Cemetery. A spade-tipped iron gate peaked at the center in an acorn shape. Hinges clung to stucco columns supporting weathered marble busts of smooth-faced saints with straight noses and pious visages despairing heavenward. He let the engine idle until a beep emanated and the gate opened in a slow arc.

He turned off the ignition.

I glanced at him. "What are you doing?"

"I can only take you to the gate. You have to be the one to cross."

"Would you stop that?"

"Stop what?"

"Stop talking like . . . like you're Obi-Wan Kenobi or something."

His cheeks drew up in a grin. "Well, my name is Ben."

"This isn't a joke."

He stared at the dash clock, then shifted in his seat. "How many times have you been here since the funeral, Aidan?"

I put my elbow on the door. He already knew the answer. I wasn't going to let him do this. But words spilled from my lips before I could catch them. "I can't. I haven't." My thumb crossed over the scar in my palm. "Not since that day."

"The day of the funeral?"

"Yes."

Cars on the road sustained a subtle hum.

"What haven't you told me about that fire?"

I shook my head. My cheeks burned.

"I see it in your eyes, Aidan. You've been shouldering a burden that's become too heavy. Whatever it is, bring it to light, let it breathe air."

Sorrow surged in my chest. I tightened my lips together.

"It's okay. You can say it."

A slow patter of raindrops hit the windshield.

"It was my fault, Ben. If we'd had just a couple more minutes . . . I remember him standing in the parking lot, like this calm vortex in a cyclone." A dull rumble traveled through the cloud cover.

"I can see James that way," Ben said. "Studying the fire."

"Always. I walked past him with a shoulder load of inch and three quarter, and he caught my eye."

"Did he say anything?"

"Yeah. 'Get in, get out, A-O.' He looked concerned."

"What did you say?"

Spike-shaped raindrops streaked the window. "I didn't say anything. I remember meeting up with Waits, who was forcing a door with a Halligan bar. I think you guys were setting up the stick."

Ben nodded. "That's right. On the other side."

"My dad was taking command until the BC got there. He had confidence in Waits and me to go on in. He trusted us. Trusted me."

"Do you think he was wrong to separate from you two?"

The rain stained dark patches of marble on the statues. "No, I don't blame him. I never have. He did what he thought was best. It wasn't his fault." The windshield fogged in the corners.

"So, Waits forced the door . . ."

"Yeah, Waits forced the door. Smoke rolls out, thick and dark and super hot. I follow my intuition and we start a long right-hand search along the wall toward the back of the building, stretching the hose line. Spats of fire break out above us, but it isn't until we are about a third of the way in that we see a distant free-burning glow, like a white star. And the place keeps getting hotter. From, like, uncomfortably hot to almost unbearable." A hollowness ached inside. "Every element in that building was fast approaching its flashpoint. I should have acknowledged that. Because nothing would be the same once it did." I wiped my eyes with my arm. "He warned me in the beginning." I strained to keep my voice level. "And I knew it.

"I . . . knew . . . it.

"I saw the outside brick walls, just like he did, the side-turned king rows and the cracking mortar between the blocks. I saw the screaming evidence of what was to come. But I wouldn't abdicate." I looked at the ceiling and took a deep breath. "I thought I could beat it. In my pride I mocked it."

I ran the back of my hand under my nose. "Waits shouts in my ear that we need to turn back. But I keep pushing on toward the glow. I think that if we can just get closer we can hit the seat and stop the spread. We can win it. We can knock it down. We get almost within striking distance, almost close enough to attack, and the low-pressure alarm sounds on my pack. Waits turns insistent. He grabs my shoulder strap and tells me we're leaving. He'd felt a window along the wall a dozen yards back. We were going to bust it out and escape that way. No more arguing."

I leaned my elbows on my knees and placed my forehead in my hands. A whirlwind of images whipped through my mind—taking one last glance at the fire, watching it fan out its clawed tips and sharp horned crown.

Ben intertwined his fingers. "You never heard James call you out on the radio?"

"Mine got bumped to the wrong channel."

"And Waits?"

"Dead battery. But we do what Waits says and find the window. We bail out and just walk away. A minute later the whole place blows."

He studied me and said, "I remember finishing our roof

cuts and climbing back on the aerial. That back wall crashed in underneath us."

"I saw you. And I stood there in the parking lot, Ben. Smiling. I stood there." Hot tears ran down. "And I thought, how indestructible we were. How the fire had tried but couldn't beat us. I was defiant and proud, and absolutely clueless as to what I'd just lost."

"You had no way of knowing he went in for you."

"I should have known."

"But you didn't."

"No."

"Because you can't control everything."

I blinked through the blur.

"This world is fallen, Aidan. Blessing and tragedy sprout side by side."

I squeezed my eyes shut.

"Fighting for what is good and right isn't wrong. But God is sovereign."

Tears overflowed.

He placed a hand on my shoulder. "Jesus loves you immeasurably. Lay it at His feet and know that He is God."

My chest shook in heaving sobs. I buried my face in my hands. Ben prayed for blessing and comfort amid everything in my life that had been twisted and robbed.

And I felt a warmth stir inside me. A timeless, familiar, and wonderful presence.

And in my heart I yielded.

You give and you take away.

Blessed be your name.

I fought the steady stream rolling down my cheeks. I sat up

and breathed in. "Okay." Ben squeezed my shoulder and smiled. I nodded. "Okay."

I stepped out of the car, the air fragrant and humid. Cloud cover blanketed the mountains, and the valley glowed with a translucent aura. The look and smell of things made new.

I walked through the gate. I followed the path to my father's grave. And there I knelt by the Celtic cross-shaped headstone that I'd only seen once before. A solitary inscription lay etched into its granite face: *Greater love has no one than this, than to lay down one's life for his friends.*

Every gangrenous guilt I had borne, every bitter root I had carried, my anger at myself, at Christine, at Blake, and at God and the seeming unfair life He'd created, I placed it all on the mantel of that rugged stone cross.

And I heard a voice, inaudible but certain, still and small.

Welcome home.

CHAPTER 38

The evening wrapped around the valley. A rare mist hovered, refracting streetlamp auras on my drive to the county hospital. With thoughts of Hartman, the lump returned to my gut. But I sensed a new strength with it. I offered a petition in faith for my brother.

The front desk had a hard time finding him at first. He'd moved on from the ER, of course, but ICU didn't have him. CCU hadn't heard of him. No less than four phone calls were made before his bed was located in the back corner of a recovery floor.

"Thanks," I told the information desk lady. She waved, her other hand holding a romance paperback to which her attention had already returned.

Save for an occasional tech, the wide hospital corridors were empty. The halls held the feel of a place that never sleeps, where someone is always moving, not caring if it's night or day, under the same humming lights and past rolling gurneys, hearing touch-tone pages for doctor so-and-so to report to the OR for a code blue.

I stood in the elevator next to a slight Filipino woman with an EKG machine.

"Slow night?" I said.

"Yes." She nodded and smiled. "We'll see."

The door dinged and opened. I stepped out. "Have a good night."

Low-lit hallways stretched in a T from the elevator lobby. I followed a sign posted with room numbers and arrows, stopping once to confer with a seated nurse before coming upon Hartman's room.

My breathing quickened. This was going to be harder than I'd thought.

The door stood propped open with a curtain drawn around his bed, the flickering blue and white light of a television the only illumination, a muffled bed speaker producing sounds of a laugh track at predictable intervals.

I stalled in the hallway. With the prospect of encountering Hartman's wife and her doubtless disdain, I found my legs locked and my heart anxious for escape.

"Aidan?"

Julianne approached from the nurses' station. "Hey, Julianne, what're you doing here?"

Her head cocked. "You don't know?"

I shook my head. "Know what?"

"Laura is my sister."

I still didn't get it.

She pointed to the room. "Laura Hartman . . . Matt's—"

"Wife." I put a hand on my forehead. "You're Matt's sister-in-law."

She glanced to the side. "Last time I checked."

"No wonder you . . . I can't believe you even talk to me. I'm so sorry. I—"

"No, don't be. I just assumed you knew. But I've only been back for a few weeks. And Matt's so new to the department, a lot of the guys have met him in here for the first time." Someone coughed down the hall. "So, you came to see how he is?"

I stuck my hands in my pockets. "I should have come earlier. I've been so self-focused." I looked at the floor and then back at her. "I met with Ben today. I went to my dad's grave."

Her eyes ran deep like the ocean.

"I've come to a place."

I saw a lifetime in them.

"And a confidence. Like a homecoming."

Her arms wrapped around my shoulders, hugging me tight. She pulled back and paused a breath away, letting her eyes meet mine. Her smile said more than a thousand words.

She moved to the doorway and tapped on it with her fingernails. "Hello?" She brought the edge of the curtain aside. "Hey, Matty. How are you?"

I heard Laura's voice behind the curtain. "Here you go, baby. Here's the pen."

Julianne glanced at me, then looked back and laughed.

"Bill Cosby's his new hero," Laura said. "It's all Jell-O pudding and reruns here, let me tell ya."

Julianne motioned for me to come closer. "Hey, I have someone here who really wants to see Matt."

"Oh, okay. I probably look like a mess."

Julianne waved a dismissive hand. "Laura, you've always looked better than me from the moment you wake up." She pulled me to her side and pushed back the curtain.

Laura stood from her chair. "Aidan."

I could tell she was surprised. I didn't know what to think, much less say. I smiled, feeling awkward. She walked up to me, expression stern like a railroad spike. Her eyes. Hazel. Deep and unnavigable. I looked away.

And found myself in another embrace.

Laura squeezed me tight. When she let go I caught my first glimpse of Matt, unshaven and gaunt in a pale blue gown. But his eyes were bright, alive and full of acceptance.

I wished I could have taken his place. "Hey, Matt."

He mouthed the words *Hey, Aidan* before picking up a notepad and pen.

Laura touched her throat. "His vocal cords got infected after the prolonged intubation. They say his voice should come back in the next few days. After the antibiotics kick in."

I patted his leg. "I can't tell you how good it is to see you awake." I shook my head. "You're alive. Despite my best efforts." I forced a grin, but the truth still stung.

"Aidan," Laura said, "I owe you an apology."

"You absolutely do not."

"No. Let me." She took a deep breath. "I've felt so bad about how I must have made you feel. You were right there with him. You helped save his life. But I was so mad at you when I shouldn't have been."

I wanted to interject and argue.

She could see it and raised a hand. "You had as much right to see him as anyone. I shouldn't have reacted the way I did. I really am sorry."

I looked from her to Matt. He nodded.

I knew I didn't deserve this. "Laura, believe me, I do not blame you one bit. I'm the one who's here to ask for forgiveness. I took us in too far. I knew better. I went against orders. If I hadn't been so arrogant and pigheaded, if I had let Matt do what the chief was asking us, then we'd both have been out in time. Him being here, right now . . ."

It took me a second to continue.

"I'm so glad you're going to be all right, and I am so, so sorry for bringing this on you and your family."

Matt nodded, his eyes reddened and watery. He scribbled words on his notepad and held it up.

You being here says all you need to. We were, and are, saved by grace.

"It's all right," he mouthed. "It's all right."

Laura squeezed his hand.

A tear dropped down my cheek, surprising me. "Thank you." I wiped my eyes. "It's late. I should let you rest. Do they think you'll be home by Thanksgiving?"

Laura looked at Matt and nodded. "The doctor is optimistic that he will."

"All right." I tapped Matt's foot. "Take care, brother."

"You too," he mouthed.

Julianne touched my arm. "Wait for me, okay?"

I stood in the hall, watching nurses down the corridor write in thick chart binders. Julianne exchanged a few soft words before waving good-bye and closing the curtain. We walked without a word to the elevator lobby. She pushed the Down button. I glanced at my watch.

"So"—she put her hands in her pockets—"guess who just got arrested?"

CHAPTER 39

D*ing.*

The doors disappeared into the walls. We stepped inside, separated by a flight team attending an unconscious patient attached to wires and tubes.

"How's that rhythm?"

"Still throwing ectopy."

"Runs of tach?"

"Little salvos. Multifocal."

Julianne made a face from her corner. I raised and lowered my eyebrows. The flight crew exited on the first floor, hurrying with the gurney toward the ER. It was already nine thirty. I felt as if I'd lived a week in a day. But tiredness didn't tempt me. My mind was spinning. Had Blake been telling the truth? Was he working alone?

I stepped out with Julianne. "So. Do tell."

She fished her keys from her purse. "Oh, come on now. You know."

"You want me to guess?"

"Do you really have to? Come on, O'Neill, this is your chance to redeem yourself."

"Redeem? For what? For not knowing you were related to Matt?"

She drew her mouth up to one side.

"Okay, all right. All right. My guess is that you are referring to one Blake Williams."

"Exactly." She searched my face. "Isn't that great news? I mean, he's just been brought in for questioning, but it still—"

A young man in dark blue scrubs steered a hospital bed up to the elevators. Julianne twisted her lips and tapped her leg. The elevator opened and he went in.

The door closed and I scratched my head. "Are they suspicious about his monopoly on the evidence?"

"And the lack of it?"

"Yeah."

"That's one rumor."

Another technician walked down the hall with a cart.

"What do you think about getting out of here?" I said. "How about some coffee? I'd love to hear more."

She glanced at the time. "Um . . . yeah."

I cringed. I saw the heartbeat of potential going to flatline. I'd make it easy for her. "Oh. Yeah, you're probably right. It's too late—"

"Oh, no, not for me. No. I could have a cup of coffee and fall asleep a half hour later."

We've got a pulse. "Wow. Yeah. Really?"

"I just wanted to make sure that you meant tonight." She glanced at the floor. "I'd love to grab a cup."

Yogi Berra was right. This night was far from over. My smile must have said it. Julianne started walking.

I came alongside. "Where to? I'll buy."

"How about Pneumatic Diner?"

"Sounds great. Which way is your car?"

She raised an eyebrow. "In the garage. How about I meet you there?"

"Fair enough."

—

We climbed a staircase to the second floor. A girl at the cash register answered the phone. "Pneumatic dot com. This is your mom."

Cool blues and pinks of neon art glowed along the ceiling—other work from local artists hung around the high walls of the otherwise compact room, the center of which was occupied by three employees preparing and serving in a U-shaped bar/kitchen.

Cash Register Girl nodded to us and put the line on hold. She led us around to the far side of the room, where we sat on tall chairs at a small square table next to a window. The lights of downtown glowed in the east.

Julianne placed her purse on the floor. The waitress returned with menus and sweating ice water glasses. We ordered cappuccinos and a piece of chocolate cake.

I drew an *A-O* in the glass condensation. "So, how is the new position going? I mean, the whole acting deputy inspector in the field . . ."

She shrugged. "Honestly, I feel a bit like a second-class citizen."

"How so?"

"Well, I'm not bona fide, to start. And the department vehicle they gave me . . . Don't get me started."

I laughed. "It's that beat up old Bronco, right?"

"Yes. Can you believe that?"

The waitress set down our coffees and cake.

I moved my water near the window. "I can't believe that thing is still running."

"It isn't. Well, barely. And apparently Mauvain thinks he's in charge of fleet maintenance now. He made me make an appointment to take it to a shop tomorrow." She sliced a small piece of cake.

"What's wrong with it this time?"

She swallowed the bite, tilted her head back and forth, and looked at the table. "Something with the carburetor . . . No, radiator. Manifold system?"

"You have no idea, do you?"

"None. Absolutely none." She grinned, then pressed her lips together. "I don't have chocolate in my teeth, do I?" She checked her reflection in the window. "Okay, good. All I know is that it smokes a lot and doesn't move very fast."

"Sounds like a lot of District One patients."

She laughed, covering her mouth with her napkin.

Chill lounge beats permeated the room from inset wall speakers.

She crossed her legs. "So about your confrontation with Blake. I heard all about that."

I rubbed my jaw. "He has a wicked right hook."

"Let me see." She reached out and turned my cheek.

Her fingers felt soft and warm. Outside, the city seemed empty and cold.

"It still looks sore," she said.

I breathed out the word *yeah*.

She pulled her hand away.

I sipped my coffee. "How'd you end up going out with a guy like that, anyway?"

She smirked. "It was just by chance. I met him through a girlfriend of mine."

"And you still wanted to go into arson investigation after that?"

She chuckled. "No and yes. My degree is actually in chemistry. A couple years into Davis and I was over him. I started taking fire prevention classes at the community college here when I came home for the summers."

She brought her arms together in her lap. "So . . . Blake being brought in for questioning . . . not good news to you?"

I felt the cold window with the backs my fingers. "I know. You'd think I'd be ecstatic, right?"

"But . . . you're not."

I shook my head.

"Why? Is it because you're just too hurt?"

I caught her eyes. "I guess you already know the whole story."

Her mouth turned, contrite. "I totally understand if you don't want to talk about it. For me, of course, it was a lot different. I wasn't engaged. But I can still kind of relate. But it's got to feel like a double whammy for you." She lifted her mug and looked away. "Sorry, that's not the most sensitive way to put it."

"No, it's okay. I'd known that things weren't working out with Christine for a while. I just didn't want to admit it to myself."

"Too stubborn?" Her eyes creased.

I shook my head. "How is it you know me so well?"

She smiled and ran her finger along the brim of her cup. "So. Back to the question."

"Blake?"

"You're getting sharper, O'Neill."

I chuckled. "I don't know. I'm this big emotional blender right now. It's not just that he cheated behind my back with Christine. It's that if he's the arsonist, then he's responsible."

Her brow tightened. "For your father's fire."

"I just don't know how to process that."

"But why?"

"I don't know. Just the thought of it. It's all so—"

"No. I mean, why would he? What motivation could Blake have? What did he have against your father?"

I shook my head. "My dad always got along with everybody. Well, pretty much."

"Who didn't he get along with?"

"Mauvain."

She leaned back with her coffee cup in both hands. "Bad blood?"

"It got to where they wouldn't speak on shift."

"Was it because Mauvain got promoted to BC?"

I laughed. "No. Definitely not. My dad never had any aspirations above captain."

"So what happened, then?"

I took a bite of cake and thought for a moment. "It wasn't one thing. They were just different from the beginning, you know? Mauvain is the type who gets his sense of self-worth from status and title. He and my dad were academy mates, but he's always had this air about him. My dad saw right through that and had fun with it, found ways to push his buttons. You know, typical fireman."

"Mauvain probably didn't see the humor in that."

I grinned. "No. Not so much."

Our waitress approached. "You two doing okay? Can I get you anything else?"

I looked at Julianne. She shook her head.

"No," I said. "Thank you."

The waitress walked off. I leaned my forearms on the table. "My dad respected guys for their work ethic, not their lapel brass. Guys like Waits who haven't flinched at running after midnight for twenty years."

"Hmm." She looked as though she was checking off a list in her mind. "Was there anyone else your dad didn't get along with?"

I shrugged. "He and my uncle would have their little arguments. Just family conflict stuff." A siren wailed. Engine Four grumbled down Ralston Avenue, light bar spinning.

"Did they argue a lot?"

"I don't know. They had this sibling rivalry thing going. Cormac had some issue with my grandfather always criticizing him and praising my dad. My dad promoted. Cormac never did. That sort of thing."

She inhaled the steam from her cup, waiting, listening.

I continued. "I don't know. Their mom left them when they were pretty young."

"Your grandmother?"

"Yeah. I don't even really think of her like that."

"Where is she now?"

"I'm not sure if she's even still alive."

"How young were they when she . . ."

"Left? I think my dad was nine. My uncle would have been eleven." I looked at the speakers. "Who is this band playing?"

"How did your uncle take her leaving?"

What's with the twenty questions? "He probably took it the hardest."

"Why him more than your father?"

"I don't know." I shifted in my seat. "I guess he was more attached to her. He'd always had a hard time connecting with my grandfather. Do you remember when my grandfather was chief?"

She nodded. "I remember reading about him in the paper. He passed away not long after your father, right?"

"Six months. It took its final toll on his heart."

I picked up my cup. An espresso-tinged crescent painted the inside. The room darkened a bit, and the conversations and clinking of plates and the scuffling of shoes and the music all faded into an audio soup. Fatigue blanketed my mind.

Julianne set her fork down. "Have you been feeling any heat from the department?"

"I'm sorry?"

"Have you . . . Do you feel like folks are pointing fingers?"

"At who? Me?"

She nodded.

"For what? Hartman?"

"No, not really. I mean more in general."

She scraped icing on the plate with her fork. "You know. With you being gone after Hartman's fire."

"And . . ."

"And . . . just the fact that you were gone for a week and that bunch of fires started up."

"What are you trying to say?"

"I'm not—" She exhaled. "I just thought that might have raised a few eyebrows. That's all."

"Is that really all?"

"You don't need to get defensive about it, Aidan."

"I don't? Well, that's a relief, because this conversation has been starting to feel more like an inquisition."

"I'm not trying to judge you. I'm just asking about how things are going."

Asking or interviewing? I leaned back and crossed my arms. I couldn't believe I'd let myself fall for it. "So that's why you're here."

"Excuse me? I am here because you invited me. I wanted to get to know you better and to lend a supporting—"

"Role in the arson investigation?"

She straightened. An offended look splashed across her face.

Nice act. I pinched the bridge of my nose. "You know what?" I stood and threw a twenty on the table. "No wonder you once fell for Blake. You two are a lot alike."

CHAPTER 40

Butcher and Lowell were whispering something when I walked into the app bay. There was a flitting moment of surprise and hesitation as I stood with my turnout bag slung over my shoulder. I broke the silence with a morning greeting of "How's it goin'?"

"Aidan. Good," Butcher said. "How's that jaw?"

I thought it curious of him to care. "A little stiff."

He twisted one side of his moustache and eyed me.

Lowell shifted his weight. "Well, hey, Mark, I'm going to make sure our new kid's fueling the BC rigs."

"Right, I've got to check the training schedule anyway."

I let them make their escape before dropping off my gear by the rig.

I took the stairs two at a time to the third floor and walked back to my dorm cube. While making my bed I noticed a thick book resting on the desk. It was soft leather bound and burgundy with gilded pages. A sticky note curled off the cover.

Aidan,

A dear friend of mine gave this to me many years ago in our academy. Thought you might want it.

Ben

In the lower right corner of the cover I read the inscription: *James O'Neill.*

I flipped the sheets and fanned the scent of old leather and binding glue by my face. My thumb caught and it flopped open, as if it had found a familiar place.

Isaiah.

A verse stood highlighted in orange, the outer end of the rectangle darker with ink.

Chapter forty-three.

Verse two.

I ran my finger underneath it.

"When you walk through the fire, you shall not be burned, nor shall the flame scorch you."

Static chirped from the ceiling speaker.

Tones.

"Battalion Two, Rescue One, Engine One, Engine Two, Engine Three, Truck One with the safety officer to multiple reports of a structure fire . . ."

I pulled up my drops in the back of the rig as Kat rolled us out, first on the apron. I kept my balance with a hand on the doorframe as we turned onto the street, my other hand pulling over a suspender. Swinging on my coat, I dropped into the jumpseat, watching the ladder truck emerge from the bay, Ben Sower in the captain's seat, working his arms into his jacket.

I caught a glimpse of dark smoke building in bulbs toward the sky, like a hellish ashy snowman. The smooth hickory of my axe handle felt right in my palm.

And then I heard it.

Quick. So fast and fine that I couldn't say if it was a word or an image, but it came in a flash of knowledge.

Four vehicles, all on fire.

I pressed the intercom button on my headset. "Cap, what kind of occupancy is this?"

Butcher held up the printout to read it. "It says Ace Auto Repair."

The city zipped by in horizontal lines.

Lowell cracked his neck. Kat swung the rig down an old industrial avenue between brick buildings girded with goosenecks thick with wires stretching to power poles. The engine bounced with potholes and broken sections of concrete. Kat brought her to a stop just past an alleyway adjacent to a single-story brick structure. Tenebrous smoke belched from its far side.

Lowell hopped out his door for the nozzle. I grabbed a hand light and a Halligan bar and circled around the engine, my father's axe hanging from its belt sheath. The city swarmed with the sounds of sirens, the balance of the first alarm assignment fast on our tail.

The auto shop sat on an elevated plot, encompassed all the way down the alley by a chain-link fence. Short of running down a full block and doubling back, our only access to the fire would be either over or through a six-foot fence standing on a three-foot retaining wall.

Lowell chucked the nozzle over, the limp hose draping down the other side. He backed up five steps and studied the obstacle. I glanced toward the engine to see if the truckies were on scene and coming with bolt cutters. I turned in time to witness Lowell hurtling through the air. He collided with the fence and clung to its crown like a cat. He somehow heaved his body up and over, crashing down onto the roof of a dilapidated Dodge. He got up, grabbed the nozzle, and worked his way through a scattering of junk to the oily curtain billowing from an open garage door.

I moved to the fence and fed the line over until I could see he had enough slack. I took several steps back, set down the Halligan and hand light, and made my best launch for it. Me and my seventy plus pounds of extra gear bounced off the chain link and back onto the road. In the corner of my eye, I caught Engine Three pulling up on the opposite end of the alley.

I saw Lowell masked and ready to go. The Engine Three firefighters would be with him soon.

I took several steps back before leaping upward again, stalling at the peak, poised for a rearward drop, when a nearby tree offered me its limb. I grabbed ahold and yanked myself over, crashing onto the car roof and rolling to the ground.

I met up with Lowell and pulled on my mask. "There's four cars on fire."

He turned. "How could you know that?"

The line charged with water. And hence she beckoned.

We crouch-walked in, Lowell tentative, stopping to pencil vagrant glows on the ceiling. He stretched his foot, sweeping for obstructions, checking for holes. Faint but familiar sounds came from above—the truck guys working to ventilate the roof. I thought of the hand light I'd left in the alley and how it wouldn't have made much difference. This smoke swallowed day like a snake with white mice.

My eyes saw blackness, but my mind made out four fiery beasts with pupils like predators, teeth to devour, claw-shaped appendages rising in flame.

Ben's voice echoed in my head. "*Maybe you're hearing the fire just fine.*"

Hissing sounds shot out overhead.

A brilliant explosion erupted above us.

Lowell shifted with the nozzle. Another blast let out behind us. Heat raged in torrid waves, and the fire pressed in, fore and aft. A third and fourth bright fireball burst deeper in. Our hose stream dissipated, swallowed by the glow and the toxic fog. The room went molten, and we stood on what felt like the one patch of solid ground. I gripped the hose and leaned my shoulder into Lowell's back. He swirled the water stream, sweeping from side to side.

It was BTUs versus GPMs, and we were on the losing end. The fire grew hotter, and closer. I felt my wrists and earlobes itching.

Lowell scooted back. I supported the hose. And then the smoke shook and whirled upward, sucking from the corners and along the floor, up and around our boots and overhead toward two glowing squares cut from the roof. The thermal strata lifted. Two-by-six rafters manifested from the haze.

Thank God for the truck crew.

We caught our first glimpse of four vehicles suspended in the air, fire still blowing out from all sides.

Lowell turned toward me, and through his ash-littered face-piece, squinted, disdain and suspicion lacing his expression.

Flames shot out from car undercarriages and up through the engine compartments, working along to the ceiling joists. We advanced, hitting the ceiling before chasing the fire around and out of engine components and steel members. A backup line from Engine Three knocked down the fire in two of the vehicles, and the truckies set fans at the open garage door.

With time the shop cleared, fire flickering down in charred vehicles, the last waving remnants of hazy gray slinking in the rafters.

CHAPTER 41

Algid air fanned the sweat on my brow. I tossed charred sections of cardboard on the pavement. The truck crew went to work with overhaul, opening walls, searching for fire extension.

Sower held the thermal imager, watching the infrared screen for signs of heat. "Not there, Sortish. To your left a bit. A little more. Yeah, right there. Feel that wall with the back of your hand."

Operator Donovan stood with a pike pole. "Try taking off your glove there first, bud."

I grabbed an armful of debris from what looked like a desk in the corner. It looked as though there could be a few legible documents in the pile. Mauvain came in, conversing with a woman holding a clipboard and wearing a fire helmet, an unbuttoned turnout coat and rubber boots over a dark pants suit.

Julianne.

Outside I dropped the debris by the pile. Mauvain strode out, looking through me as if I were an office window.

Julianne studied the license plate of the first elevated car. I could make out the *E-X* of a government exempt plate. Beside it, through the charred exterior, shone a fragment of the former paint job.

Faded red. Same as her department vehicle.

I came alongside and studied her profile. "Is this . . . yours?"

She wouldn't look at me.

I took off my helmet and wiped my brow. "You going to give me the cold shoulder, too?"

"Not here."

"Not what?"

Chief Mauvain appeared at the entrance.

She made a quick headshake. "That's what I'm going to try to determine, Firefighter O'Neill." Mauvain arrived. "Oh, hello again, Chief."

Radio traffic blared from his collar-mounted mic. He spun down the volume. "Aidan, would you mind making sure the Rescue crew shut off the utilities outside?"

Knowing Timothy Clark and Waits had already taken care of it, I switched glances between the two of them. "Sure thing, Chief." *Thanks for the invite to leave.*

I worked my way around the south side of the building, walking through a narrow path between the wall and another fence. Mustard yellow leaves blanketed the dirt. I found the gas meter and knelt down to inspect it. As expected, the petcock was perpendicular, shut off at the inlet from the ground. An antiquated electrical panel was also shut off, the large breaker switch pointing to the earth. I leaned against the fence. The buildings old brick looked porous in places, and tiny recesses pocked the mortar. Eight-pane windows were inset every twenty feet or so, the glass soot-stained on the inside, cobweb-covered on the out. I caught sight of Julianne through two broken panes.

She stood alone now, staring at charred rafters.

I looked both ways, then spoke through the empty frames, keeping my voice subdued. "Hey, Julianne."

She swiveled toward the front.

"Over here. By the windows," I said a little louder, straightening in reflex, double-checking to see if I was noticed. I felt like a fugitive.

She walked over to the window and held up her clipboard as though she were studying it. "Hey, yourself." She moved from the window and exchanged a few unintelligible sentences with someone before leaning her face back by the frames. "You still out there?"

"So you still think I—"

"I've never thought that." She put her cell phone by her ear. "I'm sorry I gave you that impression."

"Was that your department car?"

She nodded, looking around. "This is getting a little close to home."

"Explosives?"

"So far no evidence."

"Do you know how many car fires I've been on and not one of them has exploded? Your vehicle and those three others went off like bombs, right by our heads."

She scanned the ceiling and exhaled. "This building's old, but it's sprinklered. That would have kept the fire at bay."

"But it was tampered with?"

She nodded.

Leaves crunched as I shifted my weight. "What else do you have?"

"A witness said they spotted a white van leaving in a hurry about five minutes before the fire was reported."

"Did they get plates?"

She shook her head.

"How about Mauvain. What'd he say to you?"

She scribbled on her clipboard and then held it by the light of the window.

"They're looking for a scapegoat."

Out in the street, Kat walked past the engine. I crossed my arms and leaned on the brick. "They've got Blake."

"Blake's been released."

"What?"

She brought her hand up to her hair and tilted her head. "He's on administrative leave. There's not enough evidence to keep him."

"So now what? They suspect me?"

"This isn't the best place."

"That's insane. How could I even? There's so many—"

"I don't know, either. I don't know what is going on. All I'm saying is that somehow you've dug yourself a hole, and there are people out there who want to bury you in it."

"It's looking to me like someone is out for both of us."

A voice called from inside. "Inspector, you might want to take a look at this."

She nodded in acknowledgment. "I guess that means me." She pocketed her phone and went to work with her pen. She strolled away, tilting the clipboard:

"Lab tomorrow. 8 PM."

CHAPTER 42

I'd have been worried about the security cameras outside the arson lab if I hadn't known that Dan, the building maintenance guy, had been inundated lately with higher priority projects. He said the props would have to do for now and that was good enough for him. It was good enough for me, too, as I saw Julianne emerge from the shadows of the foyer, her hair pinned up, eyes poignant against the night's photo negative tones.

She pushed open the door. "What's the secret password?"

I hesitated.

"I'll make it easy." Then with a mock British accent, she said, "What's your favorite color?"

I knew where she was going. "Red. No. Blue."

"Kaboom." She animated an explosion with her hands. "Come on in."

We worked our way down a dark corridor lit by green exit signs and red smoke detector lights. We walked across the main office area to the lab door Julianne had first taken me through. Inside, Ben Sower sat at an island lit by overhead can lights.

I glanced at Julianne.

"We spoke after the fire. I invited him."

The light gave the lab table the feel of a jeweler's display, Ben, its curator, holding up a test tube in the light, studying it behind thin-rimmed glasses that hooked around his ears.

"Hey, Ben," I said.

He refocused his eyes. "Evening, Aidan." He placed the test tube next to five others on a rack. "This is a concise collection here."

I nodded. "Sometimes less tells more."

"Even as a lay observer, it seems obvious to me that the bulk of these fires point to a similar method."

Julianne stepped into the edge of a light circle. "And, subsequently, to a singular subject who has set them."

"Your name," Sower said to me, "has come into question behind closed doors."

"I was starting to get that feeling."

Julianne sat on the edge of a stool. "Ben told me that Chief Mauvain now considers you the prime suspect."

"Mauvain isn't even in Prevention."

Sower's voice was calm and direct. "You have exhibited unpredictable and, at times, irrational behavior on fires recently."

"You disappeared right when these fires started going off," Julianne said.

I crossed my arms. "Here we go again."

"Just giving Admin's point of view," Ben said.

"Devil's advocate," Julianne added.

I shook my head. "Same difference."

"The icing"—Ben leaned on the table—"is that you've managed

to cross both Mauvain and Butcher on the fire ground. You've been burning your bridges with them for some time, just for the spite of it. Then Hartman gets hurt and the hammer comes down." He sat back and unhooked his glasses. "If I'm not mistaken, Investigator Williams also happens to be tight with those two, especially Mauvain. Given your current relationship with him, Blake may not've hesitated to set you up as a suspect during questioning, especially if it meant getting himself out of hot water."

"The city is desperate," Julianne said. "The mayor's public opinion polls have plummeted."

I scoffed. "Say that ten times fast."

"I'm serious, Aidan."

"Somebody's gotta pay."

Sower interlaced his fingers and rested his chin on his thumbs. "And they're determined that it will not be the brass."

I looked at the floor. "What about Lowell? What's his agreement with Mauvain?"

Ben shook his head. "I can't see Lowell jumping in on a witch hunt."

"Then what's his deal? He's been looking at me like I'm a traitor."

"He's in a tight spot right now."

"How do you mean?"

"He's due for an interview when the next driver-operator position opens at the end of this year."

"They're blackmailing him?"

"It's possible."

"I heard Mauvain yelling at him." I rubbed my neck. "I can see that. Quid pro quo."

Julianne folded her arms. "You scratch our back, we'll scratch yours."

The pieces came together. "They want Lowell as a spy. That's why he was switched with Timothy Clark on the engine. To keep an eye on me."

"Mauvain may have left him little choice," Sower said.

I looked at Julianne. "What about your department car?"

"Seems like more than a coincidence."

"Is there anything else that would connect that shop with the department?"

"Apart from being in District One?" She glanced to the side and shook her head. "No. Not that I can think of."

Sower folded his arms. "What are you driving now?"

"My own Mini."

I rubbed my hands over my face and exhaled. "Okay . . . So now what?"

"Now," Julianne flicked on a microscope. "Now we get to work proving your innocence."

She lifted a small glass slide to the ceiling. Barely discernable gray specks sat sandwiched between the two transparent rectangular pieces. "Yeah, this is the one." She inserted it under the microscope. "I took the liberty of breaking apart one of the small pieces of char."

"From Blake's evidence boxes?"

"Yeah." She held her eye half an inch from the lens. A thin light circle shone on her iris, and her pupil constricted in a cerulean sea. "Take a look." She stepped back into the shadows.

I held her gaze, curious to know, before breaking off to stare into the microscope. At first I only saw bright light, and then an oscillating dark shaft that finally stabilized, allowing fine crystal-like granules to move into focus. "They're angled, like a crystalline solid."

"Very good, Firefighter O'Neill."

I straightened and blinked. "They seem lighter in color than the char."

"They're the remnants of what was inside, what wasn't fully burnt."

Sower came beside me.

"Here," I said. "Have a look."

He held his head about half a foot from the lens, blinking and squinting. Julianne put a hand on his and set it on the focusing knob. "Here."

He smiled. "Oh, thank you." The tray adjusted downward, and Ben leaned in. "Okay. I see."

I folded my arms. "So what is it?"

She pocketed her hands. "I can't say specifically, but I was able to narrow it down to a family."

"It's a flammable solid." Ben feathered the microscope dial.

"Yes." Julianne cocked her head. "Exactly. How did you know that?"

"Ben was on the Haz-Mat team."

He leaned back, opening his eyes wide and then blinking. "Yes. But that was some time ago." He walked over and sat on a stool. "I just remembered something Aidan told me about the look of the flame in James's fatal fire."

A flammable solid. It hit me, like the sudden heavy heat of a summer day. The bright white flame, the lightning-like appearance. I described to Julianne what I'd seen.

She leaned against the counter. "The white flame—that's hotter than most."

"Yes."

"Hot enough to separate hydrogen from oxygen."

Hydrogen plus oxygen. Water. "Right. We see it a lot in old

Volkswagen engine fires. Super bright flames. When you spray water on them, the fire explodes brighter and bigger."

"Water reactive," Ben said. "Those engine blocks have a good amount of magnesium in them. The fires burn hot enough to break the chemical bonds in the water."

"Exactly. The hydrogen burns and the oxygen accelerates the process." I pointed at the microscope. "What do you bet this is magnesium?"

Julianne nodded. "There are a number of reactive metals it could be." The can lights circled her hair. "I'll hone my testing tomorrow and see what I find."

"What time do you think you'll be in?"

"Early. I want to make as much progress as possible before lunch. Mauvain wants me down south at Station Three for a meeting in the afternoon." Subtle dark lines had taken up residence beneath her eyes. She covered her mouth and yawned.

Ben stood. "It's getting late, and I need to get on home." He patted me on the shoulder. "You two be extra heads-up. Whoever is doing all this isn't blind to the fact that they're being followed."

"Thanks, Ben," Julianne said.

He gave her a hug. "Be safe."

Patting my arm, he said, "Take care, Aidan," and walked down the hall. I heard the front door swing shut.

Julianne tilted her head. "Are you on shift tomorrow?"

"Yeah."

"Don't go picking any fights."

"Seems like they've been picking me."

She nodded. "You know, it's worse than Ben suggested. Somehow that arsonist knows it's us on his tail. By being here, by doing this, we're going down a road that we can't turn back from."

That road started for me five years ago. I would ride it to its end. "It's easy to say 'Be safe,' isn't it?" Test-tube shadows stretched long and narrow. "But there's not really a safe way right now."

"Not until this is finished."

I rubbed my eyes. Not until . . . *It is finished.* I extended my right hand to Julianne. She placed hers in it, the pads of her fingertips running back and forth over the scar in my palm. In that dim light we drew close. Our fingers intertwined. I felt her warm breath on my neck, her lips hovering by my jawline, her temple meeting mine.

We simply stood like that, guarded against time or threat, heart ties weaving bonds beyond words. And in that quiet, perfect moment lingered the unspoken understanding that with the new day nothing would be the same.

CHAPTER 43

The workday brought a lull in chasing phantoms.

I spoke little with others, methodically moving through the motions of the day. Rig checks. Morning chores. EMS training. I finished my afternoon workout and climbed the stairs, thinking of Julianne and wondering if she was back from her meeting at Station Three.

Outside, the clouds formed a soporific ceiling. Once-colored trees now stretched bare branches, wet fallen leaves plastering walkways. A quick chirp let out from the ceiling speakers.

Tones.

Kat gunned it down Mill to the freeway. Butcher zipped up his turnout coat. Piceous smoke surged from the overpass, sunlight coruscating off an overturned semi.

Lowell cinched on his air pack. I pulled on my mask, ready to go on air from the moment we got out. Kat swung around the northbound on-ramp for 395. The ladder truck ran not far behind us.

All the cars sat frozen, like an electric racetrack when the power goes out. At least half a dozen vehicles were twisted at odd angles around an overturned fuel truck, one pickup so severely damaged that the driver sat trapped inside. The semi's undercarriage pointed toward us, the cylindrical trailer atop the center dividing wall. Fire rolled from the area of the hitch and around the tractor.

Butcher got on the PA. "Pull to the right. Pull to the right."

Kat squeezed along with inches to spare. "There's nobody in some of these vehicles."

Our siren seemed excessive for the crawling pace, like a dog barking for something out of its reach. People ran down the freeway, abandoning their cars, doors left ajar, kids in arm. A wrecked car's horn blared incessantly.

Kat moved her head out her side window. "This is as far as I can get." The smell of burnt tar blew inside the cab. She snapped the air brake.

I grabbed a Halligan and met Lowell at the sideboard. We did an alley pull. Lowell took off for the front with a loop and the nozzle, his bottle breaking a sedan side mirror. I knocked one inward as I made toward the tailboard. With the line flaked out, Lowell climbed up on a hood and jumped from car to car, nozzle in hand. The smoke spread so thick that he disappeared and reappeared. I got between two bumpers to feed him more line, clicking in my regulator. Air hissed with inhalation.

Kat whipped water through our attack line. The engine revved up. Butcher weaved between cars ahead of the rig, holding his radio by the voice amp mounted on his facepiece.

Stygian smoke spurted fireballs. Lowell hunkered in the back of the T-boned pickup with the nozzle in a fog pattern, white bubbles spraying on the truck cab. Kat worked the pump panel, running the foam mixture thick through the water stream. I climbed up in the truck bed and supported the hose. The man inside threw frantic glances through the back window, shoving a door that wouldn't open. His passenger side was wedged against a car facing the opposite way, its driver gone, its rubber weather stripping already warping and bubbling.

I patted the rear window. "Hang tight. We'll get you out."

Lowell darkened one section of fire only to see eruptions of flame in another. Kat stretched three-inch supply hose toward a standpipe in the median. Butcher strode for the tractor cab with an axe in hand. Flames lapped out like a solar burst. He tucked and shielded. Smoke swallowed his form.

"You got this?" I yelled.

He nodded, and I hopped down to the street, gripping the Halligan and ducking under the smoke.

Glass shattered. Butcher backpedaled from the belching cloud, dragging an unconscious driver up the freeway.

Radiant heat beat down. From the elevated side of the tractor spilled liquid fire like a lava river. The flow hit pavement and moved toward us. The more Lowell sprayed it, the more it spread, the hose stream serving to corral, not extinguish. The fire shifted away from the pickup, back toward the center divide.

And there, trapped under the trailer and next to the wall, sat a Mini Cooper with a crumpled roof and a damaged front end. In the driver's seat, chestnut hair framed a blood-streaked face, two familiar eyes meeting mine.

I waved at Lowell. "Throw me the nozzle."

He tossed it down. I diverted the fire away from the Mini, washing it toward the rear of the trailer. A steady stream of flame followed. Lowell hopped down and I gave the nozzle back.

"Hold it away from the car."

I hopped over the fiery flow and ducked under the trailer, crouching to get next to the shattered passenger window.

"Julianne!"

"Aid—" She coughed uncontrollably.

The dash pinned her lap. A deflated white airbag hung from the steering wheel. I reached in and took her hand.

Her skin looked pale, her lips purple. "I can't—" she coughed again—"breathe."

I pulled the radio from my jacket. "Captain Butcher, O'Neill."

He transmitted back. "Go ahead."

"I need a spare bottle and mask and the extrication tools under the trailer."

"Copy that. Truck crew's making their way to you now."

I pulled off my helmet. Lowell's hose stream splashed along the car's side, cooling my boots and the back of my pants. Julianne's eyes drooped and she nodded forward.

"No. No you don't." I put a palm on her forehead and stripped off my mask, placing it on her face.

She took a breath and her eyes flashed open. She let out a shriek.

"It's okay, it's okay." I kept the mask against her.

She looked as if she were drowning.

"Just breathe. Just breathe. I'm here, okay. Just breathe. I'll hold this. I won't leave you."

The toxic brume pumped into the car. It stung my throat. My eyes watered. I hacked and coughed. My vision blurred. The myriad of colors faded into gray, and gray into a closing circle of black.

Just keep holding it.

Air fanned in my face.

Waits pressed a mask over my face, my extended arm still held my own over Julianne's.

"Let's switch." I brought mine back in place as he strapped the spare mask over Julianne.

Behind us, someone started the power unit for the hydraulic tools.

I looked at Waits. "What's happening with the fire?"

"They're chasing it around, trying to keep the tanker cool."

Timothy Clark walked over with the spreaders. Waits stepped aside and patted him on the shoulder. "Let's get this open, Tim. Doesn't have to be pretty."

CHAPTER 44

I smashed the rear window with my axe.

It was too small of an opening to fit in with an air pack. I cleared the glass around the edges, leaned my axe against the bumper, and pulled the air bottle off of my back. I fed it in first and then crawled in on my belly. Metal squeaked and popped at the passenger door. Timothy, in a crouch, worked the jaws. Julianne looked to the side through her mask, trying not to move her head.

"That's good, hold still." I twisted into a sitting position in the backseat, her spare air bottle next to mine between my feet. I leaned close and placed my gloved hands on either side of her head. "Keep looking forward. Don't move your neck."

"Okay." Her voice wavered.

"You're going to be okay."

"Aidan—"

A metallic groan let out above the car.

I glanced at Waits, who looked up at me. He shook his head. That noise was too loud to have come from the spreaders.

The groan shot out again, the car roof caving in places. Julianne screamed.

I scanned through the windshield. The trailer had shifted. Waits grabbed his radio, shouting something about support struts.

"Aidan," she said.

I reached around for a recline lever on the left part of her seat.

"Aidan, I can't feel my legs."

The groaning crescendoed. The Mini's frame strained under the weight.

I searched for the lever next to her door.

God, let me find it.

Steel whined. I knelt on the floor, leaning close. Her eyes met mine.

Where is that lever?

Steel whined. Her lips pressed tight. She didn't blink.

I found it and pulled up, lowering her seatback with my other hand.

The roof buckled.

A tornado of sounds spun around the car—tools and metal and urgent efforts.

"Get that strut in there!"

Motors rumbled with elevated voices.

We lay hard-pressed, separated by masks, only inches of clearance from the roof above. My hand rested on her hip. Her fingers grabbed my coat sleeve. Tears ran down her face. As the smoke in the air started to dissipate. I could see her legs trapped beneath the dash, the lower left one deformed midshaft at the shin.

"Can you feel anything?" I said.

She frowned. "My head. Not my legs."

Sorrow pulled on my insides. She wasn't just a patient. But

right now she had to be. "Okay." *Focus on the job, Aidan.* "Try not to move your neck."

She swallowed.

I found her fingers and gripped them. "We're going to get out of this." Through small slits in the window I saw firefighters working without air bottles. I stripped off my mask. "They've knocked down the fire." I loosened the straps on her facepiece. She winced as I slid it off.

Her jaw trembled.

"Hey." I would process my cascade of emotions later. "Come on now." Right then I was her hope. "You think this is the first time we've done this?"

The roof bent farther with a wrenching dissonance. It pressed down on my back, forcing my face next to hers. Her cheek felt smooth and hot and wet with tears. Her respirations quickened, and she squeezed my fingers like a vise grip.

She whispered something. In quiet, split sentences. "White. Van. Cut me . . . off."

"The white van?"

"It crossed. Three lanes."

Her hair matted dark with blood. It smelled of salty cruor.

The passenger door screeched and then snapped open. Outside voices and sounds poured in.

"There she goes."

"Cut the hinges."

"Get two more struts back there. Aidan?" Sower's voice.

"Right here, Cap."

"We're stabilizing the trailer. Once that's set, we'll cut the roof, roll the dash, and get you out of there."

"All right."

"How's our patient?"

"Cap . . . it's Julianne."

Silence followed. "Is she stable?"

"Conscious. Left leg fracture. Head lac—"

"Good. We'll go ahead and—"

"Ben."

"Yeah?"

"She can't feel below her waist."

A moment passed. He leaned in. "Julianne, it's Ben. We're getting you out of here. You hang on, all right?"

She grimaced. "Please hurry."

Something like large steel hinges creaked overhead, this time relieving pressure off my back. The noise repeated and the roof relaxed. The work of breathing lightened.

"What's happening?" Julianne said.

"They're lifting the trailer."

She was quiet, and then said, "They can do that?"

I smiled, fighting to keep my appearance of confidence. "Yeah. They can do that."

Sower commanded the scene. "Cut those A, B, and C posts all the way through."

Someone threw a red wool blanket over us. Sheet metal squeaked and the car jerked as tools cut through the roof supports. Beneath the covering we lay removed, in wine-colored light and humid breath and the smell of sweat. Bedlam and twisted-metal mayhem all torqued about. But within was respite, the eye of the storm.

"Any changes?" I said.

"No. I'm glad you're here."

I looked at her legs. "I wish I—"

"No, Aidan. You're here. I'm not scared now. We're together."

I nodded. "That's right."

"Lift," came the command outside. "One, two, three. Lift." The car shifted.

"There you go."

"Can you get across?"

"One second."

"Okay. Good."

Light shone brighter through the wool. My arms felt freed. I pulled away the blanket.

Sower stood and pointed. "Set it down there."

Five firefighters carried the Mini's roof and placed it on the hood of the pickup truck.

I rolled away from Julianne. "Hold still."

"Don't leave."

"I won't." I placed my hands on either side of her head. "Just keep your head still."

Waits went to work with the cutters near the open passenger door.

Julianne stared upward. "Tell me what's happening."

"Waits is making a relief cut at the base of the dash."

Timothy moved in with the spreaders. Plastic cracked and squeaked until he found a solid purchase point under the dash, widening the tool from the bottom of the doorframe up.

"Timothy Clark is working to lift the dash now."

"I can't feel it," she said.

"It's lifting. I can see it. Take my hand."

A deep groan let out from the car's front end. The spreaders grunted.

"That's all it's got," Timothy said.

Her legs looked clear. "That's good," I said. "We should be good to go."

Timothy stepped aside as guys brought over a backboard. We

slid it under Julianne's shoulders and pulled her torso straight back. Her face looked stressed but composed. We secured her to the board, immobilizing her neck and spine, and lifted her away from the car and out from under the trailer.

We wound across the freeway toward the ambulance. I walked next to her, carrying the board. She brought a hand to my coat. "Come see me. In the hospital."

I leaned down. "Of course."

She squeezed the jacket fabric. "We've got to find who did this."

"I know. I know we do."

"We have to, Aidan. It can only get worse."

CHAPTER 45

The freeway mess took hours. By the time we left, only four cars had been towed. The rest sat taped off in place with fire line, lit by a portable diesel-powered light plant for the highway patrol investigators.

We ordered pizza by phone on our way back to the station. I showered and changed and sat on the bed in my cube with head in my hands. Visions of a wheelchair-bound Julianne coursed through my mind. Sorrow melded with anguish, and from that caldron anger spawned.

Butcher agreed to let us take the rig to County. Once everyone had eaten, we took the drive and parked by the ER.

I'd begun to hate the place.

Julianne was in CT on our arrival. And the charge nurse was insistent that she not have any visitors. But Julianne had already requested that I be allowed to see her, so as my crew waited in the lobby, I made my way back and stood by the empty space on the floor where her bed had been.

A nurse pushed a gurney down the hall, Julianne in it, cervical collar still in place. I helped roll the gurney back into position.

Julianne looked up. "Hey." Her voice was raspy, her face pale. She held up a hand.

The radio clipped to my belt squawked until I spun down the volume. I took her hand in mine.

"Come down here," she said.

I leaned on the rail and she put her hand on my cheek. Her eyes looked peaceful. I wanted to ask her how she felt, but it seemed like such an inept question. I didn't know what to say. So I did what just felt right.

I brought my fingers to her hair and brushed it back behind her ears. I let my hand trail to her cheek, and she brought hers up and held mine there, closing her eyes and breathing deeply.

"Aidan." Butcher's voice startled me. I straightened and turned to see him at the doorway to the room.

I cleared my throat. "Hey, Cap."

He ran his fingers along his moustache. "We, ah, arranged for your replacement to come in for the rest of the shift. You're free to stay here as long as you need."

I felt like someone had lifted a hundred pounds off my back. "That's . . . that's great. Thank you."

He shrugged and waved. "It was Kat's idea."

I looked back at Julianne. She kept hold of my hand and smiled.

I handed my radio to Butcher. "Thank you."

He nodded and stepped backward. "Give us a call if you need us."

—

I woke in a chair and brought into blinking focus the walls of a windowless ICU room. IV pumps clicked metered drips through tubing. My cell phone vibrated in my pocket. Julianne held a yellow legal pad in the air, scrawling notes.

I stretched, sore from the sleeping position. "Hey. What are you up to?"

"One sec, I'm thinking."

"On paper?"

"Shh."

The ICU was dimly lit and calm, each room secluded.

I yawned, covering my mouth. "You should be resting."

Her eyebrows lowered in concentration. "I've got too much going through my mind."

I caught a glimpse of a wall clock. 5:55 a.m.

My cell phone vibrated again. I had a new voice mail.

It was staffing. The BC said that Engine One had left an hour earlier with a strike team of engines to a fire about forty-five miles west into California. The heavy timber was ablaze off of Interstate 80 and was now threatening about three hundred homes on the edge of Truckee. Station One needed bodies to fill spots, and I was next up on the mandatory list.

Julianne laid the notepad on her covers.

I stood by the bed. "I have to go."

Her eyes flicked a brief moment of protest. She looked to the side.

"It's mandatory. There's a big fire in Truckee. They need people downtown for anything that might crop up."

Her eyebrows pinched together. She brought her bottom lip up. "It's all right. They're taking good care of me here."

I didn't feel right leaving her. "Maybe I can find a way out of—"

"It's okay. There are some things we need to talk about, though. So I'll call you, all right?"

Those eyes held a story. "Okay. I'll talk to you later, then?"

She mustered a smile. "Bye."

I turned to leave.

"Aidan?"

"Yeah?"

"I'm glad you were here for me."

The heart monitor beeped its steady rhythm, green lines tracking across the black-faced screen. I rubbed my chin. "Funny you'd say that. 'Cause I've been thinking of it as the other way around."

—

A blanket of burgundy hung high in the clouds. The sun shone from the east, illuminating a pall of smoke that seemed to wash an apocalyptic aura over Reno. Traffic ran lighter. Folks walked with empty stares.

"It can only get worse."

I knew a time of reckoning fast approached. And even though I stood on the shore of a brand new country, with sound footing for the first time in a long time, before me lying a continent of possibilities, I considered that what I had here and now might be all that it ever got to be. That the future for me might soon be cut off, and no matter how adamantly I clung to my hopeful timeline, frayed and loose in space as it were, the end might soon slip from my grasp, irretrievable and unalterable.

I felt so ready to build. For a change. Ready to establish and root into life's soil. Had I ever really made anything in my life? Anything that would last and not burn? I'd been running for so long. Death had become my god. And I was tired of fighting. Tired of just corralling chaos and stopping loss. I wanted to lay down my arms and proclaim a truce.

My faith was eternal, I knew that much. But, as irony is fitting, just as I'd found peace in the here and now, I sensed that my life soon would be asked of me.

CHAPTER 46

At Station One the reserve '79 Seagrave sat parked in Engine One's spot. No air-conditioning apart from the wind. No heater in the open-cab backseats save for the engine cowling against your leg. No AM/FM radio. The only music it made was the mechanical grinder wailing under the weight of the captain's boot.

My dad had loved that rig.

I could hear him and Sower joking. *"Great name for a fire engine. Bad name for a boat."*

I was appointed acting captain on it. Apparently any warm body would do when it all hit the fan. I checked and rechecked my air pack, shut the cabinet door, and climbed up into the front of the cab. The dash was broad like a coffee table; the floor, flat and spacious diamond-plate steel; the grinder button conspicuous in the far right corner. I reminded myself to avoid stepping on it later when I climbed in, though inevitably, I knew I would, and it was sure to be at two in the morning and down in the app bay. I held the black cardboard-bound Central map book on my lap and reviewed the streets, their familiar grid pattern, reciting the order of roads moving south along Wells. Roberts, Thoma, Cheney, Taylor, Crampton, Burns. I wanted to be ready when the time came.

Tom Flannigan came in on overtime to drive. Despite his twenty-eight years with the department, he refused to bump up to captain. Perhaps I should say *because* of his time—wisdom coming with age. The Seagrave was familiar territory for him, an old friend, battle-tested and true. He was happy to drive and not shoulder the responsibilities of the officer's seat. As he walked past the rig and saw me flipping through the map book, he chuckled to himself.

Timothy Clark had also answered the chief's call and would be filling the senior fireman role, his jumpseat mirroring mine toward the tailboard, a simple chain strung across the side for safety. I was jealous. Guys loved to stand in back when we cruised through downtown. We'd alert each other when we saw a chief, disappearing like groundhogs, popping up again when the coast was clear. It wasn't hard to understand one of the simple pleasures of a canine once you've stood in the back of an old fire engine, wind in your face, running lights and sirens toward a column of smoke.

Sortish came in as our fourth. From the expression on his face I sensed he was about to remark, in the presence of Flannigan, on the unfavorably antiquated nature of our reserve engine, so I cleared my throat and shook my head. He wasn't sure what he'd almost said wrong but showed the good sense to keep his opinions to himself. Flannigan's eyebrows relaxed and he went about tinkering with the pump panel. Sortish continued on into the station, little knowing what onslaught he'd almost brought upon himself.

The app-bay windows collected fine soot powder. Orange and apricot beams lit the floor in long rectangles. I studied the concrete skyline, from the highest building—the forty-story Silver Legacy, which would be dwarfed in Manhattan as one among many—to the business buildings and high-rise condos and crafted parapet curves of the old Riverside lofts. Reno lay in an eddy of auburn quiet, holding true to what it purported to be, the biggest little city in the world.

The rescue rig sat unmanned. Captain Butcher showed up an hour into shift, coming in from out of town for the overtime call to staff the truck. He had his crew pull out the rig to set up the ladder. He threw me a cold and quick glance as he walked out on the driveway.

I made my way upstairs to the kitchen. The refrigerators hummed. Sortish swept. Timothy Clark sat with a plate of scrambled eggs and the newspaper. He ate twice as much as anyone else in the station but never added a pound to his sinewy frame. I grabbed a water cup from the cupboard and filled it from the pitcher in the fridge. "Feeding your worm, Timothy?"

He looked up and grinned. "The first plate was for him. This one's for me."

My phone vibrated. Julianne's number flashed on the screen.

"Hey," I said. "How are you feeling?"

"Hi, Aidan." Her voice sounded kindred but solemn. "Are you somewhere you can talk?"

"Sure. One second." I pushed through the door into the dayroom and sat on one of the reclining chairs by the windows. "Anything new? What are they saying?"

"It's not magnesium."

"What? No, I'm talking about you. How are you?"

"They have me on some anti-inflammatory steroids."

"But . . ."

"No change. I still can't . . ." She paused. "The char isn't magnesium."

"What?"

"You said that the engine fires burst into more flame with water, right?"

I looked around the empty room. "Right. Yeah."

"But that was once they were already on fire, right?"

"Right."

"This stuff doesn't need to be on fire first. It's explosive on simple contact with water."

The faint sounds of a train horn filtered up from the railroad trench. "How did you find this out?"

"I've been working on it this morning, balancing a few chemical equations. I've narrowed it in probability to either sodium or potassium. Potassium is the more volatile, so I'm leaning toward it. But get either of those metals wet in their pure forms and the results are explosive."

"Water starting a fire?"

"It's the perfect incendiary device, Aidan."

"Okay, so I'm not a chemist. But it doesn't seem reasonable that—"

"I know. That's why it's perfect. No trace."

"But how? With no heat to start it?"

"If you take pure potassium and expose it to water, a violent chemical reaction occurs. Hydrogen is released. The heat produced from the reaction alone is sufficient to ignite it. Remember the Hindenburg?"

"So all our arsonist would need is this substance and water, and then—"

"Kathwoosh."

"Ka-what?"

"Kathwoosh?"

I smiled. "How's that go again?"

She chuckled. "Stop."

"No, come on. Did you read comic books as a kid?"

"Maybe a little Spiderman."

"Get out."

"I always wanted to see if he'd get together with Mary Jane."

I laughed, forgetting for a brief moment the gravity of it all.

"Yeah," she said. "I just wanted to let you know."

"You're amazing." I wanted to be with her, to express my growing feelings. Instead I said, "Have you told Ben?"

"No, not yet."

Juxtaposed pictures met in my mind. The ring of spalled concrete, the way the fires burned fast and hot and bright, the failure of the sprinkler systems to control it. Then it all tied together like a chess game, when you see the path to checkmate half a dozen moves out.

"I think I know now how the arsonist is doing it," I told her.

"Do tell."

My palm felt hot and moist against the phone plastic. "The spalled rings, the sprinkler tampering. They're connected."

"But if the arsonist shut off the sprinkler system, then there's no water left for him to use."

"That's not entirely true. Wet systems are charged to the sprinkler head." The elevator chimed. Flannigan walked out. I lowered my voice as he walked across the room. "This arsonist has been shutting off the water where the street supply meets the building riser, right?" Flannigan tossed me a look. I could almost hear his thoughts. *"I don't know what you're getting into, Aidan-boy, but you best be keeping your distance."*

"So," Julianne's voice floated into my ear. "There would still be some water left inside the system in the building?"

"Exactly. Enough to spray a circle of potassium, or whatever."

"And ignite a wall of white hot flame."

"Consuming the evidence with it."

"But," she said, "I still don't see how the arsonist gets the sprinkler head to activate in the first place."

"He'd have to remove the fusible link somehow."

"Remotely?"

"Yeah. Some kind of small explosive?"

"That would probably leave evidence. We know we have a savvy chemist. Maybe some kind of slow-acting acid."

I nodded, picturing it all in my head. "Giving enough time to bail before . . . kathwoosh?"

She chuckled. "Yes."

"So, what then?" I switched the phone to my other ear. "Without enough evidence, what do we do?"

"We have to catch the perpetrator in the act."

"But by the time we are aware of 'the act,' the arsonist is long gone."

"Set it and forget it?"

"Right." Something still didn't connect for me. "What about the residential fires?"

"Good point. No fire sprinkler systems on the ones we've had. But potassium is reactive with water, from any source. At a residential structure it could be something as simple as automatic sprinklers or a drip system. Even the morning dew could be enough."

Tones.

"Engine One to a medical emergency. . . ."

I stood. "I've gotta go."

"Call me later?"

"I will." I opened the pole-hole door. "Bye, Julianne."

CHAPTER 47

The day flew by with medicals, minor car accidents, and an activated fire alarm that proved false. We took care of station duties and rig checks, had lunch. A few guys went down to the basement to work out in the afternoon. I sat at a computer in the captain's office, typing out reports.

The clock swung to half past four, the sinking sun a red giant in the haze. The news squawked from the thirteen-inch TV on top of the file cabinets. It switched to coverage of the timber fire, so I turned in my chair to see.

A pony-tailed reporter in a yellow fire-retardant shirt spoke into a microphone, wind whipping loose strands of hair across her face. Her voice elevated and lowered in the sing-song rhythm of professional newscasters. ". . . reporting from the point of origin of the fire. I just finished speaking with the chief investigator for the Bureau of Land Management, who has discovered a piece of key evidence related to the start of this inferno."

The video cut to footage of a bearded official pointing to a broad ring of scorched earth and saying, "As you can see, it appears that the fire began here, with a circle-shaped ignition pattern."

The reporter appeared. "Anyone having information related to the start of this fire should contact the BLM investigation hotline with the number on your screen. From Truckee, California, I'm Angelica Mann." An eight hundred number in yellow block digits flashed on the screen with a blue background.

I ran my hand over my mouth and chin. It was our arsonist. Had to be. But why out there? Under the cover of night and the banking chimney smoke of forest homes, there would be ample time to escape before anybody discovered the fire. But what did that have to do with the Reno Fire Department? Why move to thousands of acres of forested land forty-five minutes away, unless . . .

Unless that's exactly what the arsonist wanted.

A smoke screen.

The city stripped thin. Stations manned with skeleton crews. We had sent the whole world up there. If an arsonist wanted to strike something significant in town, now would be the time to do it.

Tones.

I glanced up at the speaker.

"Battalion One . . ."

My heart bounded, flush with adrenaline.

". . . Engine One, Engine Two . . ."

I slid the pole and pulled up my suspenders.

". . . Truck One to a structure fire, smoke and flames seen . . ."

Flannigan slid the pole opposite the rig. He started the Seagrave with no wasted motion. The guys in back patted twice on the doghouse cowling. Tom pulled forward and I put us en route over the radio, switching to the tactical frequency. The ladder truck rolled onto the apron.

Flannigan pulled right, heading north on Evans. "Give me some music, Aidan-boy."

I found the grinder button and stepped on it. She came alive, screaming to a pitch. I looked back to see Timothy with one hand on the roof, eyes squinting in the wind.

I worked my arms into my jacket. A fat plume lifted up in the east. I took a second look at the dispatch printout. District One. Multiple calls. Sixth and Spokane. The address matched . . .

The museum.

I felt as if a sledgehammer hit me in the chest. "Tom, this is the—"

"I know." He glanced sideways, pushing his foot harder on the pedal. "We'll get there."

I zipped my coat and flipped up the collar. We were going to be first in. "Tom, you know I didn't set—"

"I know, A-O. I never once doubted." He yanked on the air horn wire. Traffic slowed at Evans and Fourth. "Hang on, fellas."

The guys in back braced themselves as Flannigan took the corner, smooth and swift.

I flipped pages in the map book. "We've got that hydrant right at the corner."

"Son," Tom said, "you just get in there and do what you know. I'll get you water. The truck'll get you vented. Ain't no arsonist going to take our history, too." He checked the passenger-side mirrors, then winked at me. "All right?"

I closed the map book. "All right. Let's do this."

Flannigan hooked north on Spokane and pulled past the museum, giving me a three-sixty view and leaving the address for the truck to position. Smoke belched from second-story windows, many of the panes broken out. The old bowstring truss roof seemed like a lid on a pot, boiling gases spilling out at the eaves.

I clicked the mic. "Battalion One, Engine One on scene of a large-footprint, two story, unreinforced brick building. We have heavy smoke showing from the second story windows and eaves on all four sides of the structure. The parking lot is empty. We'll call this Museum Command. Engine One'll be in live-line operations."

I climbed backward out of the rig. The air carried the pungent odors of burning rafters and bubbling roof tar. Flannigan shifted the Seagrave into pump, the motor quieting and then revving with the change. The ladder truck squeaked to a stop, spotting the turntable at the corner. The airbrake hissed and the tillerman and operator hopped out, working to deploy the outriggers.

Sortish stretched an inch-and-three-quarter line to the door. Timothy Clark worked with a Halligan to force it open. The backdrop of dusk devolved into purples and grays. A glow-tinged cloud puffed from the building.

I met Timothy at the door and pulled out my axe. "Here."

He held the adz end of the Halligan near the lock. I rammed it until it drove between the jam and the door. Timothy levered the tool until the door swung open.

Smoke stormed out like a penned-up animal. I backed up, knelt, and strapped on my mask.

I put a hand on Timothy's shoulder. "Stick close to our new kid."

He nodded as Sortish went in with the nozzle. Timothy picked up the line and disappeared into the chasm. The hose slithered forward beside my boots. I clicked the light on my coat, for all the good it would do, picked up my axe, and followed them in.

Timothy's mask appeared in front of mine. "Which way?"

I sensed the fire in multiple places, one near the back. "Start with a right-hand search."

"All right."

They dragged the line deeper, and the names on their jackets, for a moment, transformed, like wavy mirages, into *O'Neill* and *Waits*. I shook my head and blinked. The *Waits* twisted, rearranged, and lengthened—this time spelling *Hartman*.

Flashes of orange spat overhead.

"Hold up," I shouted.

But they were out of earshot, the hose already angling around the front desk.

This was too familiar.

I needed to calm my breathing and get with my guys. We'd knock this down and get on out.

I progressed foward and reached out with my senses. *Where else are you hiding?*

A vision flashed strong and poignant and as clear as anything I'd ever seen.

A circle of fire stretched across the second floor. And within it stood the silhouette of a man.

CHAPTER 48

I reached down through the smoke and found the hose line. I crawled alongside it, feeling the lugs on the female couplings followed by smooth brass. If we needed to get out we'd follow that opposite pattern. Lugs to hugs.

But I wanted deeper in, all the way to the perpetrator. At the origin of this inferno lay answers and justice and closure.

Muffled sounds of machines and metal and shattering glass echoed, a chaotic din like storm thunder. My father's face flashed in my mind. His eyes stared solemn. *"In the end, Aidan, the fire always gets us."*

I shook my head. *No. No, that's not right. He never said that.* The gray-black churned.

"You going to kill another fireman, A-O?"

I whispered in my mask. "I didn't mean for you to die."

"But I did."

"This is different."

"How, Aidan? How is this fire one bit different from that fire with me? From that fire with Hartman?"

"I know what I need to do now."

"Push in too far, until it's too late?"

"No," I said, louder this time. I looked ahead. Still no one visible in the void, only the yellow python in the cloud.

I saw the Mexican doctor, his outstretched hand. It became Hartman's grasping mine from his hospital bed.

Clark manifested in orange reflective letters at the edge of the smoke, glinting from the back of Timothy's coat.

I met up with him. "I'm going to head upstairs and do a primary search."

He pulled on the hose with both hands. "You think that's . . . where the seat is?"

"This one may have multiple starts." The hint of a glow shone toward the back of the first floor. "You're headed the right way. Knock that down and meet me at the stairwell."

Concern crossed his face. "You sure?"

"We can't let it burn beneath us."

"All right. We'll catch up with you."

"Keep your radio on the tactical." I patted him on the shoulder and moved past them.

I proceeded through the haze, wandering deeper until, like murky ocean floor images, came an antique helmet cabinet, the old chemical wagon, the Gamewell telegraph dispatch board, and then the broad wood-spoked wheels of the 1917 ladder truck. I ran a glove along its side until I came to the cab, squeezing a rail.

For my father.

I turned in the direction of the stairs, following the path as I knew it in my mind. With no hose slowing me down, my boot soon kicked the bottom step.

Above, at the crest of the stairwell, beyond the double doors to the upper showroom, brilliant flames tripped the light fantastic.

The temperature rose with every step. I held my father's axe with both hands like a weapon rather than a tool, tightening and relaxing my grip on the handle. The doorway grew larger, brighter, until the top of the stairs had me crouching before the mouth of a furnace. A wall of flame stood guarding the door.

I turned, gritting my teeth. Even with a hose line up there, the water would only increase the intensity.

I couldn't see him. But I knew he was in there.

How, with the heat?

From the belly of hell, my father's murderer mocked me.

I moved to the right along the showroom wall, about ten feet from the doorway, and sounded out with the flat end of the axe until I found a space between the studs. There had to be another way in.

I struck hard. Plaster cracked. I struck again. And again, cracking through lath, busting through the void space until I breached the wall.

The same lightning brilliance met me at the hole. I unwedged my axe and pulled it back, the steel head hot even through my gloves.

No access there.

I tried the same strategy on the far left side of the door, swinging and grunting and busting through, only to find flame throughout.

My shoulders heaved. I fought to catch my breath, brimming with frustration.

The whole room couldn't be on fire. I was too close to turn back. He was in there. I was sure of it, but not for much longer. He would slip away, making his untraceable escape the way he had so many times before.

I crouch-walked back to the doorway.

Think, Aidan. Think.

It was the only natural way in or out of the showroom. Had he burned himself into a corner? He could exit any number of ways if he broke through a wall, or the ceiling, or the floor. And in the chaos of the fire scene, who would know?

Simple words, prophetic and holy, resounded in my mind.

"When you walk through the fire, you shall not be burned . . ."

I saw my father's open Bible, the words alight on the page.

"Nor shall the flame scorch you."

The doorframe flashed. Fire rippled up the lintels, lapping at the ceiling.

I was baptized with conviction.

I stood upright. The wall of flame raged. Burning buzzed at my clothing edges, grating my skin through the layers. My helmet shield warped.

"When you walk through the fire . . ."

Death and hell taunted.

". . . you shall not be burned . . ."

The price had been paid.

". . . Nor shall the flame scorch you."

There was one way to end this. One way to overcome.

I gripped the axe tight at my side. I straightened my helmet and took one . . .

Last.

Deep.

Breath.

Then I stepped into the wall of fire.

CHAPTER 49

How do I describe it?

Passing through the flame felt like walking through a curtain of light.

Heat had no effect.

Weightless. Dynamic. Paranormal.

Emerging was not unlike coming from the harried backstage preparations for a play, through the curtain and into a broad but empty auditorium, rows of seats accentuating its vacuity.

The blaze retreated, and the hollow of the room fell into focus. The eye of the tempest. Smoke waved thin, the center of the showroom lit by a glowing circumference.

And at its fiery heart stood a man with his back to me, wearing a set of old Reno turnouts.

My father's murderer. The one responsible for numerous deaths and injuries and the massive destruction of personal property. His time had come.

I cleared my throat.

His head tilted. He started to turn.

My heart beat like mad. "You've already killed one O'Neill. I'm afraid you won't be able to make it t—"

Cormac showed his face, grinning. "Make it what, Aidan? Three?"

Air left my lungs. I stepped backward, off balance. I tried to form words, but my head felt heavy and unhinged. The wall of flame streaked across my vision like flashbulb lines. I set my axe on the floor to steady myself.

Why didn't I see it before?

Cormac stepped toward me. "I was really hoping it wouldn't come to this."

"Come to what?" My voice broke. "What are you . . . You killed Dad!"

He shook his head, opalescent waves warping across his face-piece. "Your father, like you, had a special knack for being in the wrong place at the wrong time."

"He was doing his job!"

"He was never a target."

"A target?" I pulled the radio from my coat. "Command, Engine—"

He darted for my axe. I dropped the radio and grabbed the handle. We arced upward, locked like steers. His height advantage gave him leverage. He shoved the hickory into my chest. I planted my feet.

"James's death was unexpected. That's all, Aidan."

Surging adrenaline pounded through my legs. I yelled and drove him back, the two of us falling in a tumbling mass. We smacked the floor. The axe flew free, spinning toward the wall of flame. I twisted to my feet, Cormac soon after.

He shook his head. "I wanted to humiliate. Not kill. You understand that? Your dad got caught in the middle, that's all."

"He was your brother!"

"It's not my fault."

"You're a murderer!"

"Survival of the fittest, Aidan."

We revolved around the room, the smoke and flame forming a dynamic border. He'd been Esau to my father's Jacob. Now he was Cain to his Abel. Distant groans echoed overhead. Smoke swirled down from the ceiling.

"You're diseased with jealousy," I shouted. We circled in our predatory merry-go-round. "Why now? What brings you back? Grandpa's dead. Dad's dead. You want to finish me off? Is that it?"

He squinted. "Don't think I haven't tried."

I saw the ocean and the wave that drew me up. I felt the water surge beneath me, and saw anew the expression on the man who stood the closest. No concern. No fear.

Just sick pleasure.

"You let that wave overtake me."

His lips curled. "Exploitation is a natural consequence of the will to live." He tightened the distance between us. "You think I came back just for you?" He took another step in. "If your friend hadn't been snooping around in the first place . . ."

"Who? Blake?"

"His investigator came a little too close to Cardenas."

Our pace quickened like mercury. Walls of smoke closed in.

"So you framed him. What'd you use? Potassium from the mines?"

His eyebrows rose. "I'm impressed."

Lumber crashed outside the showroom. The smoke level lowered.

He drew closer. "You know, Aidan, let's cut to it. Only one of us can make it out of this." Lengthened creaks let out overhead. Fire ignited and quelled in the smoke above. A quick flash of fear crossed his face.

He wasn't supposed to be there. He'd messed up somehow. "So what happened, Cormac? Try to set two fires in one place? Trip the system too quick?"

His cheek twitched, eyes darting around the room. My low-pressure bell sounded. He noticed and smiled. He reached into his side pants pocket and with one hand pulled out a long, black semi-curved object.

With his opposite hand he unfolded a glinting steel blade.

The room darkened. Coal-colored smoke encroached like fog. It dressed his shoulders like a cloak, as if he owned the room, the fire and the darkness his stewards. I glanced at my axe. The tip of the handle pointed toward the center of the room, the head lay square in the base of a now-enshrouded and dimming fire.

The potassium had a burn period. That's what Cormac had been waiting for, his opportunity to jump past the wall of flame.

He held the knife in his fist, pointing with slicing motions as he spoke. "So many ways to disable an air pack. Cut that line there. Or that one. *Vaya con Dios*, Aidan-boy."

He sprung.

I dove for the axe, sliding across the floor.

He passed over me, staggering and then regaining his balance, inverting the knife in his fist. He started back after me.

I scrambled for the handle, one chance to lunge. One chance before the cold flint of his blade drove down into me.

I made for it with a guttural yell.

My hand met the handle.

I whipped around on my back, thrusting the hickory out in front of me. The steel flathead, warped by the heat, let loose from the end and flew through the air, hitting Cormac's mask with a sonorous *crack*. He stumbled backward, planted his feet and looked back at me. A jagged five-point fissure stretched over his facepiece.

His expression changed from surprise to anger to unadulterated panic. I shifted up off my elbows and made my feet, watching, aghast, as the inside of his mask filled with smoke.

He charged with his knife, but I shifted aside, pushing him to the floor. He scrambled to his feet and spun around. We crouched low, the smoke thickening and banking. He hacked and choked, then attacked again.

I grabbed his wrist and held the knife away. He clasped my throat with violent strength. I fought his grip and we stumbled backward, spinning like a wild gyroscope. My back hit the wall. We bounced and turned and collided with the doorframe. His hand worked from my throat up to the edges of my mask. I strained to keep him from dislodging the seal. His opposite wrist twisted under my hand, breaking free and sending the sudden stinging burn of his blade into my thigh.

I shouted and pushed him. We struggled through the doorway, his fingers digging under my mask.

Air leaked out, squeaking past my chin. We scuffled and shifted near the stairwell crest.

The stairs.

I took his weight and propelled mine with it, driving us down the open staircase. We flipped end over end, tumbling and smashing. We slammed to the floor, my helmet knocking over my facepiece.

And his grip was gone.

I lifted my helmet brim and felt my thigh. No blade, just a searing wetness. I scanned the floor and the smoke around me. No sign of Cormac. I made my knees and felt around with my gloves.

Nothing.

I reached for my radio pocket.

Empty.

My pack rang incessantly with the low-pressure alarm. Hot blood spilled from the wound in my thigh. And somewhere, swimming in that sea of black, my kinsman killer lurked.

CHAPTER 50

I stumbled to my father's refurbished ladder truck and hung onto one of its side-mounted ladders. Hobbling through the darkness, I found the hose line and knelt by a coupling to feel for the lugs. The muscles in my thigh tightened and seized. I held pressure on the wound and moved forward. The bell on my pack slowed to an intermittent ring. Only a few breaths left.

I made for the sound of fans in the distance, skip-breathing.

Breathe.

Hold . . . Hold . . .

Breathe.

Hold . . . Hold . . .

The illumined entryway met me like the surface of water. I emerged into the open air and ripped off my helmet and mask. The fire scene spun with lights and activity. Everyone was around but no one was near. I put my helmet back on, loosened the air-pack straps and belt, and shook it to the ground.

A pike pole leaned against the doorframe. I grabbed it and supported my weight, scanning the parking lot.

No Cormac.

Only one other way out.

I limped around the corner of the building, through the shadows, dragging my foot over broken asphalt. The outer layer of my turnout pant leg was soaked through with blood. I grunted with every movement, pushing off the pike pole like a gondolier.

Beyond the back corner, a motor idled. I propped myself against the wall and peeked around the edge. A white van sat on the loading ramp, lights off, exhaust steaming from the tailpipe. The rear door beside the dock hung ajar, smoke rising out and up along the building side.

I held the pike pole in front of me and worked my way to the front of the van. Biting wind burned my cheeks. My skin numbed. My resolve set. The pike pole had become my harpoon, Cormac my white whale.

The driver's seat was empty. I worked my way around the front, half expecting the van to drop into gear. But the passenger compartment looked vacant. I moved back toward the building, toward the smoke-belching door, then halted and tensed.

The door moved. Outward. Only an inch.

A scuffling sound grated inside.

The door moved again.

I couldn't let him get away. Never mind that he was my uncle. Forget that he was my father's brother.

My flesh.

My blood. Akin to that which flowed hot and viscous, coating my leg as it had coated my palm.

As it had coated the palms of Love himself.

I lowered the pole.

The door shifted.

I straightened. This had to end.

The back of a turnout coat emerged. A firefighter duck-walked, pulling something heavy. The name across the jacket bottom read *Sortish.* His arms were under those of another firefighter, who lay limp. A firefighter with old Reno turnouts and a cracked mask.

I dropped the pike pole.

Timothy Clark appeared carrying the legs. They struggled out the door and set Cormac flat on the concrete porch.

Timothy held up his radio. "Command, we've located O'Neill. We need medics on the C side of the building." He tore off his helmet and mask and ripped off his gloves. "Check for a pulse, I'll get airway."

Sortish unzipped Cormac's coat. "Strong carotid."

"His breathing's shallow. Come on, Aidan." Timothy pulled the face mask off and froze, staring at Cormac's moustached face. "Who . . . Where's O'Neill."

"Right here." I shuffled to the porch and stopped. "And right there."

Timothy's face showed surprise, then confusion and an eyebrow-knitting concern. "Aidan. You're bleeding bad."

I touched my saturated pant leg. "It's all right."

The paramedics and a truck company charged around the corner.

"All of it," I said. "It's all right now." Adrenaline receded like water in the sand. The ground started to wave.

Loss stopped.

Redemption mine.

My legs gave out, and what seemed like a dozen hands took my weight, lifting away my burden and yoke.

—

I awoke to see light bending in rainbows through large fluid bags hanging from IV poles. They were tethered by tubing to my arms. A third hung from a separate pole, shadowy sanguine and labeled *A Pos* in slanted cursive. A larger object eclipsed the light and came into focus.

Captain Mark Butcher.

I strained to sit up.

He put out a hand. "Sit back. It's okay."

Pushing down on the mattress to take the weight off my hip, I shifted upright anyway.

"You're as stubborn as James ever was." His affect softened. Something had changed in those chiseled lines, so often etched with anger. "Aidan . . . I am sorry about your uncle."

A sick feeling bored inside me. "Is he . . . Where is he?"

He swallowed and shifted his weight. "Look, you're recuping, and I probably shouldn't even be here right now."

"Cap . . . Mark. Just tell me."

"They think he'll make it. He's intubated on a vent. They're going to fly him to a hyperbaric chamber." He ran a hand down his whiskers, rubbing the ends of one side between his fingertips. "Prevention investigated the van. Loaded with evidence. They've got more than enough to pin him with serial arson."

I nodded. "And murder?"

"Sounds like the D.A. is working for multiple charges of first-degree murder." The radio on his hip squawked. He turned it down. "I'm half tempted to go pull the plug on that ventilator myself." He stared at the bed rail, then looked up. "Your father would be proud of you." He patted the bed rail. "Heal up quick. We'll miss you downtown."

Butcher turned to leave and nodded to Ben Sower, who walked in, shoulder mic clipped to his coat.

Ben smiled with his eyes. "How's the leg?"

"Feels like the worst charley horse ever." I shifted in bed.

"They got you all doped up?"

My head did feel fuzzy. "I guess they do."

"I can see it in your pupils."

I glanced at the door. "Any chance you can bust me out of here?"

He grinned and shook his head. "They just finished sewing you up. Give it a day or two."

I brushed my hand across the broad dressings that lay taped on my thigh. "How much blood did I lose?"

"At least a liter and a half."

My throat felt dry. "Well, maybe one night, then." I wondered how I could see Julianne.

A nurse entered and inserted a needled syringe into an IV port.

It held about seven milliliters of clear fluid. "What's that?"

She depressed the plunger slowly. "Dilaudid."

"You'd better get your rest," Ben said.

I nodded and lifted my hand. "Thanks for being there for me."

He took it in his. "Always."

I reclined and closed my eyes, opening them a moment later to see my mother at the opposite side of the bed. She smiled and stroked my hair.

"When did you get here?"

"I've been here, darling."

"I was just talking to Ben." I motioned to the other side of the bed. The place where he'd been standing. "I guess I'm a little out of it."

"I'm so glad you're okay." Her eyes filled with tears. "I've been praying for you." She put her hand over mine. "God let me have you a bit longer, Aidan. You're his gift to me." Her tears ran down.

My eyes welled up. "Dad was there for me. His axe." I blinked away tears. "God was with me. Just like you prayed. Just like the verse. I don't know how. But he was."

She grimaced. "He wasn't going to let another one be taken from me."

"No, he wasn't."

She embraced me and sobbed, kissing my head. I squeezed shut my eyes and shed hot tears.

She sniffled and pulled away. "You rest now."

I wiped my face. "I love you."

She put a hand on my cheek. "I love you, too, Aidan."

A deep narcotic slumber soon overtook me, vivid and surreal, people and events playing out stories like shadows on the wall.

—

The next morning Benjamin convinced the physician to release me into his care. His wife, Elizabeth, insisted that my mother and I stay with them for the next few days. I refused the wheelchair and, assisted by Ben, walked out to their car on crutches.

I tried calling Julianne on her cell but only got voice mail. The nurse who answered the direct line to the ICU said she was out for tests. I ate a light lunch with the Sowers, and then Elizabeth led me to one of the two guest rooms they had prepared. A single bed lay turned down with fresh white sheets.

She made quick mention that the small desk in the corner was mine to use as I saw fit, brushing her hand over the leather cover of a King James Bible.

"Well"—she tapped the Good Book twice—"you sure have grown since the days you climbed our old oak. You get enough sleep while you're here. And there's no excuse for not eating enough."

I slept most of the afternoon, wakened by the smell of dinner. It was warm and wonderful, succulent apricot-lime glazed pork chops, baked yams with brown sugar and butter, fresh green beans with bacon and caramelized onions.

Benjamin washed the dishes, refusing to let me or my mother help, and then sat back down for tea. The four of us talked into the night, and for a few liberating hours I felt free of the pain in my leg. I had the deep exhaling sensation that must wash over a nation when a war has finally ended.

Only one thing was missing.

One person.

I admitted that I was too exhausted to stay up and retired to the back room.

After washing up, I lifted my leg like a plank onto the bed. I dialed Julianne's cell and got her voice mail again.

From down the hall I heard the distant echoes of cheerful laughter. And it felt like the end of a long, long day, sleep coming upon me like fireplace warmth in a late-night storm.

CHAPTER 51

Getting up on Sunday morning I felt physically lighter, as if I had been traveling with a weighted pack for so long that I'd forgotten how it felt to be any other way. Elizabeth baked German pancakes, and the house swooned with the enticing scent of butter and batter.

I limped out to the table. "Nothing sweetens the air in a room like your baking."

Elizabeth waved a kitchen towel at me. "Oh, stop, you. Come sit down."

"Where's Mom?"

Elizabeth opened the oven. "Hmm?"

"Did Mom go home?"

"Oh. No, she had somewhere to go this morning. She said she'd be right back." She pulled out two round baking dishes with a towel and set them on the stovetop.

Benjamin blessed the meal with simple eloquence. Conversation stayed light, my thoughts drifting to the ache in my heart for

Julianne. Ben excused himself halfway through the meal, apologizing that he had to be going to church early to help set up chairs.

Elizabeth stood with his plate and hers. "I still need to curl my hair. You leave those dishes, Aidan."

I smiled. "Not a chance."

She feigned a cross look and walked down the hallway.

The newspaper lay folded upside down on the edge of the table. I stretched so I didn't have to get up and grabbed it with the tips of my fingers. Flipping over the front page, I read the big block letters.

"ARSONIST NABBED."

A half-page photo set beneath the headline showed Blake Williams standing beside the hospital bed of an intubated and unconscious Cormac O'Neill. Blake had one hand grasping Cormac's collar as if he had just subdued him. His other hand was on his hip, his smile sterling with camera flash reflections. All too at home in that spotlight. Happy to clear his name officially, I was sure.

The story mentioned little about the efforts of the firefighters. Mostly quotes from Blake and the brass, lilting generalities and limelight attractors. How the combined efforts of the department administration brought this serial nightmare to an end. I took a swig of orange juice and shook my head.

"Ah." I tossed the paper on the table. "It don't matter."

"You're right," Julianne's voice sailed across the room. "It doesn't."

She stood in the front doorway, hair down, with a barrette on one side. She leaned on crutches with a lower leg bound in a cast just past the knee. A dark autumn dress accentuated her features. My mom snuck out from behind her, smiling. She blew me a kiss and disappeared down the hallway.

Julianne arced over to the table, balanced her crutches in one hand, and bent down to kiss me. Her lips were supple, light and sweet.

She pulled away and smiled. "I know who the real hero is."

I choked up, managing only to say, "How?"

"Swelling reduced. Inflammation receded. Feeling came back."

I shook my head. "And no permanent damage?"

She grinned. "No."

I placed my napkin on my plate and strained to get up, leaning on the chair. "Look at us, huh?"

She laughed, lightening the room, and in that instant I knew I'd have to amend what I'd said about Elizabeth's baking.

—

Church was different than I'd remembered it. The elderly men who passed out bulletins looked at me with friendly faces, shaking my hand with firm grips and understanding eyes. Older women greeted me like a grandson. And there was something I hadn't remembered much at all from before. Not because it wasn't there, but because I think I'd barely taken notice. All throughout the foyer, families gathered—little children skittering about skirt hems, playing hide-and-go-seek in a forest of grown-ups.

Julianne saw me staring and squeezed my arm, grinning and leading me into the sanctuary. My mother was already seated with Elizabeth and Ben. We found a place in the row behind them. I sat, thankful for the respite on my leg, but no sooner had I done it than the pastor appeared on stage and asked all to rise. My mom waved her hand, admonishing us to sit, but we both stood anyway, perched on our crutches side by side, listening to the prayer.

A simple and unassuming music team took the stage, and we sat back down. The congregation sang along to acoustic guitar strumming with a bass and set of drums. Some words were old and familiar, others fresh and new. Both moved with a spirit of joy through the room. It was palpable, and apparent, like a gentle breeze in a grassy field. I rejoiced in it, and supped of it, living water deep, satisfying and healing in my core.

The musicians left the stage and the pastor walked up, casually dressed in a gray collared shirt and tan slacks. He stood at the podium and looked over his flock.

Opening the Bible, he read:

> "Then King Nebuchadnezzar was astonished; and he rose in haste and spoke, saying to his counselors, 'Did we not cast three men bound into the midst of the fire?'
>
> They answered and said to the king, 'True, O king.'
>
> 'Look!' he answered. 'I see four men loose, walking in the midst of the fire; and they are not hurt, and the form of the fourth is like the Son of God.' "

Julianne put her warm hand over mine. I looked at her and smiled, knowing that a gift had been borne, not into my blood, but into my spirit.

The assurance of what is hoped for.

The conviction of things unseen.

Acknowledgments and Thanks

To Jesus Messiah, God made flesh, and the truest, greatest story ever told.

To my wife, Sarah Beth—my first reader/editor/manager and loving confidante, from the first words scrawled on a napkin nearly nine years ago.

To our wonderful children in whom we delight—Daniel Josiah, Claire Emmaline, and Noah Connor.

To my mother—for your love of books and writing and your imagination. You've filled my storehouse with many treasures.

To my dad—for your love of reading and for teaching me about the stars.

To Dwayne—for your abundance of creativity I witnessed growing up.

To Colleen—for telling me stories when we'd do the dishes.

To Tom—for supporting my decision to go into the fire service and calling it a "noble profession."

To Ryan—for all the summertime memories.

To Barry and Gini—for loving literature and supporting me from the start.

To Bruce and Anna—for your encouraging support.

To Warren and Virginia—for being constant advocates.

To my multi-talented nieces and nephews—Joshua and

Jeremiah; David, Rachel, and Shannon; Bethany, Christopher, Michaela, and Natalie.

To Dave Long—for seeing my potential as a writer.

To Karen Schurrer—for your respectful and skilled red pen.

To Paul Higdon—for a fantastic cover.

To the marketing team at Bethany House Publishers—for all your hard work and promotion.

To the whole staff at BHP—I count myself fortunate to work with such a great house.

To Jim Bell—because every Luke needs an Obi-Wan.

To Mike Berrier—one of the finest writers I know.

To Katie Cushman—for continuing to shine your God-given talent.

To Randy Ingermanson—for paving new avenues in Christian fiction.

To Sharon Hinck—for your sunny encouragement and excellence of craft.

To Amy Wallace—for your advocacy and professional example.

To Janet Grant—for being the first faculty I ever ate lunch with at Mount Hermon, and for lifting my spirits with a generous award.

To Karen Ball—for counseling me to reach deep and write what compels a fireman to enter a burning building.

To Julee Schwarzburg—for believing in me early on.

To my brothers and sisters of the Reno Firefighters' IAFF Local 731—for your fervent support.

To the City of Reno Fire Department.

To Mike Knapp—for being the rock of C-shift downtown.

To Chaplain Steve Arvin—for your labor of love.

To Ken McLellan—for championing the book.

To the City of Reno and Artown.

To Christine Kellie and the Sundance Bookstore—for hosting the book launch.

To Jonathan Bascom and Dreamer's Coffeehouse downtown.

To the Galena Junction Starbucks baristas.

To the staff of the Washoe County Library, South Valleys branch.

To Dave Talbot and Mount Hermon Christian Writers Conference.

To Kelli Standish and the PulsePoint Design team.

To Mr. Roberts from New Haven Middle School in Union City—for encouraging me in the Young Author's Fair.

To my English teachers from James Logan High School—you are much appreciated.

To Dr. Vince Pieranunzi from Point Loma Nazarene University—for the autobiography assignment.

To Pastor Steve Hadley—for your gifted teaching and for being a constant advocate.

To Pastor Tom Tompkins—for your guidance and blessing on our marriage.

To our Bible study group—for your excitement and encouragement.

To all my friends, pastors, teachers, and mentors, and to those not mentioned who also held the conviction of things not seen—

Thank you.

About The Author

SHAWN GRADY has served for more than a decade as a firefighter and paramedic in Reno, Nevada. The line of duty has taken him from high-rise fires in the city to the burning heavy timber of the eastern Sierras. He lives with his wife and three children in Reno. This is his debut novel.

Visit his Web site at *www.shawngradybooks.com*.

Heart-Stopping Action, Hidden Motives, Political Intrigue

More Page-Turning Reads From Bethany House

When Charles Beale reacquires a rare book, he gets more than he bargained for. And he might just pay for it with his life.

According to Their Deeds by Paul Robertson

When the job of a lifetime becomes a real-life nightmare, Tessa must trust her life to a man who once betrayed her.

The Edge of Recall by Kristen Heitzmann

When a NASA space crew returns to earth, they discover the unthinkable: every man, woman, child, and animal has vanished without a trace. Yet they might not be as alone as they thought.

Offworld by Robin Parrish

Stay Up-to-Date on Your Favorite Books and Authors!

Be the first to know about new releases, meet your favorite authors, read book excerpts and more with our free e-newsletters.

Go to www.bethanyhouse.com to sign up today!

Calling All Book Groups!

Read exclusive author interviews, get the inside scoop on books, sign up for the free e-newsletter—and more—**at www.bethanyhouse.com/AnOpenBook.**

An Open Book: A Book Club Resources Exchange